PRAISE FOR THIS PACT IS NOT OURS

"Zachary Sergi once again proves he has one of the most inventive minds in YA. Exhilarating, visceral, funny, and profound, *This Pact Is Not Ours* brings to life both supernatural horror and the terror of becoming an adult with equal energy and brilliance. A must-discover read!"
- STEPHAN LEE, author of *K-Pop Confidential*.

"*This Pact Is Not Ours* is a genuinely terrifying, inventive teen horror novel that sheds light on the painful complexities of battling one's inner demons as well as the more tangible ones."
-AARON H. ACEVES, author of *This Is Why They Hate Us*

"Sergi's spooky story is certain to chill like deep lake water, but the real soul of the tale lies in the friendship and growth within the Copper Cove Core Four. A thrilling adventure about growing up and becoming your own person."
-ERIK J. BROWN, author of *All That's Left in the World*

"Zachary Sergi knows how to create the perfect mix of goosebump chills, deep emotion, and page-turning anticipation! *This Pact is Not Ours* had me clutching my heart for the characters and looking over my shoulder for monsters!"
-JASON JUNE, *New York Times* bestselling author of *Out of the Blue*

"Weaving together nostalgia, yearning, and some things that go bump in the night, Zachary Sergi's *This Pact is Not Ours* made my skin crawl and my heart ache."
- EMERY LEE, author of *Meet Cute Diary* and *Café Con Lychee*

"Pure bone-chilling, spine-tingling fun full of creep crawlies, *This Pact Is Not Ours* is simply unputdownable! Zachary Sergi smartly takes the concept of a utopia and mines its murky underbelly to create a sinister summer camp romp that explores generational family trauma and what it means to carry the sins of your parents. This is a hauntingly rich story about the bonds and boundaries of friendship that is sure to give everyone the chills!"
-STEVEN SALVATORE, critically acclaimed author of *And They Lived...* and *No Perfect Places*

THIS PACT
IS
NOT OURS

THIS PACT
IS
NOT OURS

Zachary Sergi

Tiny Ghost Press

Also By Zachary Sergi:

Major Detours
So You Wanna Be A Popstar?

For Silver Bay,
This Place That Is Ours
(And Its Heart, Mark Hudak)

PROLOGUE

My three best friends are about to die.

We were so sure we could do better, but the awful truth is revealed now, crackling and clear. How can I deny it here, kneeling in this mess? With dirt caked on my skin, flung aside in wild clumps. With my fingers broken, clawing at the ground, searing with each handful.

One of us is down there, buried alive. My favorite person, dying a custom-designed death, unable to move, unable to see, suffocating as the air is crushed from his lungs. He can't even scream, his mouth filled with earth.

So I scream for him.

I dig and I scream and I dig, desperate to defy our failure. Still, I know the truth: we were never going to win, not when we couldn't even fix the things that broke between us this summer.

Now we're all going to die, *everyone*—but first it'll be the four of us, drowned and diseased, infested and crushed…

We never really stood a chance, did we?

TWO WEEKS EARLIER

Chapter One

Every summer, it's the same.

Mom turns off the air conditioner and rolls down the windows, releasing the preserved air from the five-hour drive. There's nothing like that first breath of Copper Cove: the crisp breeze off the lake, the clean cut of the grass, the sap and pine from the trees. But it's not just the smell— what really makes that first breath so special is the flush of familiarity. The rattle of relief, to have returned.

This is my eighteenth summer at Copper Cove, one trip for every year of my life, and this stay is going to be the best yet.

It kind of has to be.

∞

Our first stop is always checking into Hemlock, the red-oak dorm that sits atop the campus hill. Every year it surprises me how Hemlock manages to feel so welcoming, with its twin-sized bunk-beds and paper-thin sheets, or the tiny bathroom that attaches Mom's room to mine. Yet somehow Copper Cove's humble accommodations only make everything feel comforting. The simplicity is calming. Being here, my ties to the outside world already melt away, stripping the traces of my normal, tattered life. For the next three weeks, this basic dorm is once again my palace.

My fortress.

My reigning perch.

"Hemlock Eighteen," Mom sighs, appearing in the doorway of our shared bathroom. "I remember standing in this very room with my own dad. I can't believe I'm old enough to have a college-age child."

"Not college age yet Mom, at least not for another month," I say. "By the way, what happens when I make it to twenty-five and the Hemlock rooms run out? Where do we stay then?"

"Make it to twenty-five and you'll find out."

We Piccones have many long-held family traditions when it comes to Copper Cove, and one of them is to always live in the present and not dwell on the future. This ends up rooting us a bit too firmly in the past, but I've never minded that much.

I drop my bags in my room and walk back out onto the balcony running along the front of the rooms, which boasts a view of the campus below. Copper Cove is the brand of idyllic you might see on a postcard, a lakeside retreat center that doubles as a seasonal vacation spot. Right now, it's all here for me, every roof tile and treetop immortalized in my memory. There are the summer cottages painted blue and red and yellow. The stained clapboard bell tower of the Auditorium, rising above the treetops. The sloping grass hill that leads down to the tennis and basketball courts. And of course, the shimmering blue bay of Lake Charlie, which stretches for miles underneath a chain of forest-green mountains.

"Okay, it's way too hot up here," Mom says, joining me on the balcony. "I'm going to get my butt in that lake as soon as humanly possible. Sure I can't convince you to join me before you meet your friends?"

"You already know the answer to that question."

"It was worth a shot." She shrugs. "I suppose I'll see you later then, figlio mio."

Mom hugs me, squeezing me a little tighter than usual. She always becomes more protective whenever we return to Copper Cove. It's like we both revert to younger versions of ourselves, and as she lets go, she inevitably gives me *that* look. A combination of love and sorrow, of adoration and…something I can't quite place. It always makes me a bit uneasy, but that's probably because of what happened to Mom during her own teenage years here, that summer one of her best friends died. Maybe I'd feel better if she actually talked to me about what happened back then, but she always freezes over when I bring it up, says we'll talk about it when I'm older.

I'm pretty sure this is just code for "We'll never talk about it," but I don't push. There are already enough ghost stories told about Copper Cove.

And I'm sick of being haunted.

"You'd think five hours of road-tripping with me would be enough exposure for you," I say, turning out to take in the view.

"No such thing," Mom answers, turning too. "But I know you have places to be and people to see."

"I think I can spare another five minutes for the woman who gave me life," I answer, leaning my head against her shoulder. "And who brings me back to the best place on Earth every summer."

"Oh, you're quite welcome," Mom says, kissing the top of my head. "Things are going to be better here. You made it through, Luca."

I feel a swell building beneath my rib cage, so I do what I always do to make it stop. I close my eyes and I imagine myself as an embattled prince, returning to my enchanted home after a long and harrowing year. Back here in this private kingdom where I am safe and loved and free, where every mundane path, every battered stone, every weathered tree is coated thick with memories.

Then, opening my eyes, I remind myself—just like any true Piccone—I have traditions of my own to uphold.

It's always been hard for me to pinpoint exactly what makes Copper Cove so special, even though I know it is just a bit *more* special than anywhere else in the world. Part of it is the campus's beauty, sure—its endlessly peaceful and restorative vibe. But for me, what really makes this place magical is the people who return summer after summer.

And at Copper Cove, I most definitely have my people.

Chapter Two

"That may very well be your finest work yet."

I hear the voice behind me on the lake beach and resist the urge to tense. Normally I hate the idea of anyone looking over my shoulder at an unfinished sketch, but this situation isn't normal—and that voice doesn't belong to just anyone.

I turn to find Hazel standing behind my Adirondack chair and leap to my feet.

"Scoops!" I exclaim. "You look positively marvelous!"

"And you're an absolute artistic smash as usual, my dear Mops!"

Hazel wags a fake cigarette and blows an imaginary plume of smoke before rushing to hug me. We acquired these 1920s wealthy-affected accents one summer when we became obsessed with *Grey Gardens*, and we picked up the stupid nicknames after exchanging TY Frizzys for one of Hazel's birthdays. Somewhere along the line these two gags merged and persisted above the sea of ridiculous inside jokes Hazel and I share.

"It is so good to see you," I say in my normal voice, my face already lost in the tangle of Hazel's curly black hair.

"You too," she answers, giving me an extra squeeze. "How is it that you always manage to smell like amber and bergamot, no matter how many years go by?"

"Because I believe things that work don't ever need changing. And because my signature scent is timeless."

"Indeed it is," Hazel says, stepping back to look me over. "And hello, shoulders! When did they get so broad?"

"I've been…swimming much more than usual," I answer, my eyes falling to the ground. My body, and my reasons for swimming, are two of my least favorite subjects. "And you look radiant as ever, my dearest darling."

It's true. Hazel has always possessed a kind of easy poise, with her copper-brown skin and the dark eyes that are her namesake, but she seems to have grown up even more in the past year. Still, I see instantly she's the same Hazel, wearing a faded hoodie and jean shorts, with the little black notebook she always carries sticking out of her back pocket. Hazel's big brain never met a thought it didn't consider capturing, like she's always hunting in her own mind—and these identical notebooks are her weapon of choice.

"You flatter me, kind sir," Hazel answers, picking up the sketch pad I left on the arm of the chair. "Drawing the beach through an archway portal view? How very *Narnian* of you."

"Yeah, I've been on a *Chronicles* kick lately. Plus, the beach where they filmed that scene is called Cathedral Cove, so it felt fitting."

"Ugh, you and your movie trivia," Hazel fake-sighs, handing back the pad. "When am I going to convince you to power down the screens and actually read some source material?"

"I imagine when hell freezes over, or some other dramatic disaster." A new voice comes from farther up the strip of sandy beach where Ariana suddenly appears, striding towards us. "We all know better than to try and separate Luca from his sacred traditions."

It isn't long before both Hazel and I are enveloped by Ariana, swept up in a fury of sturdy limbs and untamed brown hair.

"Seriously, remind me why I have to trek all the way across campus the moment I arrive here just to swim in the same old lake?"

"Because our inaugural sunset swim is a time-honored activity!" I say. "Plus, you love us damn Yankees."

"Yes, well, I'm a bit of a Yankee myself these days," Ariana says, finally releasing us from her bear hug. "I swear I love my parents, but I cannot wait to go to college and stay in one place for more than two years at a time."

Hearing Ariana's ever-evolving swirl of accents is music to my ears. She might have lived everywhere from South Africa to South Carolina in the fifteen years we've known her, but Ariana's family has never missed a single Copper Cove summer. So I know Ariana secretly loves the continuity of our traditions just as much as the rest of us.

Before I can say as much, I'm suddenly swept off my feet and carried into the lake while still fully clothed. My mind immediately flashes to my phone, but then I remember I left it in my room. There is no cell service or wireless internet to be found here, sequestered in the middle of a mountain range. Which means Copper Cove is one of the rare places where you can be truly, blissfully unreachable.

I resurface quickly, wiping my hair out of my face to find Griffin, whose own wet blond hair falls across his shining blue eyes. One eyelid is creased smaller than the other, which I know only happens when he is laughing too hard or smiling too wide. Griffin is already shirtless, standing in the shallows where he dropped me, with water running down his flexing stomach muscles. I force myself not to stare.

"I meant for my sneak attack to get us in deeper, but someone is way heavier than he was last year," Griffin laughs.

"Yeah, well, blame a late growth spurt and an addiction to gummy candy."

I'm stunned that I manage to form words over the sudden jackhammering of my heart, but I'm happy to have played this reunion somewhat cool. Standing back up with a pull from Griffin, I'm also happy to still be wearing my shirt. I could swim a million laps and know my thin, lean frame would never stack up next to Griffin's baseball-pitcher arms or his superhero chest. I'm also incredibly pale—paler than any Italian has any business being, Mom always says—but a few weeks in the sun will set that straight. My ability to tan is the solitary physical advantage I have over Griffin, whose skin only goes from shades of pink to bright red.

"Man, am I glad you guys are finally here. Copper Cove isn't the same without you," Griffin says, hugging me. "Now, if I'm not mistaken, last one to the dock pays for pizza later?"

One smile from me is all it takes to send Griffin hurtling deeper into the lake. Looking to the shore, Hazel and Ariana are peeling down to their bathing suits, so I toss my soaked shirt into the sand and set out for the dock myself. I almost catch Griffin, but he still makes it there first.

It's not long before we're sitting in a row on the dock, looking out across the lake. The deep-blue water is backlit by a purple-sunset sky, and suddenly it hits me: we're all *here*, the Copper Cove Core Four, together again for three glorious weeks. That's why we're all quiet for the next few beats—because we know we have the best weeks of the year right at our fingertips. And because whenever we're back together, it's like no time has passed at all.

"So the last few weeks before college, huh?" Griffin says, kicking his feet through the water. He never could sit still.

"Anyone else completely thrilled and completely terrified at the same time?" Hazel asks.

"Nope. Just thrilled," Ariana answers. "What's there to be afraid of?"

"Not all of us are quite so used to new places and people," I answer. "But still, I've been counting down the days until college. Or the days until Copper Cove, then college."

"Of course you have," Griffin says. "One of these summers you really should just come up early and stay with my family."

"And break the generations-old Piccone family trip?" Hazel interjects. "Blasphemy!"

Griffin splashes Hazel's leg with his foot and she splashes right back, giving him a shove. I know Hazel is right—I'm too obsessed with tradition to change anything about the three weeks we all get to spend here together. Though the idea of a month alone with Griffin doesn't sound so terrible. Maybe then I'd actually have the courage to *tell* him.

I look back over at Griffin out of the corner of my eye, stealing a glance. I hope to catch one of his megawatt smiles, or spot the scar on his left shoulder from that time we got lost in the woods playing capture the flag…

But instead, my glance falls on Hazel, looking over at Griffin with the same exact light in her eyes. And I am reminded of the exact reason why I've remained so silent— why neither of us has crossed that invisible line with Griffin. Hazel and I could never do that to each other, not after all these pining years.

Besides, I tell myself, Griffin is straight.

Definitely straight.

Probably.

"Okay, I'm starving," Ariana declares, springing to her feet.

"You're always starving," Griffin responds. "I swear, you can eat as much as me."

"And still, I look this good?" Ariana winks, striking a pose—which is easy for her, since she's practically made of curves. "Beat you back to shore?"

Never one to turn down a challenge, Griffin scrambles to his feet as Ariana jumps back into the lake. He executes a flawless dive, his back muscles flexing as he disappears under the water's slick, darkened surface. I take a moment to marvel, then turn to Hazel.

But I pause because I don't recognize the look on her face.

"Hey, you okay?"

"Yeah, I just..." Hazel begins. I can tell her mind is turning and scrolling, searching for the perfect words. "We should tal—"

Hazel doesn't finish, however, as a cascade of lake water hits her square in the head.

"I am so going to kill that boy," Hazel says, wiping her face as Griffin cackles from the lake below.

Whatever Hazel has to say, it'll have to wait.

∞

Once back on the shore of Skinny Point, we towel off and grab our clothes. I don't even mind that my T-shirt is still as soggy as my bathing suit. It makes both feel like summer, that dripping mixture of nature and freedom. The view from Skinny Point doesn't hurt, either. Copper Cove's campus hooks around a bay inlet and Skinny Point sits on a peninsula jutting into the water. There are sandy beaches along one side and patches of forest on the other, then the tip of Skinny Point stretches along with symmetrical stone ledges that end with a rectangular gazebo. The beach offers a full view of the main portion of the campus: the Inn and the Dining Hall and the Auditorium, all set into the large green hill and lit up with warm yellow light.

I close my eyes for another moment and suddenly this view becomes the Shire, or some similarly cozy village—a safe haven pinched between outer worlds, a quiet respite nestled between chapters of past danger and a future unknown. It normally does my nerves good, the wave of ease I feel...

But then I hear the scream.

I assume it's Ariana at first, because her reactions usually operate in the extreme. But I'm surprised to find it was actually Hazel.

"Sorry, I just…" Hazel tries, pointing out at the lake. "What the hell?"

I turn to look and understand why Hazel screamed. Halfway between the dock and the shore, somewhat improbably, several spiders move across the surface of the water. Each one is the size of my entire hand and covered in brown hair, their long legs outstretched. I recognize these as dark fishing spiders, a breed that lives on the underside of lake docks and that "swims" to hunt prey.

What I don't recognize is the sight of so many of these spiders at once, gliding towards us in an infinity-like formation. Copper Cove's creepy-crawlies are usually pretty easy to ignore, but these certainly aren't.

"Well, that's horrifying," Ariana says. "The lifeguards always said to avoid those nasties at night, but I always thought they were just trying to scare us."

"I hate spiders." Hazel shudders, forcing herself to look at the approaching brood. "Why are they swimming to shore like that? And don't they bite?"

"Only in self-defense," I answer. "We probably just unsettled a cluster of them or something?"

"Guys, how many times do I have to tell you?" Griffin asks. "Copper Cove is haunted. Weird shit like this always happens. And let me tell you, this summer has been downright freaky."

I resist the urge to roll my eyes. Griffin has been convinced since we were kids that Copper Cove is cursed, and so he finds signs to prove his point everywhere we go. Of course, it's absurd—animals and nature just do weird things when left to their own devices. Besides, I'm much more inclined to think of Copper Cove as enchanted, not haunted.

However, I don't feel particularly enchanted as the wave of enormous spiders ripples to shore—and starts crawling straight towards us.

"Um, what are they—" Ariana begins, stepping back.

But Ariana freezes, the same way we all do, when a sound comes tearing from the woods. It's unlike anything I've ever heard, a kind of guttural cry pierced with a high tone, like wind whistling through the barrel of a gun. It sounds tortured.

Hostile.

"What was that?" Ariana whispers, the only one bold enough to make a peep.

Griffin stands with his arms outstretched, protecting Hazel as she hides behind him. I want to inch closer to them, but I'm afraid to move. I turn my head slightly and even the dark fishing spiders have stopped in their tracks. I can't decide if that's a blessing or a curse.

"Just don't—"

Griffin doesn't finish as a patch of branches in the forest twitches suddenly. The sound may have stopped, but something is definitely there.

I want to speak, or run, or do anything—but I'm paralyzed. I can't even breathe, let alone react. What the hell? Scary stuff like this *never* happens to us here.

The forest goes dead still and silence presses in all around us, thickly layered. For a minute I'm convinced whatever is there, some wounded and stalking animal, will burst forth and devour us, tearing us to shreds. My mind reels in fits and starts—what should we do? Run away? Remain still? Nothing about my suburban life has prepared me for wildlife attacks.

My eyes twitch to the spiders, for fear they've advanced to swarm us. For a second I picture them chomping at our ankles, climbing up our legs and all over our faces...until I find they're still stopped along the shore, sitting eerily motionless. My stomach tightens and sweat pools along my brow. The only sound I hear is the hammering of my pulse against my eardrums.

There's no way to know how much time has passed when Griffin finally says, "I think it's gone. Whatever it was."

As soon as he speaks, a branch snaps in two, crackling like a rifle shot. Ariana screams, but Hazel immediately jumps sideways to clamp one hand over her mouth.

Once Ariana is muffled, we all hear it clearly—the scratching sound of something moving...

But it takes a few seconds to realize it's moving *away* from us, receding farther into the woods.

As it does, the giant spiders also return to the lake, slipping under the veil of rippling water.

I exhale for the first time in what feels like forever. Hazel steps away from Ariana, looking like she might vomit. Griffin moves to brace her.

"Since when does Copper Cove have things that go bump in the woods?" Ariana rattles. "I love horror movies as much as the next girl, but I do not want to end up in one."

"I hate to say I told you so, but..." Griffin says, arching his eyebrows.

"I'm sure whatever it was, it wanted to avoid us as much as we wanted to avoid it," I try. "And it obviously affected those dock spiders, somehow."

"Because it was clearly the Copper Cove monster, the one that causes all the inexplicable—"

"Griffin, not now," Hazel interrupts, already reaching for the rest of her clothes. "Let's just get out of here?"

"Yes, especially because I might try to eat you all instead, if you don't feed me some terrible rural American pizza soon," Ariana tries, eliciting a round of nervous laughter.

I laugh along, convincing myself that any potential danger has passed—if that's even what it was. As my pulse ramps down, I feel silly for even entertaining the thought. Despite Griffin's conspiracy theories, nothing bad has ever actually happened to any of us in Copper Cove. This campus is not only safe, it's the very opposite of haunted— it's the most restorative place I've ever been.

Still, a feeling of dread wedges its way into my gut. For our last true teenage summer, the one before everything inevitably changes, this feels like a bad omen. But I immediately suppress that instinct, reminding myself that my emotions haven't exactly been reliable as of late. And that I'm determined to leave what happened back home in the past, just like I'm determined to make this trip perfect.

Besides, I know that soon, in the light of day, the currently dark and ominous trees will seem lovely and inviting, laced with sun and warmth, and coated with that intangible Copper Cove magic.

And so will everything else, if only I let it.

Chapter Three

I'm woken at 7:30 a.m. sharp, as usual. The sun has risen over the mountains high enough to shine directly through the upper part of Hemlock Eighteen's window, which has no curtains. Even though I only got a meager six hours of sleep, I still feel wide awake, filled with Copper Cove energy. Not to mention I'm already late for breakfast at the Dining Hall, even this early.

Once dressed in my personal uniform—a blue-and-white T-shirt, khaki shorts, and a light spritz of cologne—I throw a few items into my *Game of Thrones* tote and nod goodbye to the row of fantasy figurines I insist on traveling with. The wizards and dragons and elves lined up neatly on the shelf are just a fraction of my collection, but they make me feel at home.

I've always believed objects carry special meaning, or manifested sentiment. I was a child obsessed with geotagging and finding hidden Mickeys at Disney World, always picking up and leaving behind inanimate knickknacks. From what little I remember of my grandpa, he was the same way, so I must've gotten the object bug from him. It's not something I generally tell other people—really just Mom knows about it, and that's only because I live with her.

Heading down the hill, I pass a cluster of Copper Cove's signature single-family cottages, all bearing names like *Sycamore* and *Spruce*. There are a dozen of these cottages sprinkled throughout campus, reserved for the families who don't find the woodsy dorms as charming as mine does. Ariana's family stays in one such cottage, which also means they have to cook for themselves. By all rights the cafeteria food in the Dining Hall should be mediocre, but it's actually deeply delightful. This campus is the only place I eat three tightly scheduled meals a day, in a tour of 1950s-style American comfort food. People even drink little cartons of whole milk with their meals.

Copper Cove's annual Family Week, which was so popular it became three weeks, actually started sometime during that decade. It began as a time when the campus's many facilities are fully staffed and available: boating, tennis, rock climbing, archery, shuffleboard, crafts, beaches, children's day camp—the list goes on and on. There are also dozens of free classes like painting and Pilates, plus a daily rotation of special lectures. One of the most popular ones is actually given every year by Mom: "Sofia's State of Publishing," since she's a long-standing fiction editor.

To me, part of Copper Cove's inherent magic is that it's as unglamorous as it is gorgeous, forcing everyone to live and eat together like sleepover camp attendees. It's a culturally diverse place where, at least in my own queer estimation, all of the usual barriers that draw people apart seem to fade away, blurred together in a collage of cafeteria trays and sports sandals.

As I reach the Dining Hall I'm blasted with a wave

of human-and-oven-generated heat, the dull buzz of conversation and the delicious scent of pancakes. I head directly to the tables where our family circle always eats, soaking in the smells along with a wave of nostalgia. As expected, I find Mom already sitting with the usuals. There's her two best friends, Glo and Pan, and their families. Then there's Maggie, who Mom babysat back in the day. And of course, there's Hazel and her dad.

Glo and Pan leap to their feet the second they see me, causing silverware to clang against their dishes. I don't have any official aunts, but I've always thought of these women as just that. Mom, Glo, and Pan are known in Copper Cove as the Ya-Yas, named after some old movie about sisterhood I've never seen. Glo makes it to me first, the scent of her permanently applied perfume arriving just before her body. She is a solidly stacked bundle of maternal love, whose ferocity on the tennis courts is the stuff of campus legend. Without hesitating, she scoops me clean off my feet and spins me around.

"Luca! I swear, you get more and more handsome every year!" Glo cries before placing me back down. "If only you were a few years older, I'd force you on my son in a heartbeat."

"Anything to have you as a mother-in-law," I answer, released from Glo's bear-grip hug only to be embraced immediately by Pan.

Conversely, Pan is short and wiry and made of energy, from the tip of her coiled gray-black hair down to her white sneakers.

"Pan, I see you're living up to your namesake and

aging in reverse," I say as I hug her. This elicits a burst of Pan's signature cackling laughter, which rings out across the Dining Hall.

"You always did know how to butter us aunties up," Pan says, turning to Mom. "This boy never wanted for ice cream growing up. Who could say no to that charm?"

"I wish you had said no a time or two," I say, patting the soft part of my stomach that was once rounded into a belly. "I was rocking the Augustus Gloop look until age thirteen, thanks to you two."

I make the usual round of hellos to the rest of the table, finishing with Garrett, Hazel's dad. He always manages to live up to his reputation as a handsome-yet-overly-serious bachelor-chef. I like to think of him as an ageless fixture, enduring as the world turns relentlessly around him. Part of that likely has to do with the brown eyepatch he has worn our entire lives—he lost an eye long before Hazel and I were born, to some intrepid and reckless boyhood adventure. Like my mom, he doesn't like to talk about it.

"I thought you swore off the Dining Hall forever?" I say to Garrett as we exchange a hug.

"I do every year," Garrett answers. "One of these days it will stick."

"No mere mortal can resist the pull of the Dining Hall," Hazel jokes, standing with her plate in hand. She wears white shorts and a camisole, her curly hair tied in two buns. "Speaking of, time for seconds."

I follow Hazel over to the buffet line for my own first helping, already salivating over the piles of hash browns and bacon. The diet I try to follow back home is officially suspended.

"I already saw Griffin. He went for his morning run down from his house and now he's waiting for us at Bellfour," Hazel says as she scoops more eggs onto her plate. "And lord only knows when Ariana will wake up."

While Hazel and I always stay in Hemlock, and Ariana's family rents a cottage in August Bay, Griffin is an August himself—meaning that once upon a time his family founded Copper Cove. They sold the campus decades ago and now the Augusts stay in the family's summer mansion, on the north bend of Lake Charlie.

"Hey, think we can have a minute later to talk, when we're not surrounded?" Hazel asks. "Also, do you have any lip balm?"

Hazel knows I do, just like I know she can never keep track of little things with all the bigger, more-important things thundering in her brain. I actually think it's gross to share lip balm with anyone, even Hazel, but still I dig into my pocket and produce my usual Burt's Bees.

"Sure. Though 'talking' sounds ominous."

"No, nothing like that," Hazel answers. "You'll understand when I tell you."

"Can it wait until after our opening Bellfour ceremony?" I ask. "I want to get there early to set the soundtrack, naturally."

"You do me a disservice, Mr. Mops!" she says, sliding into her accent. "I know better than to interrupt traditions on day one!"

"I do think that is the wisest choice for the day,

Lady Scoops," I bat back, feeling a swell of anticipation. Soon breakfast will end, and everyone will retreat to their designated corners: the Ya-Yas to the tennis courts, the kids to their camps, the husbands to their boats, the readers to their lakeside chairs...

And the Copper Cove Core Four to our official headquarters: Bellfour.

∞

There are many things I know Griffin hates about being an August, but exclusive access to a private clubhouse is certainly not one of them. The Auditorium was my favorite building on campus long before Griffin inherited the keys to its bell tower, which has been closed to the public since it was built back in the 1950s. Standing tall on the great lawn overlooking the lake, the Auditorium is an impressive Cape-Cod-style structure, with brown clapboard siding, white square windows, cobblestoned pillars, and sloping roofs.

As I step inside the empty Auditorium behind Hazel, I breathe in the scent of sawdust mixing with the damp morning air. We cross behind the curved rows of wooden chairs, which creak mercilessly during the annual Family Week Talent Show. I follow Hazel up the set of stairs to the balcony, where we take a moment to appreciate the morning sunlight pouring through the square windowpanes. It illuminates the dust particles dancing under the arched ceiling and I soak in the sight. I've always been one to treasure beautiful places like this, to tuck them away in my memory to be explored later, when

I'm inevitably confronted with the ugliness of reality.

Despite Griffin's haunted conspiracies and Hazel's insistence I'm not properly utilizing my imagination if I'm not reading a book, I can't remember a time when I didn't picture Copper Cove as one of the treasured movie sets I've studied. A technicolor backdrop for endless summer adventure. A secret world littered with even deeper, more secret worlds, if only you know where to look. My annual summer vacation has always been more than just that— to me, it's a trip through a secret mirror, down an endless rabbit hole, to a place where the rules make sense and my people can always be found. Sure, it's not always perfect, as we were reminded last night.

But it's mine. *Ours.*

"Do you want to use my key or yours?" Hazel asks, already knowing the answer.

I smile and pull the personalized blue key out of my pocket. Griffin, as the eldest August grandson, inherited the master set to the bell tower at age thirteen. Once he did, he immediately made four copies and distributed them to the rest of the Copper Cove Core Four. He had *C4* inscribed on each key and color-coordinated them for each of us: green for Hazel, blue for me, purple for Ariana, and yellow for himself.

I insert my blue key into the door, the heavy wood and polished brass barrier that keeps everyone else out and grants entrance only to we worthy few.

"Griffin already mentioned adding a new set of chairs, because apparently renovation runs in his blue blood," Hazel says as we climb the stairs to the second floor of the tower.

"But I told him Bellfour is perfect just the way it is."

As we finally reach the exclusive third floor and enter our hideout, I have to agree. If Copper Cove is a private fantasy kingdom, then the Auditorium is definitely its castle. That makes Bellfour the throne room, where we princes and princesses convene to scheme and revel.

"Well, I'm glad you talked him out of it. I'm not sure I could stomach any more change this year," I say. "Besides, I love all this old stuff."

I let all the familiar sights of Bellfour soak into me. It's a smallish square room covered with ancient rugs and two windows on each wall that let in a pleasant breeze. An antique letter-writing desk sits in one corner, its miniature compartments filled with treasures bought at the Inn's annual porch rummage sale.

The only outlet in Bellfour powers exactly four things: a coffee machine; a minifridge filled with creamers, sodas, and some top-shelf alcohol pilfered from August Manor; a CD-and-cassette-playing stereo; and a large TV set with a built-in VCR. C4 all agreed to this one technological distraction, since it still feels fully nostalgic to pull old VHS tapes from the plastic crate beside the TV on rainy afternoons. Copper Cove is the only place I allow myself to disconnect from my usual rotation of fantasy movies and TV series, except on such rainy days, when I insist on curating the collection of faded cardboard covers.

There's a wooden coffee table in the center of the room, laden with old board games and surrounded by four unique chairs. The walls not facing the lake are also covered with important things, magnetized whiteboards listing our traditions and holding photos, but there'll be time for those later. My first order of business, before the others arrive, is to select the soundtrack. We have a firmly established rule that each of us gets a day of musical control in even rotation—since all four of us have pretty distinct tastes—and I always go first.

I walk over to the small bookshelf, which overflows with CDs and cassettes collected over the years. Actually, if we need anything new in Bellfour, it's a second music-storage tower. Still, I know exactly where to find what I'm looking for. No matter how many times Ariana disorganizes the collection while frantically searching for some pop diva, I always re-alphabetize the entire thing by genre. Ariana hasn't yet had a crack at the shelf this summer, so I easily pull Bonnie Raitt's *Nick of Time* from my "Americana Songstress" section and pop it into the dusty stereo.

Just as the album's title track begins, Ariana appears at the top of the stairs. She holds her purple key in one hand and a binder sleeve full of the year's Top-40-burned-CDs in the other. She literally keeps an old laptop with a CD drive for this sole purpose. Ariana wears a pair of loose denim overalls, and her wavy brown hair is tied into two braids. As usual, she sports a tangle of gold bangles on her left wrist, meant to cover the secret evil-eye tattoo that marks her otherwise flawless deep-brown skin.

"Damn. I was hoping to beat you here to steal the first music day," Ariana says. "For some reason I have a Grande-sized craving this morning."

"I can't believe you're actually awake early enough to experience a morning craving," I say. "But please, everyone knows day one belongs to Bonnie, and Bonnie alone. Wait, Hazel, wasn't Griffin supposed to get here before any of us?"

"Oh, you're right," Hazel answers. "I wonder what—"

"I realized we were out of coffee, so I ran back up to the house to get the good stuff," Griffin interrupts, striding into Bellfour like he owns the place—which, of course, he does.

My whole body tenses and freezes, which is a relatively normal reaction for me when Griffin enters a room. Seeing him now, it's like someone turned on a faucet in my body and hormones are thundering over my other senses. It's both suffocating and insufferable, but any attempts to avoid this reaction will be futile today. Because Griffin wears only a pair of gym shorts, his T-shirt hanging from the waistband. Sweat trickles down the muscles of his shirtless chest and across his abs, matting down his patches of blondish body hair. I'm caught so off guard I literally lose my breath, but I try to remind myself that my lifelong friend Griffin August is the person attached to that ridiculous body. And that I myself am also a person, not just a bucket of urges.

I do the same thing I always do when I need to get a grip: close my eyes and go full fantasy nerd. In my mind, Griffin becomes August the Golden Prince of the Land, revered and adored by all common folk not for his irresistible good looks, but rather for his legendary kindness. He wears a gilded breastplate but is armed with no weapons, because he never needs any.

In the next second I force my eyes open, because I don't want to seem strange to other people. Though I quickly remind myself, with a breath of relief, that I don't have to worry about that here, not like I do back home. This is the one place where judgment disappears. These are the only three people I can be myself around, without consequence.

Unfortunately, when I do open my eyes, I see something I don't recognize...

Griffin leaning in to kiss Hazel on the lips, as if it's the most routine thing in the world.

Chapter Four

"What the flying frig?" Ariana shouts, gripping one hand over her mouth.

Hazel jumps back and so does Griffin. He slaps his forehead, as if suddenly remembering himself.

"I'm so sorry, we just got into this routine when we say hello and I forgot we haven't told you guys yet."

"Told us what?" Ariana blurts. "Wait, Hazel, did you not just get here yesterday?"

But Hazel isn't looking at her—she's looking at me. This is why she wanted to talk. This is…

"Hold on, are you two a thing now?" Ariana keeps on. "Because if you are, that is the most overdue coupling in the history of man!"

Griffin nods, his cheeks turning pink the way they always do when he steps into something without thinking. I soften at the sight, right before a hot streak of pain slices across my chest.

"I'll let Hazel tell the story because she's way better at it. But basically, yes."

Ariana jolts across the room to scoop both Griffin and Hazel up in a hug. "You two have very awkward timing, but I couldn't be happier for you!"

I want to do the same, but I'm frozen. Like my legs

have turned to ice and I'm planted in place. I must melt, I tell myself.

"Oh my god, you guys!" I say, scraping my brittle feet forward to join the group hug. "You have to tell us everything, right now!"

∞

Normally the first morning in Bellfour is reserved for a game of Low, High & Nigh, where we each recount the best and worst thing about the past year, then the thing we're looking forward to most. However, there is nothing normal about what's going on in Bellfour this particular first morning, save for sitting around the coffee table in our preordained arrangement.

"So when Copper Cove offered my dad the opportunity, he couldn't say no," Hazel continues explaining. "Running a pop-up restaurant out of Weiss Hall for the summer meant we could spend more time together before college, since I'm with my mom so much. But it was kind of a last-minute thing, and we weren't sure it was going to work out, so we didn't really tell anyone. Plus, it's not like there's a way to post or anything up here."

"Well, that explains your social media blackout this summer," Ariana says, bobbing in the rocking chair from the Inn porch. "I just assumed you were detoxing. And let me tell you, I had zero idea what articles to read without your regular posts."

"Don't worry, I've got a backlog I can give you."

Hazel and Ariana share a private wink—those two

have always had their own separate rituals, mysterious "girl stuff" Griffin and I haven't been allowed in on since we were kids.

"Anyway, we all know I'm up here all summer with my family, so Hazel and I got to hang out a lot more," Griffin adds from his beanbag chair borrowed from the Children's Pavilion, his shirt placed mercifully back on. He rolls an old baseball between his palms, twirling its frayed stitching.

"And I don't know, it was just the two of us and… it kind of just started happening," Hazel continues, leaning forward in her Auditorium chair from downstairs.

"Anyone with eyes has known the two of you were into each other," Ariana says from her plush recliner. "I'm just surprised it took you this long."

"Yeah, well, living in Connecticut and Philadelphia and only seeing each other three weeks every summer didn't exactly help." Griffin grins. He can't seem to stop. "But when we realized we'd have the whole summer together…"

"We couldn't not give it a shot," Hazel finishes, finally turning to face me. "Hey, you okay?"

I do not know the answer to that question.

There have just been so many unspoken things I've accepted as fact. Like, sure, maybe Hazel has feelings for Griffin, but she never actually said so—just like me. And sure, maybe Griffin flirts with Hazel, but he flirts with everyone—including me. This is the way things have always been, and we all choose to remain just friends, summer after summer.

But maybe what Ariana said about this being

inevitable is true, too. Maybe I've kept my eyes closed to that particular bit of reality?

"Yes, of course I'm okay!" I cover from my Cove Beach Adirondack chair. "I'm just trying to process it all, but I'm with Ariana—this is such good news."

Hazel visibly relaxes, hearing me say this. I'm very thankful she accepts my explanation at face value. I'd never want to take away an ounce of her happiness, no matter how I really feel.

"I wanted to tell you later today, so we wouldn't have to break any traditions," Hazel says to me. "But Griffin and I already agreed, we don't want anything to be different between the four of us. So we can totally still do Low, High & Nigh. In fact, that could be my High for the year—getting to date Griffin August."

Hazel slides her hand into Griffin's and suddenly I can't help but think about the two of them, my favorite people, here all summer. Without me. Here in this very room, the room that was supposed to be all of ours, doing the things I've dreamed of doing for years.

Together.

I feel a lump of emotion knot in my throat…then I feel that familiar numbness tingling in my fingertips.

No, I tell myself.

I've already resolved I won't let *that* happen at Copper Cove. Those episodes belong purely to the past.

"Then let the grand game of Low, High & Nigh commence!" I proclaim, in my best jousting announcer voice.

Yes, I decide. We will still do the same things we do every year. So what if Griffin and Hazel are dating? I will still have my invaluable annual retreat, because I will find a way to be happy for my friends. So what if my heart might be cracked along a fault line?

That's been true for months already, anyway.

"Anyone up there?"

We all turn towards the window when we hear the new voice, but Ariana is the first to make it there.

"Who dares interrupt the sanctity of our first meeting?" Ariana shouts, because she already knows exactly who it is: Blake, the director of the talent show.

"Is now a good time to talk about my favorite finale's act?" Blake calls up.

"For you, any time is a good time," Ariana answers, turning away from the window. "Well team, it's been real, but I'm afraid the people have demanded some face time with their reigning pop princess."

I stand next, actually happy for the interruption. Usually my brain would privately spin out over the prospect of one of our rituals being interrupted like this, but I'm already properly spun. I need to get my head right—and there's no better way to do that than an impromptu performance by my favorite singing duo, Ariana's August.

∞

Hazel and I settle into front-row seats in the Auditorium beside Blake, while Griffin perches on the edge of the stage with a guitar in his lap. Ariana sits with her feet dangling off the stage, her attention fully focused on Blake. Everyone knows she had a thing for him when he first arrived last year, mostly because Ariana is subtle about almost nothing.

Blake is an employee, aka an "Emp," the majority of whom are college students, many from abroad, exchanging their various summer-long services for room and board. Blake took over the talent show, managing the many recurring talent show acts, including Ariana's August, who've been the grand finale every year since we were ten years old.

Even though the show is still nearly two weeks away, Blake has requested a preview of Ariana's August's act, knowing they tend to work on it right away. Despite Griffin's initial objections—they'd only talked about their performance once, last night—Ariana never turns down the opportunity to put on a show.

I always find it equal parts unfair and mesmerizing that Griffin and Ariana are both such good singers, considering Griffin is also a baseball-scholarship star and Ariana is a science prodigy destined for *Grey's Anatomy*. My one talent is drawing and I'm mediocre at best, while Griffin and Ariana bathe in excess talent.

"We'll figure out the harmonies and chop up the verses later," Griffin says, turning to Ariana. "But for now, just come in when we talked about?"

Ariana gives him a thumbs up, so Griffin begins strumming chords. I recognize the song instantly since it happens to be one of my absolute favorites. My own first musical loves are American female singer-songwriters— Carly Simon, Lana Del Rey, Patty Griffin, and the like— while Griffin loves their male counterparts: James Taylor, John Mayer, Billy Joel. The duet that Griffin just began playing is one of the most iconic collaborations between two artists from these categories: "Stop Draggin' My Heart Around" by Tom Petty and Stevie Nicks.

As Griffin's voice rings out, I'm reminded how perfect his lean and clear tone is on Tom Petty's verses. Then once Ariana joins him, her smoky and muscular runs sound a bit mismatched for Stevie Nicks—until the song suddenly mashes up with a different pop duet: Sia and The Weeknd's "Elastic Heart."

Ariana's August is known for their mash-up duets, so as the new chorus continues, I close my eyes and let the sound wash over me. I know exactly what Griffin will say afterwards: that it's just the start of an idea, that they still have to work out more original parts. He'll say it all with that same embarrassed, rosy flush that always shows up on his cheeks. Griffin has every reason in the world to be confident—cocky, even—but still, he's never so sure of himself.

It's his principal charm, as far as I'm concerned.

So as Griffin and Ariana continue dragging their elastic hearts around, I remind myself that I possibly have the coolest and most talented friends in the entire universe. I vow here and now that nothing—not even some ancient, all-encompassing crush—will ever make me screw that up.

Chapter Five

Chocolate sprinkles drip onto the photo album from my spoon, and I'm relieved for the plastic covering, otherwise Mom would kill me.

"Why don't you just eat ice cream like a normal person?" Griffin asks, biting into the last of his vanilla waffle cone. "I swear you're the only one in all of Copper Cove to ever order frozen yogurt."

"Don't ice-cream shame me. You know better than anyone how I used to suck these things down. I'm trying to show some self-restraint."

It's a nightly ritual to convene at the Store after dinner, a classic diner-booth spot with one counter for ice cream and another for pizza and bagels. Under its fluorescent lights and ever-spinning fans, everyone plays cards or trivia games and eats too many scoops of hard ice cream—everyone except me, apparently.

Though tonight Griffin and I got our orders to go, because he's sleeping over in my room. It's another one of our most beloved traditions—Griffin staying at Hemlock as much as possible during Family Week.

"If you're really trying to restrain yourself—which you shouldn't in the first place—don't go for your typical guise-of-health nonsense," Griffin says.

"I don't know what you're talking about."

"Frozen yogurt. Fruit-juice gummies. Granola parfaits. Spinach pie. Fig bars. Flaxseed tortilla chips. Veggie pizza," Griffin lists. "Shall I go on?"

I hide my smile with a look of faux outrage—those are indeed most of my favorite foods, all typically chosen in the name of finding a "healthy alternative." I flick a few rogue sprinkles at Griffin in retaliation, but the volley scatters, flying in several directions.

"Nice shot, Legolas," Griffin laughs. "You better watch the album though, this photo is too good to ruin."

Griffin reaches over and uses his thumb to wipe an errant sprinkle off my chin. The touch doesn't last more than a second, but it's enough to send a lightning bolt crackling through me. I'm painfully accustomed to infusing these little gestures with infinite meaning, latent expressions of some secret Griffin and I share. But tonight, I've been trying to ignore the warmth of Griffin's arm against mine as we sit side by side on the bed, or the scent of his clothes, which still smell like clean laundry even after a full day of activities. I try to ignore all of these little things I usually cherish, because now they belong to Hazel.

I was so sure I could breeze by this earlier when the news was still fresh. But now a searing missile of emotion breaks through my chest, threatening to detonate. Before it can explode, I force myself to focus on the photo in Griffin's lap instead. He insisted on us looking through the ancient Piccone Copper Cove photo album, which Mom hauls with us every year. Griffin claimed to want to look because he's working on finishing an incomplete family tree project leftover from his senior history elective—and while that might be true on the surface, we both know the real reason.

Griffin has remained obsessed with proving something spooky is hidden within Copper Cove's peaceful campus, perpetually digging up old news clippings of fires and disasters or fielding urban legends and ghost stories. He believes Copper Cove has its very own Loch Ness Monster or Casper the Unfriendly Ghost. It's all ridiculous of course, but I try to be sensitive to Griffin's complicated relationship with his family and their long legacy with Copper Cove.

We've paused our tour on a photo of Griffin and me at age twelve, wearing triumphant smiles as we clutch either side of a large trophy. That was the year we broke the Van Wie brothers' fifteen-year winning streak at the annual shuffleboard tournament. While Griffin might be used to performing in front of eager audiences from his tenure as a baseball star, I'm most definitely not—this shuffleboard championship still ranks as the crowning athletic achievement of my life.

"Why did we ever retire from shuffleboard?" I ask, willing my heartbeat to settle back to an acceptable pace.

"I recall you wanting to end your shuffleboard careers 'as Copper Cove legends,'" Mom answers, suddenly appearing in the bathroom doorway. "What precocious little shits you two were."

"And whose fault is that?" I ask.

"Touché," she responds. "What prompted this little walk down memory lane?"

"I'm working on finishing a family history and wanted to see if I could find anything useful in here," Griffin says, trying to sound as casual as possible. "Speaking of, I actually have a question for you."

"Shoot," Mom answers, yawning and stretching out her flannel-pajama-covered limbs. She might seem casual enough, but I know the truth.

All our parents, Mom included, don't like to talk about their Copper Cove pasts. Wendy, Griffin's mom, Garrett, Hazel's dad, and my mom, Sofia, were best friends in their own summertime youths—Ariana's parents only started coming when she was three. Garrett and Mom were even a couple, same with Wendy and another friend named Tommy, who died in some freak accident when they were eighteen. After that, the couples broke up. Wendy stopped speaking to Garrett and Mom, and never set foot on Copper Cove's campus again.

Mom and Garrett have remained friendly, but neither like to talk about what happened between them. I get it. If something unthinkable like that ever happened to C4, I'd probably never want to talk about it either. Except, my grandpa was equally evasive about his Copper Cove youth, so somewhere along the way I just chalked it all up to some inherited, repressed Italian-Catholic guilt thing. Mostly I don't like the idea of Mom having to dig into her past trauma, so I leave it be.

Griffin usually does too, especially since he and Wendy have a pretty distant relationship to begin with. She hates that he spends so much time at the Cove with us every summer. I always thought Griffin wanted to know more about Copper Cove's history in general because of his family's former ownership, but this new push feels more...urgent?

"Well, you know Luca and I were born in the same year, and I'm sure you know that you and my mom were, too," Griffin begins. "But I looked it up and our grandfathers, your dads, were also born in the same year. How weird is that?"

"Oh, really? That does sound familiar," Mom says, rubbing her eyes. "It must be something in the Copper Cove water. Our families have always been connected up here, and things like that tend to sync up sometimes. You know, the circle of life. I bet you boys might end up having kids around the same time, too."

"Yeah, maybe," Griffin says, trying not to be deterred by this invisible roadblock. "I can't find the exact records because of that fire back when Copper Cove was Morrissey Village in the 1920s, but as far as I can tell, I think my great-grandfather and Luca's great-grandmother were also both born in the same year. Do you know what year Luca's great-grandmother, your grandmother, was born?"

"Hmm...1908, I think?" Mom answers. "Does that match?"

"No, it would have to be 1906," Griffin says, frowning. "Are you sure? Could you maybe—"

"Okay, I know it's only 9:30, but this old lady is beat," Mom interrupts through another yawn. "That would be interesting though, if it did line up, Griffin. Now see you two in the morning. Good night, figlio mio."

"Night, Mom," I say, feeling Griffin's disappointment radiate beside me. "Hey, close the door?"

"As if I want to be left open to the wafting nighttime

emissions of two teenage boys on Dining Hall meatloaf and ice cream," Mom laughs, closing the door behind her.

I turn to say something to Griffin, but find him wearing another familiar expression: the *god I wish I was close to my mom like that* look. I've seen this face all too often over the years...and I know it's one of the many reasons Griffin prefers to sleep in Hemlock. Just like I know, deep down, this is the real reason he occasionally gets obsessive over the history of Copper Cove and the tragedy that haunted our parents as teens. Because maybe it would help him understand his family, or his mother, a little more? Or maybe it would help explain why she is so cold and distant. Believing in supernatural spookiness is a lot more appealing than the rich-repressed reality. Fantasy-me can certainly relate to that brand of escapism, at least.

"Don't take it personally. You know my mom hates dredging all that past stuff up," I try. "Plus she really doesn't like talking about my grandpa much since he died."

"Hey, if that's your version of not talking about things, you should spend a day in August Manor," Griffin almost laughs.

I would actually very much like to spend a day in the manicured grounds and fully staffed walls of August Manor, but Griffin never invites the rest of C4 there. On rare occasions he offers us a glimpse of what goes on inside the mansion's walls, claiming his mom is inexplicably warmer to his younger siblings, or that his own grandfather gives him weird lectures about "The August Duty" every summer. Mostly, Griffin seems to have inherited the Waspy tendency to avoid talk of family matters, except in the past tense.

"This does nothing to disprove the obvious fact that our parents are hiding some grim secret about Copper Cove," Griffin follows up.

"I choose to think of our parents like the characters in *The Magicians*—former kings and queens of Copper Cove, broken apart by the pressures of their reign. It's way more fun than your grim fairy tales."

"So how do you explain away that thing in the woods from last night?"

"That was probably just a wounded raccoon or something," I answer. "Though no one would love it more if it turned out to be a queen spider calling forth her minions, or an ancient dragon trotting out to be vanquished."

Griffin looks at me then, in the way that always melts my insides. Like the full focus of his river-blue eyes is on me, and no one else in the world exists. He wraps one arm around my shoulder and I forget about anything and everything else.

"Sometimes I really wish I could see this place through your eyes," he says. "It's why I love having you around."

Staring at Griffin's pure-sunshine smile and half-crinkled eyelid, feeling his bicep curl against my back, and smelling the soap-bubble scent of his hair, I might disassemble. I just can't fathom how these giant little gestures don't mean the same thing to both of us, deep down…

How will I ever get over Griffin if he keeps doing things like this?

But then I reground myself. Because Griffin doesn't

even know how I feel, underneath it all. And if I really wanted these affections to end, I realize I have the power to stop them with just a few words. But I'd never risk that—not when it could mean changing so much.

So instead, I close my eyes for the usual moment and picture myself leaving a floating château, one that has shuttered up its beautiful stained-glass windows for the winter. If anyone gets to live that sky-high, it's...

Not me.

My heartbeat races a little faster and suddenly I feel anxiety creeping up my sides, like water staining paper.

No. Not here.

"Oh please, there's a reason I see Copper Cove this way," I say, standing and resettling on my own twin bed. I need to create some space between us, some room to breathe. "It's an escape from my life back home. I need as many of those as I can get."

"I can't imagine going to a Catholic school, let alone an all-boys one," Griffin says, pulling the sweatpants he wears as pajamas out of his duffel bag. "I'm guessing you still haven't come out back home?"

I shake my head. It was only last summer I told anyone I'm gay—first Mom, and then Griffin, Hazel, and Ariana. Beyond that, I've been staying in the closet back home in my small Long Island suburb. I've never really fit in there, but at least I've been able to stay pretty invisible at school by keeping to myself. There's only one person back home I trusted enough to come out to, and that ended in disaster.

"Well, at least you have Frances, right?"

Speak of the devil. No—I most definitely *do not* have Frances.

But I most definitely *will* have one of the crippling panic attacks she left me with if I talk about what happened in this already-heightened moment. So I fake a yawn and walk towards the bathroom.

"I know it's early, but I'm wiped. Mind if I get ready for bed?"

Griffin frowns a little—he hates spending time alone. Still, he stands and pulls off his shirt, making his own moves towards sleep.

"I guess I've got enough to keep me busy," Griffin answers, stretching so that every muscle in his torso flexes at once. I try my hardest, but I cannot bring myself to look away. "Hey Luca, you good?"

I take in the sight of Griffin, the genuine concern on his perfect face, and suddenly I want to let it all flood out. I want Griffin so badly it aches—literally. My body betrays me again, a jet stream of hormones and longing and desire burning my blood.

"Yes, totally good," I lie, with a smile. "Just tired."

Then I turn away, before Griffin can see the smile fade.

∞

An hour later, I'm still painfully awake. I'm completely exhausted, but my body also feels supercharged. My mind won't stop churning. No matter what I try to think about, I can't escape the reality that Griffin is sleeping just across the room, after another year of having to make do imagining him nearby. His latest oversized American history biography sits open on his bare chest, lifting slightly with each breath, and his hair falls perfectly across his tilted forehead.

For me, realizing I was gay didn't come all at once. It was something I'd always known deep down, but not something I understood until my sophomore year—and then not something I accepted until my junior year. But there was one thing I understood, once I did become aware of my sexuality: that I was in love with Griffin August. In my mind, the two realizations were inseparable. I am gay, and I love Griffin. I realized one the same time as the other, or perhaps one because of the other.

Only then did it become clear to me, the crush I'd had since we were kids. It was easy to miss because everyone naturally gravitates towards Griffin. He's always been wealthy and attractive and good at sports, but all these things that should've made him a jerk didn't. Griffin's wealth makes him generous, he never really thinks about his appearance or what he wears, and he is kind to everyone as a default.

This outer Griffin is easy to adore, sure, but for me it goes much deeper. My emotions are all wrapped up in the times Griffin would beg Garrett to take us to the batting cages to work on his swing, when really it was only because I was too embarrassed to ask to go to the gaming store next door, the one with the rare *Lord of the Rings* imported merchandise section. Or how Griffin insists on making everything a competition to pass the time, like life is one long series of games to be won. Or how he'd push the other day-camp boys straight to the ground if they ever made fun of me for being quiet and seeming gay. Or how Griffin only ever reads his biographies about obscure American politicians when we're alone in Hemlock, or how he scribbles song lyrics in a composition notebook he never shows anyone.

I get to see the private Griffin, and in turn he's one of the only people aside from Mom and Hazel that I'm comfortable flying my fantasy-nerd flag around. Back home, not even Frances is allowed into my room, which is plastered with my favorite sketches and a vast model castle collection. But Griffin never comes close to making fun of my miniature figure display here in Hemlock, instead asking earnest questions about each one's origins.

I've always had a hard time believing a boy so thoughtful could be straight, but I realize that's the patriarchy talking—not all straight men are repressed douchebags. Exhibiting a properly expressed emotion or having a kind streak doesn't automatically make a guy gay. I know I have to accept that I've misread any potential signals from Griffin— that I'm still misreading them, even tonight.

Still, that doesn't keep me from the fantasies. All the magical, fictional ways Griffin might return my secret feelings. I've imagined it so many times, the ways it could happen—during one of these sleepovers, for example. Griffin would wake up and slide into bed beside me. His lips would find mine and they'd taste exactly like he smells. I wouldn't believe it at first, but then my hand would reach out and I'd finally be allowed to touch the lines of his stomach or trace the invisible blond hairs on his chest. Griffin wouldn't say a word about what we were doing, especially not as he reached his hand into my sweatpants...

I force my eyes open. Then I glance over again at Griffin sleeping and feel the waves of desire drowning me, causing me to lose control in exactly the way I hate most. I know there's only one way to clear the singular thought pulsing through my brain, to stop the skipping track stuck on repeat.

So I climb out of bed and tiptoe towards the door. I manage to slip out soundlessly, even with one arm draped over the erection I have tucked under my waistband. It feels like such a violation, my own body insisting I'm a thing of instinct and urge, first and foremost. Thankful that no one is awake, I rush down the balcony hallway, cool night air breezing against my skin. The communal showers are home to many harmless moths and daddy longlegs. Neither are high on my list of favorite things, but I ignore that thought as I slip into one of the dark stalls.

I've been able to privately rewrite so many of the old Catholic rules once ingrained in me, but I still have a hard time thinking about masturbation as anything other than something to be guilty about. Still, once puberty overtook my body, it became a physical necessity—like a sneeze expelling an allergen. Once I do it, my hormones recede and my body leaves me in peace, if only for a little while. I never knew how to relate when I'd overhear guys at school talking about loving to jerk off. For me, it's more of a lifeline, a source of temporary respite from all of the things I'm constantly reminded I can't have as a closeted gay teen.

I pull the stall curtain closed, and it only takes a few seconds before I finally sputter with relief. A rush of clarity, then inevitable shame, fills my hollowed brain. I reach for a towel, hoping my desire will leave me alone long enough for me to finally fall asleep.

That's when I hear it—the steady *tap-tap-tap* against the window above my head. I freeze in place, latent adrenaline surging into my system. Was that sound always there, or did it just begin? I exhale, convincing myself it's just the wind rattling a tree branch against the window or something. It's most definitely not some Copper Cove monster stalking me, or the semi-public masturbation police coming to arrest me.

But that's when the tapping turns into a full, sliding scratch—one that sounds like it might shatter the glass.

Alone in the dark, I resist the urge to scream, but just barely. I know I have to get out of here. Especially as something soft and hairy brushes against my ear.

I lurch forward, slapping my hand madly against my head. My bare feet slip against the shower floor, and my legs swing out from underneath me. I reach for something to brace myself, but only grip the plastic curtain.

I twist and fall to the floor, landing on my side more noiselessly than I expect, buffered by the curtain wrapped around my body. I'm not hurt, but whatever brushed against my head is still there.

Until it slides into the canal of my ear from the momentum of my fall.

I feel only panic as my ear clogs with the soft thing, writhing and wriggling. Each of its movements suddenly sounds like thunder, banging against my eardrum. I spin on the floor to try and shake it out, but only further tangle myself in the plastic curtain, trapping my arms against my body.

For a moment, I consider calling out for help, but then I remember the stained towel on the floor beside me.

A gurgled sob chokes out of my mouth as the thing in my ear shimmies madly. It's probably trying to work its way out, but instead it feels like it's burrowing deeper, attempting to invade my brain stem.

Cold fear somehow manages to sharpen my limbs, and I react. I roll back out of the curtain to free myself. Then I pop to my knees and reach my fingers into my ear. But they're too big to grasp the...

What is it?

My mind flashes with horrifying images of roaches and parasites, but I push those as far away as I can manage. Instead, I try shaking my head, the way I do when water gets trapped inside my inner ear after swimming. The thing bumps and loosens, and I try to ignore how enormous it feels.

After a few vigorous shakes, I can tell it's actually working. I bob my head even harder, the world spinning and my lips shaking, spewing spittle. Just when I think I might pass out from the thrashing, the thing finally dislodges and shakes to the surface of my ear. I reach between the cartilage with my fingers, pinching desperately.

Finally, I pull the thing out like a feeding tube from a dry throat. I throw it on the floor and, impossibly, it's just a small silverfish. It scampers across the floor and slides into the darkness, as if it was just as frightened as me.

I. Hate. Bugs.

Especially ones that try to get in my head.

I want to kneel for a few minutes to catch my breath, but I want to get the hell out of here much more. Lifting to my feet, I wonder how this possibly could have happened. Did the banging scratch against the window spring the silverfish forward, then when I fell it slipped into my ear? There's no way it could have been trying to get in there…right?

No, I tell myself. Though I know exactly what Griffin would say if I told him about this—that I'm being haunted, or that we're somehow cursed. So it's a good thing I will never tell him—or anyone—what happened here tonight, while I was half naked and alone in the dark.

I shudder at the thought as I emerge back onto the balcony hallway. Barring the supernatural, what could have been scratching against the window like that? And what if the silverfish had gotten stuck in my ear? Or if I had pinched it in two and lodged its halved body in there?

Nerves rattle in my system like needles, poking holes in a sea of acid exhaustion. Walking forward, I experience a head rush that makes me dizzy and blurs my vision. I lean against the railing and blink, waiting for it to pass. As I do, I swear I see something farther up the balcony. It's crouched and blurred, putrid and misshapen. And it…hisses.

I step back and gasp, pressing my eyes shut to further clear them. But when my vision returns to normal, there's nothing there. Exhaling, I realize my eyes, and my imagination, must be playing tricks on me. Like with the rogue branch against the window, or the invading silverfish.

I tell myself that everything just seems scarier at night. I return to Hemlock Eighteen so quickly, I don't realize I've been holding my breath until I'm back in bed.

Unfortunately, I do not fall asleep for a long time.

At least I'm not thinking about Griffin August anymore.

Chapter Six

Swimming laps in the lake is always harder than in a pool. The relentless churn of motorboats generates uneven, choppy waves to navigate. Staying within the buoyed lap lanes requires constant course correction and angling. The water itself is filled with distractions: the occasional darting fish, scattered plant formations, craggy piles of rocks, the odd discarded artifact lost in the clay confines of the lake floor.

Swimming in the lake is harder, but it's also better. The water remains crisp and cold stroke after stroke, unlike the preheated swaddle of most pools. Slicing through the surface at my usual speed demands more effort, and swimming straight requires more attention, but I don't mind. Because swimming in the lake always feels like a feat to conquer. Like I'm taming an unruly beast, hammering chaos into order with each clean repetition.

Just like every other activity at Copper Cove, swimming laps wears me out. Last night notwithstanding, I usually sleep like the dead here, my typical vortex of thoughts and anxieties drowned by the flowing tides of exhaustion. This physical exertion is a large part of the reason I swim in the first place, even back home. I've always hated sweaty workouts and the sterile smell of the gym, so I just assumed fitness would never be my thing. But when a YMCA opened in my neighborhood, I discovered swimming. Unexpectedly, I became an exercise person.

Of course, it does nice things for my otherwise-scrawny body—Hazel was right, suddenly I have *shoulders*—but that's not even the most important part. For me, swimming has become almost entirely about mental health. It feels like therapy and meditation and church all rolled into one. It's the rare time I get to be completely alone with myself, without the distractions of music or TV or homework or my phone. When I swim, every one of my senses is completely dulled: waterproof earplugs, fogged goggles, a feeling of complete weightlessness, and being locked into a repetitive rhythm. It's like, with all of my many inputs occupied, I'm free to fly.

It's strange I didn't discover swimming laps earlier. I've always loved oceans and lakes more than most. I feel connected to the water, where I can be clean and spotless, strong and sleek, lifted and simplified—all of the things I never really am on land. I have also harbored a lifelong fear of drowning, but swimming regularly has helped me confront that particular dread too.

So if swimming is my daily relief from reality, and if Copper Cove is my annual escape into fantasy, then swimming here is something close to nirvana. And today it is just the reminder I need—I can't let *anything* ruin this summer.

Instead, I focus on my breathing. On the air bubbling out my nose as I face the lake floor, then on sucking in through my mouth as I turn out. I catch a glimpse of the scenery as I do, the expansive blue sky scattered with puffy white clouds, set against the deep green of the mountain trees. Along the darker blue of the lake, a yellow sailboat billows by and water splashes onto the dock over at Skinny Point. Then the world disappears under the surface as I turn to repeat the process all over again.

It's so easy to feel like this place is enchanted—and not just in my mind.

The familiar burn in my lungs and the ache in my arms indicate I'm nearing the end of the day's swim. I don't necessarily want to stop, but dinner will be starting soon, and I have to shower and change. So, I swing around the final buoy in the rope-chain lane to head back to shore... until I spot something. An object I can't believe I missed during my previous laps.

On the murky lake floor sits a pair of the flat black stones I've come to covet. These stones are part of another of my Copper Cove traditions—a private one I inherited from my grandpa. I can't believe my luck finding two stones at once. It's got to be a sign of something good. After last night's close encounter of the silverfish kind, I could use a good omen. It turns out I was completely right: everything about last night's experience seems far less spooky in the light of day. Traumatizing, yes—but certainly not intentionally sinister.

Gulping in a mouthful of extra air, I dive down to retrieve the stones. My ears clog with pressure as I reach the lake floor, but I grab the two stones easily. Their smooth surfaces are cool and satisfying against the skin of my palm, even underwater. Then as I turn to resurface, I spot something else: an imprint in the sand, just beyond where the stones rested. I've seen this hooked, broken-in-half infinity symbol many times before in the lake's claylike bottom. Although it always strikes me as strange, I assume it has to be some kind of naturally occurring phenomenon, twigs or something settling in an odd-but-perfectly-normal shape. I always tell myself I'll ask someone about the broken infinity imprints later, but it's one of those things that's not pressing enough to ever really get around to.

Wading back to shore after my final lap, I slip the rocks into my pocket. They add to the weight of my soaked bathing suit, sagging the waistband lower across my hips and exposing more of the almost-muscle there, which only shows when I'm breathing heavily post swim. I'm particularly aware of this fact when I realize the lifeguard's attention has fallen solely on me, as the last swimmer at this hour.

I don't recognize this lifeguard, which means he must be one of the new Emps. I've looked up to the Emps since I was little—they always seem like a fraternity of cool older kids having the best summers of their lives, filled with dormitories and dollar beers and drama. It still doesn't compute that I'm pretty much the same age as most of them now.

This new lifeguard is slim and young-looking, with thick black hair and almost-black eyes that seem unusually fixed on me. It's…a strange thing.

"I thought you might keep me here all night, at the rate you were going." The lifeguard's voice comes out with a slight accent—Spanish, maybe—despite his flawless English.

"Actually, one more lap and I might've needed actual saving," I laugh between heaving breaths.

"I wouldn't have minded."

I'm sure it's just in my head, but that sounded almost…flirty? As I approach the lifeguard stand, I examine the new Emp more closely. He seems pretty short, and he's even skinnier than me. But his tanned skin shines nicely in the sun, his smile is bright, and his stomach is made entirely of muscle in the way only naturally thin bodies can be. He looks nothing like Griffin, but there's no denying the lifeguard is still cute.

Then I remind myself that probably isn't even the point here.

"This your first summer at Copper Cove?" I ask.

"Yes. You?"

"Eighteenth."

"Damn. That explains the swimming, at least."

"What do you mean?"

"You looked…I don't know, at home out there."

I'm taken a bit aback by this observation, though not in a bad way.

"Oh, well actually, swimming is more like prayer to me than anything else," I say without thinking.

"Prayer?" he asks. "Isn't that something you're supposed to do kneeling beside your bed at night?"

"Ha, yeah, I guess. But I went to an all-boys Catholic high school, so there was a lot of very-mandatory praying at very-mandatory masses."

"And so this school of yours held mass in a pool?"

"No, but that would've been awesome." I laugh again. "I meant, to survive all those mandatory, non-watery masses, I figured out a system that worked for me."

"And that system involves swimming?"

"You really want to know?"

The lifeguard nods. I take a deep breath, trying to steady my racing post-exercise pulse. Endorphins burst to life in my system, buzzing like sizzle sticks and overpowering the usual reservations I have about talking to complete strangers.

"Well, my school was run by Jesuits, and they have the whole education thing down. As underclassmen we studied world religions, then as upperclassmen we were encouraged to develop our own spiritual practices based on what we learned. I liked the challenge. Many things about religion never made much sense to me, but the central point of most is to make you a better person, right? Kinder, more selfless, less judgmental. And if that's the case, then shouldn't the concept of god be about that process?

"Anyway, I ended up realizing that to me, god isn't a fatherly old man in the sky who is angry or loving or vengeful or forgiving. I mean, how egocentric is it of us to think the thing that governs the entire universe is somehow human? It makes way more sense to me that god is an energy, the kind of intangible flow that connects everything and everyone. The thing that guides us towards being better."

"So you think god is the Force from *Star Wars*?" the lifeguard asks, grinning.

I laugh, but only for a moment before carrying on.

"That's one way to put it—it turns out there are a lot of different names for it. But basically, I think god is grace, the guide that helps us learn lessons. If that's true, and if prayer is supposed to be about connecting to god, then any process of reflection, of trying to make yourself better, counts as prayer, right? I mean, if repeating psalms or talking to some heavenly father during a mass is your way to reflect, then more power to you. But I think most people do that because they're told they have to. For me, swimming is the only way I've ever really cleared my head. It's the best way for me to process things I've done and set goals for myself. You know, connect to the source. Thinking of things this way was the only way I survived high school. Because even if I'm not a religious person, that doesn't mean I can't be a spiritual one, right?"

I look up at the lifeguard and see the expression on his face. Suddenly I realize how long I've been talking, and that I entirely bypassed his *Star Wars* joke. I'm mortified by my impromptu monologue. It's just been so long since anyone new asked me a question like that. Or since anyone new cared enough to listen.

"I guess as a lifeguard, that kind of makes you like my priest," I joke, my eyes falling to my feet. "Sorry for the spontaneous confession. I haven't even asked what your name is yet."

"Manny." He smiles at me, looking both puzzled and amused. "And I'll be happy to hear you confess your sins any day of the week."

If I wasn't sure Manny was flirting before, the look on his face makes it clear he is now. And that makes me feel…

Exposed.

I force a smile and nod, crossing my arms over my bare chest and the patch of hair that's grown in there. I hope, as I continue walking towards my towel, that the gesture comes off as coy and smooth, instead of awkward and abrupt—which it likely is. I just don't know what to do with being seen like that, not after…

"Hey, do I get to know your name?"

I stop and turn, forcing myself to reply: "I'm Luca."

"So will I be seeing more of you here, Luca?"

"Probably more than you want?"

I turn and grab my towel, heading back up the grassy hill before Manny can respond.

Stone One

My secret tradition goes like this…

Some nights I gather the flat black stones I collect from the lake and etch my initials into their soft surfaces.

Then, throughout my days at Copper Cove, I hide these rocks in special places around campus.

My grandpa was the one to start this tradition, back when he was my age: leaving eight stones each summer, in the places that mattered most to him.

He said it was his way to ground himself in Copper Cove, to pay tribute to important things.

Of course, the practice of leaving personal totems appealed to my childhood self, like I was scouting locations in my own fantasy kingdom, or leaving behind a personal treasure map.

Grandpa also said, just like anything else that was special, Copper Cove had broken parts—and that the stones were a way to heal these parts.

My current self could definitely stand for some healing, too.

So when the mood strikes, I explore campus until I find the home that feels most right for each stone.

On the morning of this fourth day, I leave my first stone in plain sight: the hill behind the Auditorium, on the top step of the cracked and weed-filled stairs.

I know these steps must have once led somewhere, but now they lead nowhere.

It is my tribute to things forgotten, and to things foretold.

Chapter Seven

I'm a few minutes early to meet Hazel this morning, so I hang a left past the faded yellow panels of Melody, the music-practice cottage, and bound up the stairs of the Inn porch to soak in the scene. The Inn, crown jewel of the campus, is a massive Victorian-style building painted mauve and white, with an angled copper roof for which the Cove was named—though this roof is no longer copper-colored, having long ago turned as green as the Statue of Liberty. Most of the Inn's wraparound porch faces the lake, and it's made of white picket fencing, creaky wooden floorboards, and hanging flowerpots.

The Inn porch is already populated with dozens of morning readers enjoying novels and newspapers over cups of coffee, cradled by rocking chairs that are likely older than me. As I walk through pockets of space, the floral couches and cracked leather armchairs eventually give way to a trellis-lined outdoor hallway. It's overgrown with thick green vines and leads down to the Boathouse.

I find Hazel there in a lawn chair on the second-floor deck, writing furiously in her little black notebook. It rests against a larger novel—likely number thirty-something of the year. According to her Instagram, Hazel is attempting to read fifty-two books this year, one a week.

She's worried starting college might interfere with her flow, but I suspect Hazel will end up reading three times as much, aiming for her English major with a double minor in Women's and African American studies. True to form, Hazel is reading a graphic novel collection of *Bitch Planet,* an intersectional feminist dystopia.

Hazel seems oblivious to the spectacular lake view, her eyes laser focused and her freckled nose crinkled the way it always is when she's lost in thought. I think I might be finding Hazel in her most pure state, so I hate to interrupt. However, our solo kayaking session is another important tradition and I already postponed it by a day, blaming a cloudy-afternoon sky instead of the truth: I had to get myself together before talking to Hazel, especially about Griffin.

Instead of dwelling on this, I decide to call up an old joke we haven't revisited in years. I duck behind Hazel's chair and say, in my best cartoon voice:

"Hmmm NuNu."

Hazel startles and almost drops her pen, until she realizes it's me.

"Hammm HeHe," she answers, in her own goblin voice. "Wow, I haven't heard NuNu-HeHe in years! How did we even come up with that?"

"I honestly have no idea, except for sugar rush gibberish," I laugh. "But that whole summer we pretended it was a greeting in our own private language?"

"I remember clear as this fine day, Sir Mops-A-Lot." Hazel slips into her accent, standing and stretching out.

"Shall we commence our morning of boating leisure, Lady Scoops-A-Loops?"

"Indeed we shall!" she answers, hooking her arm around mine. "Griffin is meeting Ariana at the Craft Shop, so we have the whole morning to ourselves. How that boy developed a skill for stained glassmaking I will never understand."

"Yeah, his whole Renaissance man shtick is pretty annoying. Leave something for the rest of us?" I joke. "But since Griffin said he's making something for your dorm, I asked Ariana to paint something for mine."

"Yeah, she's another annoying one. An international Pre-Med prodigy who can sing and paint? Positively greedy!"

Hazel smiles and hands back the pen she must have borrowed—another thing she can never seem to keep track of—to an older gentleman sitting on the deck. We walk down the steps to the first floor of the Boathouse, which is made entirely of wood—the stairs, the walls, the many racks holding canoes and kayaks and various oars. The water of the lake lolls against the motorboats moored to the extended docks, lapping against their permanently wet edges. We walk by several pillars filled with colorful life vests before arriving at the boat-rental desk.

"Well, I'll be, if it ain't Hazel and Luca, in living color," Coop says, the thick Southern drawl rolling out of his mouth.

Coop the Boatman has become a permanent fixture in the last five years. After a few military tours, he left his Mississippi roots behind to live and work full-time in Copper Cove. He's the boating supervisor in the summer months and the snow-activity coordinator in the winter, and the surprisingly riotous emcee of the talent show. I always have a hard time imagining Coop the Boatman anywhere but Copper Cove, as if all six feet of him just sprouted here fully grown.

"Coop, I've been looking forward to seeing you all summer," I say, reaching across the desk to shake his hand.

"Day four is late for y'all," Coop replies, shaking back so vigorously that the bait and tackle on his beige fishing vest shimmies and shakes. "But don't you worry, I've got one blue and one green kayak stashed away with your names on 'em."

I've never really met anyone like Coop in my East Coast suburban life. It always amazes me how slowly and methodically he speaks, like he has all the time in the world. Despite only being in his late twenties, Coop has the spirit of a languishing senior citizen, resigned to riding out his twilight years in the snug embrace of Copper Cove.

"How has your year been?" I ask, despite already knowing the exact answer.

"The world hasn't ended yet and I'm still kickin', so I can't complain," Coop says, repeating the response he gives every year. "Now Luca, you as excited for college as Hazel here seems to be?"

"A little nervous, but mostly excited," I say, turning to accept one of the life vests Hazel has plucked from a nearby pillar rack.

"You know what they say about nerves," Coop begins. "If you don't have butterflies in your stomach, you're nothin' but an empty cocoon."

∞

I run my hand through the water, creating swirls as my fingers drag along. My kayak slices through the lake's dark surface, which appears rather menacing if I look ahead, all black and choppy. However, if I look to the side of my kayak, the streaks of sunlight make the water clear all the way to the bottom.

As I so often forget, it's a simple matter of perspective.

I tried to remind myself of that when Hazel asked if we could paddle in a new direction instead of heading to our usual destination of Gulley Island. The shift in our tradition pinged me at first, but I told myself things were already different this year—and that more shifts were likely coming. So as we paddle, I try to rehearse the resolutions I set during my latest swim. It began with acknowledging that I might actually have some private right to feel betrayed by Hazel. In my own mind we'd made a silent pact, but Hazel went behind my back and took Griffin for herself.

Then, after this indulgence, I forced myself to face the reality that I can't actually be mad at Hazel for violating feelings I never expressed.

I cycle through these thoughts until we arrive at the small inlet near Onita Cove. Its curved banks are occupied mostly by untouched woods. Hazel chose well—this is the perfect place for a private catch-up session. I rest my paddle across my lap, allowing my kayak to drift with the water and the breeze.

"Okay Lady Scoops, time to spill. How did this whole Griffin thing go down?"

Hazel hesitates a moment, glancing down at the ever-changing surface of the lake.

"There's no big romantic story, honestly," she begins. "We were both here and it was just the two of us, without you and Ariana, for the first time. And…I don't know, all the things standing in our way seemed to disappear. We were both single at the same time and together for the whole summer. It took a week to adjust, but then all of a sudden hanging out just started feeling…easy. Then our second week we were playing a dumb game of Candyland on a rainy night and he just kissed me. The rest happened pretty naturally, from there."

I fight to keep my face even, but each word wages a war inside me. I want to be happy for my two favorite people, I really do. But I also want to know what it's like to kiss Griffin on a rainy night.

How can it be Hazel, of all people, who gets to?

"Luca…" Hazel starts, searching for the right words. When she gets like this, I always imagine the letters scrolling behind her eyes, cracking some personal code. "Are you really okay with all this?"

I freeze. I was hoping Hazel wouldn't ask this, at least not so directly. I really don't want to lie to her, but the truth won't help either. Still, this is Hazel—she'll be able to tell something is wrong with me, no matter what I say. So I look down at the water again, trying to decide what won't drive an invisible wedge between us.

"I mean, I know how much Copper Cove and our traditions mean to you," Hazel adds. "They mean a lot to us, too."

I exhale. Because Hazel has just provided me with a precious escape.

"I forget what it's like to be around people who know me so well," I finally say, pushing a smile through. "Yeah, I guess if I'm being honest, I am a bit afraid that you and Griffin being together is going to change things. It's weird, thinking of you two as so close all of a sudden. Like, are you going to tell each other everything we talk about, now? And I don't even want to think about what would happen to us if you two…you know, broke up, or something."

"We don't want anything to change either," Hazel answers the moment I stop talking. "Griffin and I promised not to let anything that happens between us mess with C4, no matter what. And if it makes you feel better, Griffin and I already talked about it and we're going to try to stay together when we go to college. UVA might not be super close to Dartmouth, but that's what FaceTime is for, right?"

Nothing about what Hazel just said makes me feel any better, but I keep smiling and nodding all the same. This will get easier, I scream in my head. Over time, I probably won't feel so…

Left behind.

"Don't worry about me, I think I'm just extra sensitive to change with college coming," I say. "And also, after the last few months. I was just kind of hoping this summer would be one for the ages…but it still can be. It *will* be."

"Hell yes, it will be," Hazel answers. "But first you're going to have to explain these cryptic allusions you keep making to things being tough. And don't give me that Luca crap and say it's nothing. I can tell your gears have been grinding."

I feel my chest pull into a tight knot. I don't really want to relive what happened, but I also know telling someone will probably make me feel better. Besides, Hazel is still the person I trust most in the world—that can still be true. In fact, that's what I'm fighting so hard for—to keep this true.

I take another deep breath as our kayaks lilt and bob, steadying myself before starting.

"All right, all right. So you know how I'm not out back home to anyone except my family, and Frances?"

Hazel nods—of course she knows. She was actually the one to make sense of my friendship with Frances for me in the first place. When we met our freshman year at a brother-sister school event, Frances and I seemed like polar opposites: life of the party versus wallflower. But Hazel's writer brain was the first to break down why Frances and I complemented one another: I grounded Frances, while she pushed me out of my comfort zone.

It seemed so obvious once Hazel said it that way, but it hadn't occurred to me. Frances was just the only person back home who seemed to get me—or who took the time to, anyway. She was also the first person to call me out about being gay and in love with Griffin, who I apparently talked about way more than I realized. Once I finally admitted both to Frances, she tried to convince me to come fully out, or at least hook up on the DL with the few other out kids in our neighboring towns. I never could muster much interest. Apart from the terror of being potentially outed, I just didn't feel ready.

"You know how Frances is always trying to get me to 'live that gay life'?" I continue. "In a weaker moment, she convinced me to make a faceless Grindr profile, with all these private pictures and some of me shirtless. I know, so dumb."

"Not dumb if it's what you want," Hazel says.

"Well, it turns out it wasn't. I met exactly one guy and learned that random hookups are not for me. Shocking, I know."

The truth is that one random hookup made me realize all I really want is Griffin August, but that isn't a particularly helpful detail to include right now.

"I deleted the app and Frances dropped it for a while. Until we got back from Christmas break, and this senior at the public school, Kevin, came out. He's on the football team and super-hot—like, Michael B. Jordan hot—so naturally I constructed an entire personality for him in my head based on his social media before even meeting him."

"As one does," Hazel follows. "Let me guess: Your version of Kevin was really kind and soft-spoken, despite being one of the popular guys. He loved movies, played video games, and preferred tallish Italian Catholic boys."

"Something like that," I sigh, cringing at my own predictability. "So I kept picturing ways to run into him and played out all the conversations we'd have, about our favorite TV shows and being closeted in a small town and not really having anyone to relate to. Anyway, I guess I must have talked about that kind of thing a lot, because Frances got super-annoyed with me. She kept saying she wanted me to stop daydreaming and actually do something about it."

"What did she do, Luca?" Hazel asks, her face growing grim.

I want to pause again, but I decide it's just better to charge through.

"She got into my phone one night during a sleepover, after I passed out. Then she re-downloaded the Grindr account—because she had set it up—and started a conversation with Kevin. He seemed interested, so Frances unlocked all my photos."

My throat goes dry, thinking about what happened next.

"I guess seeing my photos, Kevin lost interest. I don't really know how this next part happened, if Kevin was at a party that night and left his phone somewhere, or if he actually gave it to... Whatever. Either way, this idiot girl with a stupid gossip account posted screenshots of the whole thing."

I still can't fathom how someone could do something like this, reduce my biggest and most embarrassing moment to clickbait. Still, that was precisely what it ended up being. I still shudder remembering the post title: "Closeted Catholic Boy Swings Above League + Strikes Out Hard (Well, Soft)."

"Oh my god," Hazel whispers. "There's an account like that at my school too, but..."

I remember the feeling the first time I saw the post, after it had already bounced around the corners of social media: The blood rushing from my face to my head, the way the world seemed to tilt on its axis. The...powerlessness.

"Everyone in a three-town radius saw it, including

all the guys at my school. Life there got…difficult, after that. The pranks and the bullying died down after a few weeks, but then I just went back to being invisible, eventually."

"What about Frances?" Hazel asks.

"She insisted she was only trying to help. That yeah, it sucked, but now I was free to be myself. She called it tough love. She didn't even apologize. I think deep down she was mortified, but like, admitting even a shred of wrongdoing would unravel her whole self, or something. I don't know… I haven't spoken to her since."

"And this Kevin guy? Or the blog girl?"

"I never tracked them down. What would be the point?"

I can tell Hazel has several points, but I can also feel the pinpricks of panic stabbing at my hands and feet. It's still so hard to understand how my best friend and another gay guy—the ones who are supposed to protect me most— were the ones who cut me down the quickest. It would be one thing if I had been brave, if I had taken this swing on my own and struck out—but this had all been done behind my back. So for the rest of senior year, I retreated inwards even further: Swimming. Inhabiting fantasy worlds. Sketching. Counting down the days to Copper Cove, then to college, where I could reinvent myself.

Of course, alongside all that came the devastating panic attacks.

I don't want to think or talk about those most of all, because sometimes just contemplating one can be enough to trigger it. I refuse to give the panic that power now that

I've gotten it under control. Especially not in a place that means as much to me as Copper Cove.

"Luca, I'm so..." Hazel tries. "I can't imagine how hard that must have been. Or how alone you must've felt. I wish you'd called, or something."

I honestly thought about it more than once, but C4 mostly texts when we're back home. Besides, I'd never want anyone, let alone C4, to see me that way. That...*damaged*.

"Well, I'm really glad I told you now. But honestly, I just want to leave it all behind me. So I don't think I'm going to tell Griffin or Ariana, if that's okay?"

"Yeah, I understand that, I guess," Hazel says. For a few beats she processes another thought with silent fury. "Luca, I know you didn't come out back home because you didn't have a lot...because you didn't think it was important to tell relative strangers. But you're not going to do that at college, right? I mean, maybe if you put yourself out there from the start..."

"That's my plan," I say, hoping—no, *knowing*—I'll have to be braver when the time comes.

"Good," Hazel sighs. "Because we love you—I love you—just the way you are. And more people deserve to see the real and true Mr. Mops."

I smile a genuine smile, hearing this. At the same time, I feel kind of hollowed. Like I've just purged a little bit of this nightmare by telling Hazel, but that doing so also took something else out of me.

"Hey, what do you think that is?" I ask, intentionally shifting the subject by pointing at the shore.

The water has pulled our kayaks around another

bend, towards a small peninsula housing a mini stone castle. It looks like it must have one day been manicured and lovely but has since crumbled and cracked with age.

"That's actually why I wanted to paddle out here," Hazel answers. "Back when the Weiss family still lived in Weiss Hall, apparently this was where they held afternoon tea. At night, young couples who were guests would sneak onto its roof to 'look at the stars.' So they nicknamed it The Spoon Holder. Scandalous, no?"

"Positively salacious. How do you know that?"

"Griffin told me when we kayaked out here the other day. You know him, always the history buff, especially when it comes to Copper Cove. I thought you'd get a kick out of it, too."

I picture Griffin and Hazel together, there in The Spoon Holder, and suddenly I want to know so much more. I want to ask if they've had sex yet. Hell, I want to know what sex is like in the first place, even though it will be different for me. I want to ask if Griffin's mom knows about them dating, given the lingering weirdness between all of our parents. Or if Hazel has gotten to see the inside of August Manor or spend any real time there. I want to ask what Griffin's skin feels like or what kind of kisser he is, but instead I let myself drift.

I close my eyes, trying to change my vision of Hazel in this moment. I imagine her not as Griffin's girlfriend, but instead as Evergreen the Wise, Scribe for the Ages. Contemplator of thoughts and seer of great truths, whose glowing eyes glimpse all, despite having been blinded long ago.

But I come crashing back into reality when Hazel starts screaming.

I can't fathom what might make her shriek so loud, until I see the first spider crawl across her kayak. It's thick and black and immediately followed by a second, much smaller spider.

Then a third.

And a fourth.

Then dozens more, all crawling out of the inside of the green kayak in a haphazard parade.

Terror rises in Hazel's eyes as the baby spiders stream out, some across her arms and legs. She tries to shake them off, but they cling to her, their sticky legs digging into her skin and clothes. I paddle furiously to get my kayak closer, but the spiders keep moving faster than Hazel can swat them away, climbing all the way up her neck. Before I can reach her, Hazel jerks wildly, trying to get out of the coated kayak. I watch her in horror, trapped in the middle of the lake, covered in frantic clawing spiders. Then the kayak tips, sending Hazel into the lake with a desperate splash.

Even though I'm terrified and disgusted, I instantly bail into the water to help. My head springs out of the lake beside Hazel's, both of us buoyed by our yellow life vests. She gasps and chokes, kicking her legs and pumping her arms to get away. I maneuver my body between Hazel and the infested green kayak, as if that might make a difference.

"What the hell?" I shout. "Are you okay?"

Hazel can't speak, so she gives a weak nod instead as she keeps shaking out her limbs underwater. Everyone knows we both don't love bugs, but Hazel especially hates spiders. Something about the way they move, she always says, their terrible little legs skittering back and forth.

The same legs that just covered her entire body.

"Was there a nest in there or something?" I ask. "Do spiders even have nests? Why didn't they come out before?"

Neither of us have any answers. So I just bob beside Hazel in silence while the spiders thrash in the lake, not drowning but not quite swimming either.

Stone Two

For my second stone, I take another kayak out on the lake the next day instead of going to breakfast.

Gliding through the water as the sun continues to rise, I try my best to avoid being seen, fancying myself a covert explorer.

The lake is not yet filled with its usual recreationalists, so this task is not impossible.

When I reach Onita Cove, I beach my kayak on a slim strip of sand littered with little rocks.

Then I climb onto the outer banks on my hands and knees.
I leave my second stone in the window of the crumbling castle.

It is my tribute to loves past.

Chapter Eight

The days eventually fall into a familiar pattern, the usual rhythms punctuated by strict mealtimes and activity plans. It always amazes me how it only takes a few days to return to one's Copper Cove routine, or any routine for that matter. Now, at the end of Family Week One, C4 is very ready to celebrate one of our most special traditions: Hazel's birthday. And for her eighteenth, Garrett has arranged a particularly lovely night.

"So how did everything taste?" he asks from his seat at the head of the dinner table, the whites of his chef uniform crisp against his eyepatch and deep-brown skin.

Hazel might get her eyes from her mother—who divorced Garrett right around the time my dad moved out—but Hazel's intellectual curiosity comes purely from Garrett.

Ariana answers first by lifting her empty plate, which she has literally licked clean. Griffin is the only one still eating, thanks to the upper-crust manners that make him an overly polite dinner guest. Then again, Griffin was also the only one to ask for a third helping, hoping to score some extra points with Garrett.

"Everything was five-star, by any standards," Mom says.

"It helps that Hazel's favorite meal happens to be

eggplant tagine," I add. It also helps that Garrett happens to be a chef of some renown, and that for Hazel's birthday, we have his pop-up restaurant in Weiss Hall all to ourselves.

The old Weiss Hall mansion is a dark, Gothic structure located on the outskirts of the campus. Its relative distance makes it an unpopular place for guests to stay, though not as much as the almost-confirmed fact it is haunted as hell. Griffin often confuses my resistance to his spirited conspiracy theories with disbelief. The truth is I acknowledge Copper Cove has its share of creepy history—I just don't think that lore makes it any less fantastical. This particular bit alleges that the Weiss's teenage son was murdered in this mansion in the 1920s and that his spirit hasn't allowed anyone else to rest here properly since.

While Weiss Hall might not be a great place to sleep, it turns out to be a fantastic place to feast. In celebration of Hazel's eighteenth year of life, we spend the night eating risotto rolls and squash samosas over lengthy conversations about immigration rights and the role of Beyoncé in the narrative surrounding American Black women. The soundtrack, carefully curated by Hazel, shifts between Lauryn Hill and SZA, Boyz II Men and Kehlani. By the time I have to undo the top button of my jeans to make room for more food, we're onto a hearty debate comparing RuPaul's and Oprah's respective legacies as media moguls.

It's like a piece of Hazel has broken off and sprouted into this little pocket dimension: a melting pot of coziness and good food, lofty intellect and grounded soul. She practically radiates joy—which is especially nice to see after the now-infamous kayak mishap from earlier this week.

Understandably, Hazel was traumatized by the experience—and Coop has since apologized profusely. His best working theory, after a painstaking investigation, is that a spider must have laid eggs inside her kayak and they broke open while she was using it, perhaps because she disturbed them with her feet. In the wake of this natural disaster Coop checked all the other boats personally and has implemented a new system of routine sweeps to prevent this from happening ever again. If Coop the Boatman takes anything seriously, it's his duty towards recreational safety.

This has contributed to another recurring topic throughout tonight's dinner: our bad luck with wildlife this summer.

"Well, if anyone deserves an especially epic birthday dinner this year, it's Hazel," Griffin adds. "Between our first-night brush with the dock spiders and her kayak freak nesting, it's nice to have a slow night in a haunted house."

"I'll take intangible ghosts over tangible creeps any day," Ariana says, shuddering. "My dad found *another* dead racoon with its insides ripped out stashed behind our cottage. And I told you I keep finding those flowers I hate blooming around campus, the ones with those visible seedpod circles."

"Right, the ones that remind you of diseased flesh," I reply. "You know, you'll probably have to get over your trypophobia if you're ever going to become a doctor."

I suppress a shudder as I finish, remembering my own shower stall slithering earful. I already decided that's a secret I'm taking to the grave, plus I don't want to add more fuel to Griffin's conspiracy theory that Copper Cove has its very own Demogorgon running around, haunting us all with miniature disasters.

"I think this is actually a fitting dinner setting given our summer so far," Hazel says. "Weiss Hall is the perfect example of how historical detail can become myth. I bet fifty years from now, the tale of the girl in the spider kayak will be embellished with an ending where I get eaten alive or drowned by the spiders, becoming a ghost just like the Weiss's son."

"This conversation is ruining the ambiance," Garrett says next, effectively shutting down this topic—and not for the first time tonight.

I notice his eyes shifting to Mom. It makes sense, given their own far-more-severe Copper Cove teenage disaster.

"Everything about dinner has been absolutely perfect, Dad," Hazel responds, also seeming to note the shift in our parents.

"After the day Hazel put us through, I feel like I've earned dessert," Ariana says. "Is it just me, or does that hike up to Gabe's Pond get longer every year?"

"Forget the hike, I always forget how grueling archery can be," Griffin adds, pushing his finally empty plate away. "My arms and back are aching."

"Yeah, well Katniss Everdeen over here looks completely unfazed," I say, nudging Hazel. "She wasn't even winded once during the hike, and then her archery scores blew the rest of us out of the water."

"On any other day I'd be mortified by all this praise and attention," Hazel proclaims. "But not today. So please, keep it coming."

"In that case, I'd like to raise a toast," Garrett says, lifting up his glass of Cabernet Sauvignon and prompting everyone to raise their own. Mom insisted on letting us kids "live a little," at least under their careful watch.

"To my little girl, who never misses a target she sets her sights on."

We all connect our glasses and drink to Hazel, whose smile looks especially bright in the candlelight.

"This seems like a good time for presents. If you don't mind me doing it before dessert, Mr. Hart?" Griffin asks, before adding, "I mean Garrett. Sorry, habit."

Garrett nods, the traces of a smirk crossing his otherwise-impassive face. It's obvious Garrett likes intimidating Griffin, especially now that he's dating his daughter.

"I thought I said no presents?" Hazel says. "Forcing you all to participate in my ideal day is present enough. Seriously."

"Well, these technically aren't from me," Griffin answers. He stands and collects a tote bag stashed in the corner of the dining room. "My mom actually sent them along, as an apology for not being able to make it to dinner tonight."

With Griffin's back temporarily turned, the entire table tenses. Every year when we celebrate Hazel's birthday, Griffin's mom always declines her invitation, finding excuses in various unmissable galas and likely fictional summer flus. However, Wendy has never felt the need to send along a present before. And judging from the look that passes between Garrett and Sofia, they too find these presents to be the only strange thing about Wendy's absence this year. They both eye the stack Griffin places on the table like a potential time bomb.

"She wanted to do something special because this is an important birthday," Griffin continues. "If I'm being honest, she left the actual buying to me—though she'd kill me if she knew I told you that. She instructed me to get something charming and personal, which I think I did. Hazel, I know you don't love the fuss over getting gifts, so I actually got one for all four of us."

"Griffin, that's so sweet. You really..." Hazel begins, before eyeing the presents more closely. They look like they've been wrapped by a toddler—an impatient one, at that. "Wow, you really shouldn't have. Who taught you to wrap presents?"

"Hey, I could have just asked one of the housekeepers to do it!" Griffin replies. "But I thought this would be a more unique touch."

"Unique, indeed," Hazel laughs, kissing Griffin on one of his blushing cheeks.

Ripping through the haphazardly taped paper together, we unearth four matching hoodies, made of some very upscale fabric. Though what makes them truly special are the matching block letters written across the front: *C4*. Griffin has chosen four different colors, to match our clubhouse keys: forest green for Hazel, navy for me, dark purple for Ariana, and pale yellow for himself. I get a whiff of the unworn sweater as I unfurl it and it somehow it smells like Griffin. It gives my heart an aching jolt, especially as I see the look on Hazel's face...

I can't recall a time I've ever seen her happier.

A pulse of panic snaps alongside the envy in my chest, but I take a deep breath and will it to evaporate. I will be *happy,* damn it.

"Griffin August, I forgive you for the wrapping massacre," Hazel says, standing to give him a hug. "They're perfect, I love them."

"I am so never taking mine off," Ariana says, pulling hers over her shoulders and causing her gold bangles to jangle. "What do we think? Fit for a queen?"

"This is the classiest hoodie I have ever seen," I add, putting on my own. "Thank you, Griffin-slash-Griffin's-mom."

"Yes, please send our thanks as well," Mom says, in that overly polite tone I know means she's annoyed. "It really is very thoughtful, since she couldn't be here."

"Actually, she sent me something for you both, too," Griffin says, his voice full of caution as he produces two small envelopes.

I think the sight of these pastel missives might knock Garrett and Mom clean over. Still, they both take their envelopes with a silent nod, their eyes meeting for a tense glance. Sometimes I really can't stand not knowing the full story of what went down between our parents. The emotion they exude is nearly palpable.

"It's an invitation for all of us to a dinner party at August Manor," Mom says, keeping her voice even as she reads. "For tomorrow night. How lovely. Did your mother say what the occasion was?"

"Oh, you know my mom, she's not exactly forthcoming," Griffin sighs. "She just said it was about time we all got together, especially now that I'm dating Hazel. As if we don't all get together all the time without her..."

Mom forces a smile, but I can see something in her eyes—especially as she flashes Garrett another look. She suspects there's some other reason for this unprecedented dinner invitation. A reason that fills them both with visible...dread? What's that about?

I know neither parent will tell us, even if I ask directly. They'll find some circular answer, then change the subject. As usual, the details of their Copper Cove past remain locked away. So maybe it's time I took more of an active interest in Griffin's historical research project... especially if somehow we can use this upcoming dinner party as a way in?

"Oh hey, Ariana, you're invited, too," Griffin says.

With all my focus on the parents, I hadn't noticed the expression on Ariana's face. I don't recognize it, either.

"It's fine," Ariana says. "I'm surprised your mom even knows who I am."

"Of course she knows!" Griffin tries. "It's all weird, if you ask me. Even weirder because my grandpa is coming to dinner too. He hasn't attended a social function since I was in diapers, or so I'm told."

Ariana smiles and shrugs. She's been friends with us since before we were old enough to remember anything, so it's easy to forget her family doesn't have the same history at Copper Cove. Her parents are friendly enough, but their annual three-week vacation to their cottage in August Bay is a rare respite from their usual travels, so her parents tend to spend a lot of quiet time here.

I make a mental note to talk to Ariana later, but it turns out there's little time for anyone to further comfort her. As the song changes to "Waterfalls" by TLC, Hazel leaps out of her chair.

"Okay, we are so having a dance party. And no one can say no because it's my birthday," she announces, before breaking into the first verse of the song.

Ariana immediately follows suit, jumping out of her chair to dance around Hazel. Garrett takes this as his cue to slip into the kitchen and prepare dessert, but Mom is never one to stand down from a dance challenge. Grabbing my hand, she pulls me out onto the faux dance floor first, then does the same with Griffin.

"Ah, I always forget dancing is the one natural talent that eludes Griffin August!" Hazel laughs as Griffin bounces, terribly off the beat.

"Please, just stick to the lakes that we're used to," Griffin contends, executing a pop-and-lock maneuver that would make a Muppet look coordinated.

I do my best to ignore how painfully charming it is.

∞

"Griffin, where are you taking us?" Ariana asks. "It's way too dark out here."

"Almost there," Griffin calls back from his spot leading the pack. "I found this place while poking around campus the other day."

"You know, the hot guy leading a group of friends into the woods to show them something cool—that's how so many slasher movies start."

While I'm usually all for deeper Copper Cove exploration, I have to agree with Ariana. I'd much rather be waiting for Mom and Garrett to finish cleaning up in the well-lit parlor room—not scaling down the hill behind Weiss Hall. I can see the lights of the Children's Pavilion below, illuminating the old wooden pirate ship that doubles as a playground. That's where Hazel and I first became friends with Ariana, letting her join our intrepid, mermaid-capturing crew. Normally this sight would fill me with nostalgia, but at the moment it only serves as a reminder of how steep the fall down the hill would be if we slipped.

"I have hiked more in this one day than I have all year," Ariana groans.

"Hey, you lived in LA for a while, doesn't that mean you're supposed to love hikes?" Griffin teases.

"Sure, the kind where you can pose in your yoga pants on some gradual incline with a cityscape in the background," Ariana sighs. "But I guess it's good we're giving Sofia and Garrett some alone time, to rekindle their romance."

"Don't even joke," Hazel answers. "Luca and I spent way too much time trying to *Parent Trap* them together when we were younger."

"Indeed. Sadly, expert matchmakers we were not."

As we finally reach a somewhat flat landing, I can just barely make out Griffin turning right up ahead. Looking down, I'm slightly reassured to find we're on some kind of path, hooking back around Weiss Hall.

"Griffin, how did you even find wherever it is we're going?" Hazel asks.

"I was reading an old history of Copper Cove and

there was this section on the Weisses. They lived here before my great-grandfather bought the land and—"

"And I'm sure this has nothing to do with your unending quest to prove Copper Cove is actually on the Hellmouth or whatever?" Hazel interrupts.

"Just wait until you see this, you're going to—oh, here."

Griffin stops suddenly, causing the rest of us to bump into one another in the semi-darkness. As far as I can tell, we've arrived at a stone wall set into the face of the hill, perhaps even as part of the mansion's foundation. Griffin turns up the flashlight on his phone, which he brought only for this purpose. We see the wall is actually a door, with words engraved into its cracked face:

THE WEISS CRYPT.

An involuntary chill rolls up my spine.

"Griffin, what the hell?" Ariana yells, slapping his arm. "What makes you think we want to see a crypt in the middle of the night?"

"Relax," Griffin says. "As much as I'd like to say this place is full of dead bodies killed by the Weiss spirit, according to the book the Weisses didn't actually use this as a crypt. They just called it that to keep people out."

"Then what did they use it for?" Hazel asks, stepping up to examine the door.

"No one really knows; the key has been lost for decades," Griffin answers, pointing at a rusty padlock. "It's generally assumed the place was emptied out, but the more exciting theories say it was some kind of secret clubhouse, or a wine cellar, or maybe even a panic room. I was actually thinking we could all come up with our own theories, but then I looked at the padlock. There's something written on the underside."

"What does it say?" I ask, a bit more eagerly than I intend.

"Go look for yourselves. You wouldn't believe me if I told you."

Under Griffin's instruction, we gather around the tiny padlock. Griffin angles his phone, shining the light onto the padlock as Hazel lifts it away from the door as far as she can. Leaning in, I'm just barely able to make out the letters scratched into the metal:

TOMMY.

"Holy crap, isn't that the name of your parents' friend, the one who died when they were our age?" Ariana asks, peering from the back.

Hazel and I are too stunned to answer. All my excitement immediately shrivels. Something about this just got a touch too real, standing at the doorstep of a long-dead teenager. My desire for answers disappears. It's like picking at a scab I won't be able to cover again. Could Griffin be right? Have we all been willfully closing our eyes to some dark mystery right in front of us, lingering under Copper Cove's serene surface?

These are not thoughts I want to entertain, but that's the thing about ideas: they're insidious once they've been implanted. The sense that this particular idea might change things for all of us already gnaws at the back of my mind.

"I know, I was just as stunned when I saw it," Griffin says excitedly. "Do you think this is where Tommy is buried? I was wondering, now that we found this, do you think maybe we can ask one of your parents about—"

Griffin stops speaking, because he hears the same thing we all do: a faint sound, coming from behind the stone. My bones freeze and my breath catches in my throat as I try to make it out. It's a kind of high-pitched ringing tone. It sounds a little like wind whistling through the cracks in the door, or maybe even like something...

Whimpering?

"You shouldn't be here."

This new, deep voice causes me to actually jump, along with Griffin and Hazel. Ariana shrieks and I feel a burst of adrenaline flood my system, but I can't make out where this voice has come from. Griffin frantically points his flashlight outwards, illuminating the dark woods until he shines it down the path...

Where Garrett stands, his arms crossed and his expression stoic.

"This path is dangerous at night," he says. "And there's nothing to see in that crypt."

"How do you know?" Hazel asks, the only one who'd dare question Garrett when his tone is this stern.

"I got a full report on Weiss Hall when I took it over for the restaurant," Garrett answers. "Now follow me. This way back is longer, but safer."

"Dad, there's a name on the padlock," Hazel tries again. "Tommy."

"Sofia is waiting for us," Garrett says, his back turned.

"But we know you had a friend named Tommy when you were all—"

"I told you to follow me."

The words are delivered finitely, with a chainsaw-rattle intensity. They silence Hazel.

In all my years knowing Garrett, he's always been reserved, perhaps a bit distant, but never *harsh*. And he might not have raised his voice just now, but he didn't need to.

We walk back without another word.

As unsettled as I feel—as ruffled as we all likely feel—I can tell something else just shifted. That, despite Garrett's attempt to sever our interest, he just uncorked something that can't be rebottled.

It's why Griffin almost smirks as we trudge along. He can feel it, too.

It's time we got some better answers.

Chapter Nine

Hazel is lost in heaven. Her heaven, at least.

I watch absentmindedly as she floats around Mom's Hemlock room like a moth to flame. As usual, the floor of Mom's room is covered with dozens of stacks of books. All year-round she amasses a personal arsenal of galleys and free copies from work and saves them to bring to Copper Cove. Then every summer she donates them to the Library and the Inn Porch Sale—but not before she gives Hazel first dibs for her birthday. Hazel has managed to suspend her feelings about our little crypt creep to enjoy this tradition, so I try my best to do the same.

"It's like watching a caged animal being returned to its natural habitat," Ariana whispers, standing by the bathroom beside Griffin.

"I'm going to make you leave if you can't be quiet," Hazel says. "This is my own personal Christmas, and I will not have it tarnished by your taunts."

Mom stands in the doorway, yawning. She looks exhausted, but also like she's savoring every second of this. The book rummage has always been Mom and Hazel's special thing, but still, something about how Mom hovers feels particularly...eerie? Usually, she's on her way to sleeping in Hazel's room by this point.

Another annual birthday tradition is Mom and Hazel swapping Hemlock rooms for the night; this way Hazel and Ariana can sleep in the adjoining room to Griffin and me for a good old-fashioned slumber party. It's always a night filled with eating junk food, listening to vintage girl groups on the stereo, and telling ghost stories. Though right now there's only one story I want to hear. While Garrett might have remained a closed vault all the way back up here to Hemlock, I have a feeling I can get Mom to budge. Especially given the combination of Wendy's envelopes of doom, the crypt we just unearthed, and her obviously sentimental vibe.

"Hey Mom, before you head to Hazel's room…" I start. "We didn't mean to upset Garrett earlier, when we went down to that Weiss Crypt place."

"He knows," Mom answers, clearly wanting to end the conversation—but also not leaving the way she normally does.

"On that padlock though, do you think it was the same Tommy you were friends with when you were our age? Is that, like, where he's buried? Or was it just, you know, a coincidence?"

Mom sighs, as everyone turns to her—including Hazel, despite the book bounty before her.

"Neither," Mom begins reluctantly. "That crypt was actually Tommy's favorite place in Copper Cove. He loved scary stuff and horror movies and pranks, so he would always spook the other kids by bringing them there at night and telling them stories he made up about what was in there. He never actually got inside though, so he scratched his name on the padlock to try and lay claim to it."

"Oh," I say, trying to build to the question I really want to ask. "I know you hate talking about what happened with Tommy, and I get that... But you always said you'd tell us what happened when we were older."

"And let me guess: you're going to argue you're the same age now as when it happened to us, which means you're old enough to at least hear about it?" Mom fills in. "And with this August dinner party reuniting us, you all deserve the full picture?"

Mom tries to smile, but she can't. It makes me feel guilty for taking advantage of her weak spot, for capitalizing on us finding her dead friend's secret hideout...but not so guilty to let her off the hook. Because while Ariana's interest is only mildly piqued, Griffin hangs on every single syllable. Even Hazel suspends her interest in the surrounding books, listening just as eagerly.

"I guess you're right. You're old enough to know, this year of all years."

Mom looks physically pained. It's almost enough to make me relent, until she finally opens up. "The four of us—Garrett and I, Wendy and Tommy—were going for a hike up to Diver's Rock, because that's where we had gone on our first double date. We'd all started dating the same day the summer before, so it was an anniversary of sorts. Gross, I know, to think of your parents as hormonal teenagers once upon a time."

Mom tries to joke, but it doesn't land—she's too nervous, too emotional to defuse the tension that has seeped into the room. We all force a laugh, just the same. I feel almost faint. I can't believe she's really telling us.

"Anyway, like I said, Tommy was always planning these pranks. We brought a picnic up there and Tommy thought it'd be funny to hide a tiny, harmless garter snake in the basket, because Wendy was petrified of snakes. Though she actually happened to love a good scare, given how 'predictable her trust-fund life was'—her words, not mine." Mom tries to remain impartial, but she can't help the touch of disdain that leaks into her voice.

"When Wendy opened the basket and saw the snake, she freaked out. I still don't know how, but she slipped and fell down the side of Diver's Rock. Not the jumping ledge, but the steeper ledge they've since sectioned off. Wendy was alive, thank god, but she fell onto some of the big rocks above the water and broke her leg. We should have gone to get help. I begged the boys to, but Tommy was so mortified he'd caused this, he went down to save Wendy himself. The climb down on that side is steep and slippery, and..."

Mom pauses, swallowing hard.

"Tommy lost his footing and he slipped, too. He hit his head on a rock on his way down and fell into the water, unconscious. We panicked. Garrett and I tried jumping off the normal ledge of Diver's Rock and swimming around, but there were more big rocks blocking the alcove where Tommy and Wendy were trapped. I couldn't even climb up, they were so slick with moss. Garrett tried and made it farther than me, but he slipped too and...

"Hazel, that's how your dad lost his eye, hitting his face while falling off that wet rock."

I feel a net of pain radiate out from my tailbone,

which sometimes happens when I hear about something physically horrific. The idea of losing an eye that way... Did it get pierced by a jagged rock? Or was it knocked out from the impact of the fall? On second thought, those are details I don't need to know.

"He never told me that," Hazel whispers.

"I know... Well, I swam Garrett back to shore and we went to get help. But by the time they got to Tommy, he'd drowned. It was all so...stupid. And senseless. After that, Copper Cove excavated all those rocks and fenced off that part of Diver's Rock, but the damage was done. Wendy stopped coming to campus and stopped talking to us entirely. To this day I don't know if she blames us. Anyway, it's hard for us to make sense of. Which is why we don't talk about it."

Mom finishes and when she does, I'm speechless.

It has happened very rarely in my life—and perhaps that's why I'm able to detect it so instantly. But I just *know* that Mom is lying.

Perhaps not about the larger story—that steep side of Diver's Rock is fenced off now with caution signs, and the emotional fallout to our families tracks. But she is definitely lying about the particulars. I don't really know how I can tell, but I can. It's like back when she'd tell me about Santa Claus or the tooth fairy. It's too rehearsed, too effortful. But I don't dare look to Griffin or Hazel to see if they agree, nor do I dream of calling Mom on this when she seems so raw. So...frightened.

But what is she so afraid to tell us?

"Garrett and I decided some years ago that we

wanted to remember Copper Cove as a happy place, especially because that's what Tommy would have wanted," Mom concludes. "And we wanted this place to be as special to all you kids as it was to us. Still, the three of us deal with his death in our own ways. Hazel, I know your dad doesn't show it, but he is the most sensitive about Tommy. They were like brothers. With you turning eighteen this year... just, don't take it personally if he seems off, okay?"

Hazel nods, and Mom forces a weary smile. Her eyes look like they're still brimming with a sea of unexpressed thoughts, but her face remains composed. I'm so overwhelmed by the truths and the maybe half-truths, I don't know what to say. But in this moment, I do decide something: I'm going to find out what really happened to Tommy. If not for myself, then for all these people I love. And for Copper Cove, because someone needs to close this chapter.

"We've avoided telling you because we don't want you to worry about it. Just have fun, you four. And happy birthday again, Hazel," Mom says finally.

She pauses again, seeming like she wants to say more—or like she wants to stay here with us all night? Instead, she closes her eyes and exhales.

"We're just down the hall if you need us, figlio mio."

With that, Mom turns and heads towards Hazel's Hemlock room, looking like she has to force every step.

We're left in stunned silence for what feels like a long time. I can only imagine Griffin and Hazel are processing very different thoughts and questions. *Is this why my mom is so closed off? Is this why my dad always seems like he has a secret burden to bear?* Meanwhile, all I can wonder is, What really happened between the four of them on Diver's Rock that awful summer day?

"You all look like you've seen an actual monster," Ariana says, breaking the silence. "Does that little revelation count for our ghost story hour?"

"Actually, I'm pretty wiped," Hazel adds, snapping out of her trance. "I'm not sure how much room I have left for candy—or ghost stories, for that matter. Ariana's right. I feel like I got quite a bit to process right there."

Despite feeling the same way, I still experience a pang of disappointment over the thought of another broken tradition.

"Whatever the birthday girl wants," I try, in my cheeriest tone.

"Well, let's all just change and see how we feel?"

Everyone nods, so I turn to walk through the bathroom back into my room. It probably won't be the worst thing to have some time to process what Mom has just revealed, or to figure out a game plan on how to dig for the deeper truth. Then I realize Ariana has followed me.

"Um, where do you think you're going, my dear?"

"Oh, the happy couple didn't tell you?" Ariana answers. "Griffin wants to switch with me so they can room together this year."

Another shot of disappointment cracks through me, and I'm too tired to hide it. Or at least that must be the case, since Ariana registers the look on my face.

"What, am I not good enough company?" she asks, her tone somewhere beyond joking.

I know Ariana must feel a little left out, especially after all the evening's dredged-up parental history. But I can't help but feel a little left out myself. When I turn back to Griffin and Hazel, they both wear guilty looks on their faces.

"We've never actually gotten to spend the night in the same room together," Hazel says, looking past me instead of at me. "I thought it would be nice, for my birthday?"

I pause. Because what am I supposed to say?

No, I'm going to argue with you on your birthday because I hate that idea.

No, I don't want anything else to change.

No, I don't want to be right next door while you get to be with Griffin.

These sentiments seem so silly compared to the story we just heard. But that has all made my emotions more heightened, not less.

"Of course it's fine!" I say instead. "But only if you admit you're just doing it to avoid Ariana's monster snoring."

"I do not snore!" Ariana shouts, slapping me on the back.

Hazel and Griffin smile too, relief playing across their faces. There, with one joke, I've made it better for everyone else.

But as I swallow my feelings again, this time they explode in my chest, instantly and messily. My heart seizes and starts pumping overtime. I feel dizzy, like I might vomit. I know I will have a panic attack right here and now if I don't find a way to calm myself down.

Somehow, I still manage to force a smile when Griffin says, "Thanks, buddy. And hey, I'll do some digging on this whole Tommy thing tomorrow, see what I can find? Something tells me there's more to the story."

I nod, or at least I hope I do, before I turn to walk back into my room. Maybe if I just lie down in my bed, I can breathe the attack away. Except now, of course, Ariana is going to be there. What could I say to justify lying in silence, without seeming like a total freak? Or without making Ariana feel shut out, like I'm alienating her even more?

I feel trapped—and that only makes everything worse. I don't want C4 to see me spiral like this, so thoroughly and rapidly out of my own control. If I break down here, then they'll all know just how messed up I really am. All of those fun, idiosyncratic neuroses they once found endearing will suddenly become blinking hazard signs. They'd never look at me the same way again.

No, that can't happen. Not here. This is supposed to be my happy place. Hemlock. Copper Cove. I'm with my favorite people, on one of my favorite nights of the year. It's impossible to imagine I could have a panic attack here.

"Speaking of ghosts, you look about as pale as one," Ariana says, entering the room behind me. "Wait, Luca, are you okay?"

"Totally," I manage. "I think I'm just overwhelmed by everything tonight, especially this Tommy thing. Do you mind if I just go to bed?"

It's a miracle I'm able to speak with some measure of calmness, a placid surface hiding all the churning underneath. I suppose it only works because what I said is true enough—it just isn't the whole truth.

"Oh. Sure." Ariana's answer makes it clear she's hiding some churning of her own, probably thinking I don't want to spend time alone with her.

I wish I had it in me to tell Ariana this isn't the case, but right now it's all I can do to just keep myself together. I crawl under the covers without another word, praying my body will find some way to shut itself down.

∞

Mercifully, I do fall asleep. However, as it turns out, not even my dreams can do much to ease the riptide of my thoughts.

I find myself in a hospital bed, keenly aware that I'm dying. Sick—something about a blood clot traveling fast through the pathways of my body, streaming towards my heart. But the prospect of dying isn't as frightening as the reality that no one has come to visit.

My heart will kill me and no one can stop it. No one even wants to try.

Then suddenly there's someone at the door and my spirits lift...until I realize it isn't so much someone as some*thing*. Some heavy presence lurking outside. Then under the door slide two long, slippery antennae—the kind that belong to a cockroach or a water bug. The wiry antennae probe and twitch, like the thing is trying to escape a drain. The thin appendages, slithering and curling like hair follicles, sweep across the length of the floor, feeling and groping.

I dare not make a sound.

The antennae keep moving, impossibly, deeper

and deeper into my room. Eventually they reach the bed and that's when I realize I made a mistake playing dead. I try to scream, but no noise comes out. Somehow the thing outside the door hears me anyway and the antennae wrap around my bare ankles, their grip so frigid it burns.

My body jerks forward as the hidden thing bucks. It pulls me towards the door, which cracks open violently. As air rushes around me, I realize I'm falling, inexplicably, through open air towards water—like I've just jumped off Diver's Rock. Hazel is falling too, along with Ariana. Griffin has jumped as well, all four of us together. Except now we realize, too late, we've jumped off the wrong ledge. We're going to die when we hit the rocky water.

I look for something to grab onto, but all I see is a small crowd gathered on the ledge above, gazing down at us. It's Mom and Garrett and Wendy, all watching silently as we fall. They seem oblivious to being watched themselves—by something above them, perched even higher. It's all rotten flaps of muscle, with too many eyes and too little body, shorn and striated, flayed. Something about it is fundamentally...incorrect. It makes me shudder in a way I didn't think possible. Especially because, rotted deeper in the side of its head is the broken infinity symbol, the one I've seen on the lake floor.

The thing shrieks and the sound that comes out is too high-pitched for me to hear, but it somehow still curdles my blood. I look to my friends for answers, but their faces are no longer there, ripped away by the impossible force of the wind.

In the next moment I find myself on the ground beside Hazel, and we are digging...but I don't know why. Dirt cakes under my fingertips as I fling it away. It covers my clothes and my skin, it flies into my mouth, but that doesn't matter.

Because somehow I know Griffin is somewhere in the ground below us, buried alive.

Griffin—our Griffin, my Griffin—is trapped underneath several feet of tumbled, packed earth. Unable to move, unable to see, suffocating as the air is crushed from his lungs. This moment fills me up and I swear it's so real, it feels like history...but also like tomorrow? I know somewhere in the back of my head that I'm supposed to remain in the present, to not dwell on...whatever this twisted moment is, where everything I care about most is on the line.

So we keep digging, Hazel and I, even as my hand smashes and breaks against something solid. And cold. And...

My eyes open before I can unearth Griffin's corpse. I gasp out loud, hurtling into wakefulness. I grip the sheets and find they're completely soaked through with sweat.

It takes a few seconds for me to catch my breath. By the time I have it, most of the details from my nightmare have already slipped from my memory. All that remains is a lingering fear, buried deep in my chest. That, and the image of our parents looking on as we fell.

I kick the wet sheets off my body and roll out of bed, careful not to wake Ariana. My heart still slams about in my chest, so I hope some night air will help cool me down. Slipping out the door silently, I step onto the balcony...

Only to find Mom standing a ways down, staring at me. The sight is startling.

"Sorry, I was out here and saw your door opening," Mom whispers, just loud enough for me to hear. "Can't sleep either?"

"Oh. Just a bad dream, I think," I say, trying to pull myself together.

"We all get those," Mom sighs, walking up beside me. She places her hand on my wrist and it nearly makes me jump, though I'm not sure why. "Want to sleep in Hazel's room with me tonight, in the other bed?"

"Oh no, I'm okay." I'm not necessarily okay, but I think I just need some space. "It wasn't a panic attack or anything."

"You sure?"

There's something in Mom's face as she speaks that I recognize. Some distant, faraway look that's somehow... pleading? But I only have one mom, so I assume it's a general maternal thing, some potent mix of worry and love and protectiveness. Then I remember Tommy and know that's probably part of it. Some residual and all-too-legitimate fear of my senseless, premature death.

It's another reason telling her about this particular dream isn't a good idea.

"Really Mom, I'm okay."

She half smiles, resigned to my answer.

"Okay. But come get me if you need anything, figlio mio?"

"Sure," I say, already beginning to worry about how I'll fall asleep again. I need for this day to end and for tomorrow to come.

I don't think much of it when Mom squeezes my hand one more time, a pained expression on her face. She turns and returns to her room, moving as if leaving my side is physically difficult. Like she wants to say more but can't find the words.

I know the feeling.

Chapter Ten

The next afternoon, with a blanket between me and the damp grass, I sit in front of the Auditorium and reimagine it as a grand castle. I haven't sketched one in way too long— this past year I've been much more drawn to wilderness landscapes. The summer after freshman year I went through a real-world-castle phase, thinking architecture might be the best way to transpose the ideas in my head into the world. But I quickly found that field way too constricting, too steeped in math and bogged down by reality.

It was that summer I also came to understand one of the deeper reasons I love fantasy so much. It isn't just the beauty or the splendor or the brutality of the genre; it's the way the rules work. Braveness is always rewarded, while wickedness is punished. Good and evil are clearly defined, color coded in bright and shadowy lights. Anything is possible because everything is charged with wonder and magic. There is balance, always, and limitlessness.

Not like the real world, which is jagged and uneven, cast in grays and bound by the inevitable. Where braveness most often only invites heartache, and where most things cannot be undone.

It's why I sketch the Auditorium as a castle, the kind I've always believed it to be. I've added a drawbridge leading down to the lake and a turret on the tower, but my attempt at avoiding reality isn't exactly working. I've absentmindedly doodled that broken infinity symbol on the bell inside the Auditorium-castle. Last night's supposed revelations and fever dreams clearly remain burned in my brain. Unfortunately, our efforts today to find any answers have only turned up more horror.

"I've been looking all over campus for you, but of course you're here," Griffin says, suddenly appearing above me. "How people ever got on before cell phones, I'll never understand."

The usual warm pulse I feel seeing Griffin rushes through me. I also suppress the urge to flip my sketch pad closed, reminding myself I don't have to hide things here.

Well, not everything, anyway.

"Shouldn't you be rehearsing with Ariana?" I ask.

"We wrapped up early. Our song is in pretty good shape already, but honestly, I'm still hungry to dig deeper into this whole Tommy thing."

Griffin has already spent most of the day digging. I woke up late this morning to find the rest of C4 departed from Hemlock. By the time I made it down to lunch, Griffin and Hazel were coming out of a full morning of research.

The results of this currently sit underneath my sketch pad, in a neat stack of photocopied news clippings—though only one new article pulled my focus. According to it, Thomas "Tommy" Kastan did indeed die the summer of 1990 when he was eighteen years old, in a freak accident off Diver's Rock. The article reports the incident in less detail than Mom did last night, just echoing the same story. This new Diver's Rock detail was actually the only thing that allowed Griffin to find the lost article for the first time, since it was filed by place instead of by date in the Copper Cove Archive.

Griffin's discovery inspired him to go back into his own personal folder of articles from over the years, some even pulled secretly from his grandfather's study at August Manor. Most of the reports from the past century are terrifying: horrific fires claiming the lives of dozens, unthinkable animal attacks, unexpected building collapses. These disasters seem mostly random and pretty infrequent, but each one is as tragic and inexplicable as Tommy's death—assuming Mom told us some version of the real story. Seeing all these bits of history at once, I can't make up my mind. On the one hand, sporadic tragedies like this are normal anywhere, especially somewhere with as much history as Copper Cove. On the other hand, why can't I shake the feeling that we're missing something?

Sitting here now, with the sun in the blue sky and the lake breeze on my face, it feels silly—and slightly narcissistic—to connect these threads to our own history. Though of course I'd never say as much to Detective Griffin.

"I dunno, the stuff you already dug up is terrible," I reply, sliding over to make room for Griffin on the blanket. "Though one upside is deciding to cancel our annual hike to Diver's Rock. I never understood wasting all that energy just to watch you all risk your necks jumping off some giant ledge. That's maybe our only tradition I don't mind breaking."

"Yeah, I'm not sure Diver's Rock will ever be the same.

I'm shocked our parents ever let us go up there in the first place," Griffin answers, settling next to me on the blanket.

I'm hit with the smell of Griffin's sweat and the sight of his round biceps pressing against his knees. Suddenly I feel light-headed.

"You said you were looking for me?" I manage.

"I was about to head back home to prepare for the big dinner," Griffin begins. "But yeah, I was hoping to find you first. I wanted to ask you…something important."

The list of important things Griffin could want to ask me is quite long right now, but something about his tone feels aching. It makes me wary. It doesn't help when he sets his blue eyes on the lake down the hill, suddenly looking far away.

"I guess I just wanted to make sure you really aren't mad about me dating Hazel or anything," Griffin says finally. "I could tell last night you were a bit put off."

My insides seize.

"Well, we only discovered our parents' dead friend's secret crypt and learned he died in a horrible freak accident, scarring them forever," I rattle off, a smile on my face. "But what about that could possibly make me seem put off?"

I don't know if it's a flimsy cover, but it's the only one I have to work with. Thankfully, Griffin breaks into one of his killer smiles, his eyes crinkling.

"Yeah, okay, I just wanted to make sure," he says, sighing. "I just… I would never want to do anything to…I don't know."

"There's nothing to know, Griffin." The lie stings on its way out, but I keep smiling anyway.

"Good. Okay." Griffin inhales, once again looking sentimental. "Hey, you ever wonder if we were meant to be together?"

I nearly choke. What does *that* mean?

"I mean, like, if our families didn't have all this history or whatever," Griffin goes on. "Do you think we would have met each other and been friends anyway?"

Before I can exhale properly, Griffin turns away from the lake. His eyes connect with mine, and for a moment, everything is perfect. For a moment, I can see all the love he has for me. For a moment, I believe Griffin actually sees me. It feels so intense, I don't know what to say.

Then Griffin blinks and shakes his head.

"Don't mind me," he says. "Last night just churned up a lot. And I'm more nervous about dinner tonight than I'd like to admit."

I reach forward, placing a hand on Griffin's shoulder.

"We'd be friends no matter what," I say. "And I, for one, could not be more excited to finally get to spend a real night in August Manor. After you crowding my room all these years, it feels very overdue."

Griffin laughs.

"I don't know, the grand August Manor can feel pretty confining," Griffin says. "I actually got trapped in our elevator earlier this morning."

"Come again?"

"I was being lazy about going from the basement up to the third floor where my bedroom is, so I got in the elevator—which barely has room for one person my size, honestly. I never usually take it, and of course the one time I do it gets stuck between the first and second floors. The thing totally stalled, and all the lights went out. It was pitch black in there, and like twenty minutes passed before anyone heard me shouting."

"That sounds horrible," I offer, also confounded— and intrigued—by the idea of a house so big no one can hear you shouting for that long.

"Yeah, it was like being in a...coffin," Griffin says, his last bit barely audible. "I almost freaked out. Especially because there was this strange sound coming from the elevator motor, from it trying to turn back on. This weird whining and scraping. Not great for someone who is claustrophobic."

"Or for someone who believes Copper Cove is haunted, especially after last night," I return. "Though technically speaking, this wasn't in Copper Cove. This was in your *Richie Rich* summer mansion up the road. Which I am still dying to explore, broken elevators and all."

"Well, I don't think you're quite ready for what's in store tonight," Griffin says, a smile breaking across his face. "The house might be named August, but to put it in terms you'd appreciate most..."

Griffin stands, the sun shining on his blond hair and pale skin.

"Winter is coming."

∞

"Does anyone have any idea why the Augusts really invited us over tonight?" Ariana asks as we get out of the car outside August Manor.

The girls insisted on driving separately in the Hart Toyota just in case C4 wanted to stay later after dinner, so Garrett rode with Mom in the Piccone Subaru.

"Who knows. Griffin didn't seem to know when I asked him," Hazel answers, adjusting the little black dress she wears under a jean jacket. "His mom doesn't just hate Copper Cove. Apparently, she only brings their family to August Manor every summer because it's a stipulation in their trust funds, as a way for Griffin's hermit grandfather to force them all to visit. Griffin said he thought this dinner might actually have been his grandfather's idea, weirdly."

"Whoa. Way to glimpse behind the veil, Lady Hart," Ariana says, lifting the bottom of her flowing, almost-caftan dress as we walk up the driveway.

"Well, I've been especially curious about tonight, to see for ourselves if Griffin's perspective checks out. Everyone kind of has blinders on when it comes to their families. I'm also dying to see if we find out anything else about this whole Tommy thing."

Hearing all this, I can't stop myself from feeling anxious instead of excited. Maybe it's the unprecedented nature of tonight, coupled with the Hazel of it all. Maybe it's because this is the first time our parents are going to be together like this in years. Or maybe it's just my bent brain and broken nervous system dancing their own panicky dance.

I try to ground myself as I step to push the bell, but the door is opened by a butler before I can. From the outside, August Manor is all manicured hydrangea bushes, crisp white panels, and deep-blue shutters—three stories told in restraint and repression. On the inside, the whole place is done up to look cozy, but everything is so perfectly arranged it looks more like a staged house than an actual home. Even the family pictures look rehearsed—posed and airbrushed to perfection.

We are ushered into the parlor by the butler, who then quietly vanishes. The room boasts crisp beige armchairs, a driftwood coffee table, and floor-to-ceiling bookshelves filled with bound volumes. The white ceilings are creased with stained beams, and the floors are a wood the color of sand. I should be spellbound by the lush room, but I'm far more entranced by the sight of Mom, Garrett, and Wendy all seated in the same place.

Then I'm surprised by the sight of Griffin here too. Somehow he looks like a different version of himself, one I've never seen before. He wears a button-down shirt and sweater-vest, looking so proper—but somehow still hot as hell. Longing pangs in my chest, crystal clear and sharp as a knife.

Griffin moves to hug Hazel first, which does nothing to dull my ache. Ariana is greeted by Mom and Garrett, which leaves Wendy to me. I try to re-ground myself in reality, but I blink and all I can see is Wendy the Frost Queen: dripping in beige shades of cashmere and droplet diamonds, her blond hair set as rigid as her reign.

"Luca, I can't believe how much you've grown," she says, leaning in to hug me, stiff as a board. She smells like green apples and vanilla.

I force myself to smile and say, "Your home is beautiful. Thank you so much for having us."

Wendy offers a tight smile before moving on to greet the girls.

"Where's Mr. August?" Hazel asks, accepting a tall glass of Arnold Palmer.

"Eric took the other kids to the movies tonight," Wendy answers, returning to her glass of white wine. She takes a generous sip, mainlining the golden liquid like it's medicine. "I thought it would be nice if it was just us, tonight."

A look passes between Wendy, Mom, and Garrett. A lightning strike of knowledge, impossible to miss.

"Is that why you didn't invite my parents, too?" Ariana asks, stepping up to a coffee table laid out with appetizers and popping a maroon olive into her mouth.

Wendy purses her lips into a shape resembling a smile, then nods. She clutches her wine glass so tightly it seems likely to shatter. I get the distinct sense she'd rather be anywhere in the world but here. So why set up this dinner in the first place? Is there some other trust-fund stipulation in place here? Griffin did say his grandfather was supposed to be here.

"I had the hardest time sleeping last night," Griffin says, obviously trying to shift the small talk.

He seems so unlike his usual easy self, too uptight and polished, just like everything else in the land of August. Winter has come, indeed.

"Oh my goddess, me too!" Ariana exclaims, kicking her feet up on a nearby ottoman.

Wendy's eyes dart to it in a way that implies it's meant to be purely decorative, but she takes another tense sip instead of correcting Ariana.

Wendy is acting like she's at a funeral. But so are

Garrett and Mom, sitting in equally heavy silence, looking uncharacteristically joyless. The sight hits me sideways.

My gaze slides to Hazel and I can tell she notices it too. In fact, she must have sensed it from the moment we entered—I probably would have, too, if I wasn't so preoccupied with Griffin. What the hell are we all really doing here, in this beautifully appointed house of obligation? It's like the protective bubble of Copper Cove has suddenly burst now that we've stepped outside the borders of its realm.

"I had the weirdest nightmare," Ariana continues. "I was locked outside of a house. I could see you all hanging out inside, but I couldn't get in. And something was stalking me, but no matter how loud I screamed, no one could hear me."

"I had a nightmare, too," Griffin says. "Something was coming after all of us at Skinny Point and everyone was counting on me to stop it. I had this bat in my hands, but I couldn't remember how to swing it. Anyway, once the thing finally got us, all of a sudden we were falling off Diver's Rock."

"Wait," Hazel says. "I had the same nightmare about Diver's Rock. At least, I think. I knew I had a bad dream last night, but I couldn't really remember it."

I should say next that I had the same nightmare, or some version of it. But all I can see is the look on our parents' faces. They gaze blankly at the floor or the nearest wall, seeming to know exactly what we're talking about. A flashback from my own nightmare comes to me, of our parents watching us fall. Then I remember the way Mom had been standing out on the balcony, almost like she *knew* I'd be having a bad dream.

Dread bursts open inside me like a depth charge.

"Wait, what's going on?" I finally ask. "Why are we really here?"

The room falls silent under the weight of my question. Griffin and Ariana appear dumbstruck, but Hazel clearly wants the same answer. Wendy takes another gulp of wine, and that's when I notice Garrett is gripping the arms of his chair so tightly, his knuckles blaze beige.

My eyes fall on Mom last...

And the look on her face scares me more than anything has in my entire life.

"You're here because I asked you to be."

I turn, along with everyone else, to find an old man in the doorway sitting in a wheelchair. I assume this must be Cecil August, the infamous hermit and benefactor of the August fortune. But I can't imagine the man sitting before me is Griffin's grandfather—he seems like a man made of stone and anvil, not sun and soap.

And this man is not well. His skin hangs off his bones, spotted with age. An oxygen tank is attached to his wheelchair, and silvery strands of brittle hair cross his skull. He looks like he should have died long ago...

But that he somehow willed himself to live until this very night.

Chapter Eleven

Cecil August wheels into the parlor, his frail hands spinning him forward. He turns and swings the door closed behind him—and locks it.

"What the hell?" Ariana startles, springing to her feet. "Seriously, this is starting to feel very *Get Out*."

"No one can disturb or overhear us once our conversation begins," Cecil answers, turning back to the assembled group. "And no one can leave before we are finished."

I want to turn to Mom, to search her face for an answer, but I'm too afraid to look at her again.

"Grandfather, what's in your lap?" Griffin asks, his attention laser focused on the square thing.

It's a glass case preserving a very old piece of paper, but Cecil has it turned inwards so none of us can see what's written on it.

"This is the single most important part of our family's legacy," Cecil begins. "Of all our families' legacies. And it is inescapable."

"My family doesn't have anything to do with—" Ariana tries.

"Stop interrupting me, girl," Cecil says, his voice searing hot. "And you will come to understand your place in all this."

I'm stunned that, instead of challenging this old white man, Ariana takes a seat in silence. Clearly, she's just as spooked as the rest of us.

"As you already know, our families have been bound together for generations by Copper Cove," Cecil continues, wheeling himself to a more central spot near the mantelpiece. "However, there has always been a part of our history you do not and could not know. Tonight, you will learn your true place in the legacy of Copper Cove."

The words make no sense, but also all the sense in the world. I want to look over at Griffin or Hazel or even Ariana, but I'm too riveted by Cecil's speech.

"Every generation, it is the job of those who come before to pass along their wisdom, their knowledge, and their traditions—but also their burdens. Burdens which tonight, you inherit."

I open my mouth to ask a question, but Cecil turns to me with such sharpness in his cloudy eyes, I understand why Ariana fell silent.

"Surely you know by now that Copper Cove is a special place. It's more beautiful, more peaceful, and more restorative than anywhere else on Earth. You've enjoyed this glow all your lives, but today you learn the true reason this place is so special. And the price we must pay to keep it that way."

Cecil pauses to suck a shallow breath through his lips, as if building up the strength to say what comes next. "Every generation, the progeny of four Copper Cove families are bound by an ancient and unbreakable pact."

"This is a joke, right?" Ariana interrupts again. "Will someone tell this—"

"Ariana, let him finish." To everyone's surprise, this time it's Hazel that causes Ariana to fall silent.

Cecil collects his hands to rest on the artifact in his lap, breath escaping his mouth in labored wheezes. He probably needs a shot of oxygen, but he clearly wants to finish what he's started.

"Nothing this beautiful can exist without a counterpart: a corrupted force, equal in its potency. Just like Copper Cove, this corruption takes physical form. And to call it a monster would not do it justice."

Hearing this last part finally jolts me to look around the room, to make sure I haven't lost my grip on reality. Our parents stare off in different directions, unable to make eye contact with anyone. Hazel, Ariana, and I all find each other to share a stunned glance. Then we turn to Griffin, whose grim face remains set only on his grandfather, all too ready to believe this unbelievable revelation.

"While the Pact fuels Copper Cove with love and abundance, the Impact absorbs its fear and emptiness. This Impact, as our families have named it, wants only one thing. It aims to destroy Copper Cove and everyone in it."

For a moment I wonder if I've tumbled headlong into one of my fantasy stories. I desperately want to write this off as some kind of bizarre rich-person game, but I can't help but soak in the way our parents all listen with their heads slightly bowed. Like this is a secret truth they've known longer than we children have been alive.

It would certainly explain why I've always felt that

there's something truly different, truly special about Copper Cove. It would also explain why our parents have always been so cagey about their pasts. And why we've all felt like there has been something creeping around the edges of our experience this summer. I've been so desperate to ignore it, so desperate to keep everything perfect, to blame the coming changes and my panicky past...

But could this truly be why Copper Cove is so full of brightness, because this "Impact" absorbs negativity like some curdled sponge? Could Griffin have been right all along?

"The demands of the Pact are simple," Cecil carries on, before any of us have a real chance to respond. "In order to safeguard Copper Cove for the next generation, the Impact must be kept at bay. And this requires a sacrifice."

These revelations hang in the air for several moments like poison fog.

"What do you mean, a sacrifice?" Griffin finally asks, taking the words out of everyone in C4's mouths.

"A human sacrifice," Cecil answers, cold as stone.

He then turns around the flat glass case in his lap, obviously wanting to finish before any of us have a chance to interrupt again. But it's like he moves in slow motion as my brain struggles to absorb the phrase he just uttered: *human sacrifice.*

It's an idea so unthinkable, I can't bring myself to look anywhere but straight on. I need to know more, the full story. Given the complete silence that has enveloped the room, I guess everyone feels the same way.

So I place all of my focus on the scroll Cecil

reveals. I want to devour its words, desperate to latch onto something that makes sense, but instead I'm stopped cold in my tracks. Handwritten in old, faded ink at the top of the page is the title:

∞ *The Copper Cove Pact* ∞

It isn't the title that freezes me, but rather the broken infinity symbols etched into either side of the paper. My eyes fix on one, its curves searing my retinas like a white-hot brand. Like...

Proof.

I look up and close my eyes for a moment, trying to imagine Cecil as someone fallible. The Rotting Monarch, barking mad decrees from his feeble throne of senility. But all I can do is open my eyes and read the sentences written farther down the cracked page.

To seal the bonds that keep the Impact at bay, in their eighteenth year, the eldest-born children of the Pact families must choose to sacrifice one of their own.

To keep the Impact sealed, the Pact families must abide by three rules:

1.) *The Pact must be kept secret, save for the passing of the Pact to the next generation three nights before the sacrifice.*

2.) *Once bound to the Pact, the three survivors must return to Copper Cove every summer at the sacrificial anniversary, as tribute.*

3.)   *These three survivors must birth or adopt*
        children at age thirty-three. Their success
        is guaranteed by the Pact.

If any of the aforementioned rules are broken,
the Impact is released to prey upon Copper Cove for a
duration proportionate to the severity of the breach.

Thoughts tumble through my mind in an avalanche as I try to grasp the meaning of these words. They seem impossible, the stuff of grim fairy tales. But at the same time, it's like a light has been shone on something I've felt but never seen clearly. In either of my worlds, this makes a terrible kind of sense.

"Where did that paper come from?"

Griffin's question isn't the first I'd ask, but it'll do.

"My father, your great grandfather, saved this after the Pact was revealed to the first generation ensnared in Copper Cove," Cecil explains. "This contract came to them in a dream, just like the nightmare I presume you all had last night. But this decree was not transcribed by him. That was done by Grace Piccolo, Luca's great-grandmother."

This information sends a shock through me, and I instinctively turn to Mom for confirmation. She nods, with that same pained expression once again on her face. Dread twists in my chest like a peach pit, shriveled and dense.

Ariana begins to laugh, loudly, making me jump. Once the burst rattles through her, she looks at everyone like we're insane.

"Okay, I don't know what Puritan, evangelical, witch-hunting nonsense this is, but it has nothing to do with me."

She stands to leave, but Wendy places an icy grip on her shoulder before she can take another step.

"I'm afraid it has everything to do with you, young lady," she says. "Every cycle, the Pact chooses a new fourth member to replace the sacrificed. Hazel, Luca, and Griffin were born into the Pact, but you were bound to it when you became close with them."

Even given everything else, that's a particularly horrifying notion.

"But...I'm... I'm not..." Ariana sputters as the defiance leaks out of her.

"The Pact only pertains to you. Your family knows nothing of it, and they never can," Cecil says to Ariana, before turning to address the rest of us. "What matters now is that it's up to the four of you to save Copper Cove. As it was up to your parents before you, and me before them."

"How do you know any of this is real?" I ask, finally finding my voice. "I mean, how do you know any of these rules work the way you say they do?"

"I... We believe you've all already encountered the Impact?" Mom asks as an answer, her voice struggling to remain even. "For some reason, on the year of the Pact renewal, the Impact's bonds weaken enough for it to reveal itself. Like it wants you to know it's there, as...evidence."

Instantly, this tracks—not just with me, but also with the rest of C4. Although it's little consolation. Our parents have known about this, known what's been happening to us all along? And they...Mom...no one has uttered a thing?

"What Sofia says is true," Cecil adds. "And we've learned the hard way that if you break any of these rules, the Impact is temporarily freed to wreak even more havoc. History is marred by the times our families have tried to break these rules. The deadly fires of 1924. The lost children of 1956. The Overlook Hall collapse of 1976. The pregnant murder of 2019. Dates that none of us will ever forget."

Cecil pauses and allows us all to scroll through our memories. I certainly remember the last one, since a pregnant woman was killed a few summers ago on a hike. She was deathly allergic to bees and stepped on a fallen hive, causing a series of stings that claimed her life—at least, that's how the story was told. Could that awful tragedy really have been because of this Impact thing? Because our parents somehow broke these binding rules? That's...

Unthinkable.

I turn to look at Griffin and can tell from the expression on his face: these dates check out. After all, he dug up the reports reminding us of these terrible incidents this morning. We just didn't know—*couldn't* know—they were all connected.

"And those are just the big ones. Copper Cove's past is littered with smaller tragedies, accidents caused by lesser infractions," Cecil says. "Bizarre-but-explainable freak accidents. They've been few and far enough between to keep under wraps."

"The pregnant woman, that was my fault," Mom says in a small voice, fighting back tears.

"Our fault," Garrett adds, before turning to look at Hazel. "When you kids were fourteen, Sofia and I, we decided we had to tell you, consequences be damned. But that same day, before we could, word started spreading that…"

Garrett stops, as if what comes next is too much for him to speak out loud.

"Luca, you have to understand, I wanted to tell you about this, to warn you, every single day," Mom says, unable to stop herself from crying. "I wanted to take your place, we all did. But the Pact doesn't work like that. All we could do was protect you, allow you to have a normal life for as long as possible. We couldn't do much, but we could do that—shoulder this burden for you all. Until today."

My whole body flushes. Why didn't I listen to Griffin sooner? Why didn't I listen to my own instinct—why did I shut it down, tune it out, over and over? But then I think: We've all been willfully misled. We've been lied to our entire lives. So really, how could we do any better? I know I should feel furious, or grateful, or betrayed, or something…

But all I feel is numb.

"I don't belong here," Ariana says, to herself more than anyone else. She walks farther towards the door. "This is… I need some air."

"You're free to go, now the Pact and its rules have been revealed," Cecil says, before Ariana can move too far. "But tonight, this precise moment, has historically been the only time the elders are allowed to talk to the next generation about the Pact without consequence. So if you have any questions, you'd better ask them now."

It's obvious Ariana only wants to leave, to escape this haunted, foreign room. But something, some basic instinct, makes her stay, if only a little longer. I can't imagine how lonely she must feel. Though I'm not sure if it's better or worse for the rest of us, having our parents here.

"This...Impact. That's what's been terrorizing us this past week?" Hazel asks, remaining analytically calm. "The spiders and the sounds in the woods?"

A look passes between the parents, a kind of ripple.

"For us, the Impact didn't haunt us, at least not that way," Mom answered. "It just destroyed things, or maimed people. I don't know why its behavior would—"

"It doesn't matter," Cecil interrupts, impatience bleeding into his voice. "The Impact is a thing of fear and despair, and it imprints on each generation differently. The Impact of my day scorched forests and ate things it shouldn't, but the incidentals of the Impact are inconsequential. All that matters now is stopping it for another generation."

"Okay, so you're telling us we have to sacrifice one of our own to save Copper Cove?" Griffin asks, the words seeming to burn on his tongue. "What does that mean, really?"

"It means three nights from now, one of the four of you must die," Cecil answers.

A sharp pulse snaps across the room, thick and foul.

Because there it is, the ugly truth that lives at the center of this surreal nightmare.

And it's all completely...

Unimaginable.

Chapter Twelve

"How did you handle it? The sacrifice?" I ask, right before the revelation hits me. I can't believe none of us arrived at it sooner. "Oh my god. That's what really happened to Tommy, isn't it?"

Wendy crosses the room, but not to answer my question. Instead, she lifts a bottle of sauvignon blanc out of an ice bucket and pours the remainder of its contents into her empty glass.

"Tommy sacrificed himself for the rest of us," Garrett answers, his jaw clenched so tight it might crack.

"But Mom, you...you told us the story of what happened at Diver's Rock, just last night," I say, fully realizing the ease with which my own mother can lie to my face. I knew something hadn't been right, but now I don't know what's worse: that this lie is so much bigger than I could've imagined, or that I just let her get away with it.

"It's the story we've all told as a cover, since the day it happened," Garrett answers for Mom, who can't seem to lift her eyes to meet mine. "We had to keep the lie, the truth—all of it—a secret from you, to protect you. The consequences of telling anyone, especially you four, about the Pact, they're..."

"Preferable to letting one of your best friends die?" Hazel asks, her voice finally charged with emotion. "How do you expect us to believe you? What really happened to Tommy?"

"Don't you dare question him! What Tommy did was noble!" Wendy shouts suddenly, on the verge of slurring.

I try to remember, once upon a time, she might have loved Tommy.

Wendy swallows another mouthful of wine, then mutters: "And it's better than what we Augusts have done in the past."

"What does that mean?" Griffin asks, his face both hesitant and frantic.

"We August men have always done what we must to protect what is ours," Cecil answers for Wendy. "I did what my father was bold enough to do before me."

"Oh, why not just call it what it is, father?" Wendy shoots. "Murder. And it's not something to be proud—"

"Of course it is!" Cecil fires back, his voice thundering. "Do not forget you are here because of me, child. Or because of what that foolish Tommy boy did to protect you, for your Pact. Our legacy lives on because of what this family has done for Copper Cove, for the entire world—because we were brave enough to answer when called. Now Copper Cove and the August legacy will live on because my grandson, Griffin, will also do what must be done."

"And what is that?" Griffin chokes out.

"You will bring order to the Pact. You will establish a rule that will protect the three surviving families for generations to come," Cecil announces. "I've carried on to this day to deliver this message. You, Griffin, must set the precedent that ensures the fourth member of the Pact—the outsider—is sacrificed from this generation on."

As the meaning of Cecil's message settles in, my face twists with horror—which matches the looks on Griffin's and Hazel's faces. We all turn to Ariana, expecting fire and fury...

But she's silent. Catatonic.

"And if we refuse?" Hazel asks instead.

"If there is no sacrifice, the Impact is free to destroy Copper Cove and kill everyone in it," Cecil answers.

"What happens once it's done with Copper Cove?" I ask, trying not to tremble.

"Presumably it will be fully freed to prey upon the world. There's no telling how far the Impact's wrath can spread once its chains to Copper Cove are broken. And it's thanks to our families this apocalypse has never come to fruition."

"Because you've always obeyed the Pact, always killed one of your own," Griffin says, stepping up beside Hazel. "Because you always took the easy way out, instead of fighting back."

"How spoiled you are, how spoiled you all are!" Cecil spits at us, gasping. "Your generation believes you are free from the responsibilities of your birthright, despite all it affords you. The idea you can ignore the past and be free to shape your futures, unencumbered? It's a modern, privileged illusion. The reality is that we are all born into situations out of our control, with burdens or sicknesses. It may not be fair, but this Pact is your cross to bear. This is your sacrifice to make, to earn what you always believed to be free. To fight for the future and the freedom you assumed were owed to you. You are soldiers, called to make the sacrifices necessary to defend your home and all who inhabit it."

"But why?" Hazel asks. "Why did this pact happen? Have any of you tried to figure out even that much?"

Mom looks like she is about to answer, but Cecil cuts her off.

"You might as well ask why the rain falls, or why the sun shines," he says.

"But we know *how* those things happen," Hazel responds. "It's what science is for. There must be a reason for the Pact, even if we can't understand it yet."

"Can we ever understand why anything exists?" Cecil counters. "Or why we have to die at all? Some things are simply beyond our grasp."

"So you just give up?" Hazel is defiant now, on fire. "How could you not spend your entire lives learning how to stop this?"

Hazel turns her focus from Cecil to Mom and Wendy, but everyone knows who she's really talking to. Garrett doesn't flinch, but he doesn't defend himself either. Beside him, Mom looks like there are words burning on her tongue, but Cecil doesn't leave room for anyone else to speak.

"Many of us have, including my own father," Cecil answers for the parents. "We've tried everything you could think of. Nothing ever got us closer to slowing this storm—in fact, we only succeeded in making it stronger. Fighting the Pact is futile. You must accept it, then find a way to endure it."

"Cecil is right," Mom says finally, her voice willed into steadiness. "We learned the hard way that the more you fight this, the worse it gets. You'll see someday, hopefully sooner than we did. There's no escaping."

Mom looks at me for a moment and her tone changes. "We know this is a lot to take in. But if there was some other way to stop this, we would have found it. Trust us."

"No," I say, anger suddenly finding me. "How can you ask us to trust you when you've been lying to us our entire lives?"

My question echoes across the room, stinging Mom with each syllable.

"If the Pact is real, if it happens here in Copper Cove, that means it probably happens somewhere else, too," I continue. "Someone has to have answers. We'll find them, no matter what."

"Even if it costs the lives of others? Maybe even people you love?" Mom answers. It's like she's tapped into some maternal force now, as if our lives depend on her every word—which they very well might. "You can't imagine what it's like, to have lost lives on your…"

But Mom can't sustain, and her voice finally cracks. It threatens to crack me, too.

"Whatever you think, you didn't give us time to have a fighting chance," Hazel says. "You just decided what was best for us because it's what was best for you. And for what? To live in fear your entire lives?"

"No. To live. Period," Cecil answers. "People die every day, every second, for far less meaningful reasons. This is a hero's death. One life for all of Copper Cove, for the generation to come, for all the world. It's a small price to pay."

"You mean *my* life is a small price to pay," Ariana says.

Cecil turns to Ariana, resolve burning in his eyes.

"Yes, I do mean your life," he says, without a trace of remorse. "It's nothing personal. You're simply in the wrong place at the wrong time."

"How can you say that to my face?" Ariana asks.

"Because apparently he's a murderer," Griffin interrupts, the sentiment grinding through his teeth.

Cecil attempts a deep breath, then turns to Wendy instead of Griffin. "I believe this conversation has moved beyond the point of usefulness."

"Yes. I don't know about the rest of you," Hazel says, turning towards the door, "but I've heard enough."

"After tonight, you're on your own," Mom tries. "We can't help you without—"

"Honestly, I think we're okay with that," I say, cutting her off.

Mom recoils, like a wounded animal.

"I know it goes against all your teenage instincts to listen to we who are older and wiser, but you have the opportunity to learn from our...from us," Cecil announces breathlessly, before we can leave. "But go ahead, ignore our warnings. If you do, be prepared to carry the consequences for as long as you live."

Cecil pauses to lock eyes with Griffin, then me, then Hazel, and finally Ariana.

"However long that might be, now."

∞

The four of us ride back to Copper Cove's campus in silence, too stunned to speak. There will be time for words when we return. More words than we can handle, likely. C4 understands. We'll go to Bellfour and we'll...what?

Decide?

Defy?

Die?

Is the choice really even ours to make?

Stone Three

Once back in Copper Cove proper, we all agree to take thirty minutes to ourselves, to try and process what just occurred.

Unsurprisingly, that doesn't feel like nearly enough time.

I still feel weighed down.

Or maybe untethered.

Either way, I know I need to try to re-center myself, to root myself in something real.

So I figure planting a stone in the ground might help.

Now that I know the truth, or some of it anyway, there is only one place to go: the small memorial garden beside the Chapel.

It's where my grandpa is buried.

Of course, now I can't help but wonder if there is more to this tradition I've inherited from him, to these stones my grandpa has me dedicate to Copper Cove.

Was he trying to send me a message, somehow?

I can't know yet, but I can leave my third stone there

anyway, next to the cracked slab of rock that serves as my grandpa's tombstone.

Maybe it is my tribute to my ancestors, who I feel more connected to than ever.

Or less connected to?

Chapter Thirteen

Perhaps it's because I'm surrounded by graves, but I feel somewhat dead inside. My mind is so full, I feel compressed. I'm a dulled edge, a folded funnel. How can I possibly retain anything else, after tonight?

Still, I have to get myself together, because our thirty solo minutes are almost up. There are decisions coming, big ones, and I need the clarity to make them.

But all I feel is clouded. My land of fantasy has ruptured, its ground split open to reveal a rotting underbelly. Everything about Copper Cove now appears warped through the distorted lens of this familial pact. Is it the realest reason Mom and Grandpa came back every year, out of obligation to this twisted curse? Is the Pact the reason Mom got married and had me in the first place? Has my whole relationship with her been a lie, given everything she's been keeping from me? How did our parents live with something this heavy hanging over their heads? How could they have kept it secret from literally everyone? Is this what broke my parents apart? Hazel's, too?

Surely these questions are too big to answer in one night.

As surreal as it all is, something deep in my bones

tells me the Pact is real. That's what I hate most. I want to feel blindsided and betrayed, to maintain innocence and defiance. I want to hate Mom, to hate our parents, our grandparents, to kick and cry and scream: *Why didn't you find a way to protect us from this?*

But then I think about how this past week, I've willfully blinded myself to what's been happening. Ignoring all the strange little things that haven't added up, Griffin's suspicions, the sense Mom was lying. Am I to blame for not recognizing the signs, for burying my head in the sand, for being so thoroughly focused on my own traditions?

Then I consider the nature of the Pact, how it's designed to keep its captives complicit, to keep others unaware. Everyone in C4 was kept in the dark on purpose, even Detective Griffin. Entering the Pact is like signing some twisted, cosmic NDA with the devil. I'm still not sure how it can be possible, how any of this can be possible...but if the consequences of breaking the Pact truly are deadly, can I really be mad at our parents? They've been trapped in a hellish Catch-22, damning the world if they do and damning us if they don't. Every time I start to get mad, I consider my own future, my own potential child. Would I be able to do what our parents have done?

I know this much, at least: no matter what rules our parents laid out and what precautions they set, C4 will have to see for ourselves. If our options really boil down to slaying an un-slayable dragon, destroying a sacred space that inhabits thousands, or killing one of our own...I have no idea what we'll do.

Actually, that's not true.

If I'm being honest, I already know exactly what we should do. I felt it in my gut the moment we left August Manor, but I had to be sure before facing C4. Even if I haven't quite cleared my head, I've made up my mind.

I know what to do about the Pact…and the sacrifice.

∞

We sit in a circle in Bellfour around the coffee table, all of us staring at a box of pizza Hazel bought from the Store. Dinner was never served at August Manor, but still, we don't seem to have much of an appetite.

"So, I hate to say it, but…" Griffin starts. "I deeply, thoroughly *told you so*. Copper Cove is haunted. I've only been saying it for our entire lives."

Despite his attempt at levity, there's no satisfaction in Griffin's voice. After all, this is far worse than some ghost story or monster hiding under the bed.

"Okay, yes, now that we've gotten that inevitable moment out of the way," I sigh, "does anyone else feel relieved we can't talk to our parents about this anymore? It's like, every time they opened their mouths everything got worse."

"I know," Hazel exhales, as if for first time all night. "I keep thinking I want to call my mom, to tell her how unfathomable it is that Dad kept this from us our whole lives. And then…well, has anyone else waded into the deep pit of *I wasn't wanted* yet? Like, I know my dad came to love me, I know that. But now I also have proof that I was an obligation. A burden."

Tears begin streaming down Hazel's cheeks, against her will. Griffin wraps an arm around her as she wipes at her eyes.

"Sorry, I didn't realize how much I've been holding in until just now."

"No, it's okay. I thought the same thing about my mom," I add, tears pooling behind my own eyes. "I mean, I feel like I know her better, like the picture of her is complete for the first time in my life. But I also feel like that makes her more of a stranger?"

"Well, my mom was always a stranger to me," Griffin says. "And she's always treated me differently than my younger brothers. Now I finally know why. I'm a walking, breathing reminder of this person she lost, of this terrible thing in her life. And hey, if there's a 25 percent chance your kid is going to die at eighteen, it's easier not to love them in the first place, right?"

Griffin's question hangs in the air for a while, because no one knows what to say. Hazel takes her turn at wrapping her arms around him.

"I can't stop thinking about having my own kid someday," Ariana says eventually, her voice smaller than usual. "About whether I even want to have a kid. And what it means to have that decision made for me. Oh, and what I did to deserve this, aside from loving all of you."

"Ariana, we..." I try, and fail. "We love you, too. We're in this together."

"None of us deserve this," Griffin adds. "Well, maybe except for us Augusts, now that I know my grandfather and great-grandfather are murderers."

"Okay, but do we know that, really?" Hazel follows up, wiping her cheeks clean and switching into processing mode. "I was going to say, before anything else, we have to figure out exactly what's real."

"Unfortunately, I have some answers on that front already," Griffin says, leaning forward to open something on the coffee table.

It's a leather-bound book, one I can't believe I didn't notice before. Then again, everything that was once familiar about Bellfour suddenly feels foreign. It's like nothing can be trusted to be what it once was.

"My grandfather gave me this before we left," Griffin explains. "He wasn't sure if it's technically against the rules, but he also said the Impact never appeared when he recorded stuff in here. And yes, that's a sentence I just spoke out loud.

"Anyway, this is a listing of every time one of the Pact's participants claimed to break a rule and the consequence that followed. Evil mastermind my grandfather turned out to be, he also made notes of all the times he paid off reporters or falsified stories, to conceal any obvious patterns in Pact-related deaths. This book contains the actual details—including what really happened with Tommy and our parents."

Griffin is silent for a beat, shaking off a chill. "I spent the last half hour going through it and checking what I could against the other records I had. I can't necessarily confirm the rule-breaks, but everything else checks out."

I picture Griffin, our historian, sitting here, scribbling furiously through his thirty minutes. I was so shell-shocked when we got back, I didn't even ask where Hazel and Ariana went. Did they spend their time alone... or together, walking to get the pizza? Should I not have stayed alone? Could the two of them have already promised to protect one another, or—

No, I think, stopping myself. I will not let my brain go to that paranoid place. At least...not yet.

Instead, I lean in to look at Griffin's work along with Hazel. As Griffin said, it's a collection of handwritten accounts and newspaper clippings, but Griffin turns purposefully to a particular page.

"I made a timeline, to summarize the biggest details," he says, pulling a paper from the middle of the book. "Here, I'll pin it up."

Griffin grabs a couple magnets to hang his timeline over one of the whiteboards. For a moment, everything almost feels normal. Griffin geeking out over some obscure, spooky facts from Copper Cove's history, Hazel and Ariana feigning interest while I listen intently. Except there's nothing normal about these facts, so Hazel and I both begin to pore over the timeline with rabid interest.

COPPER COVE PACT FAMILY TIMELINE

1906: First Generation Born

1924: PACT ONE

Grace Piccolo - *Marries*

John Weiss - **Sacrificed**

Stephen August - *Marries*

Anne Perrone - *Adopts*

1939: Second Generation Born/Adopted

1957: PACT TWO
    Gino Piccone - *Marries*
    Sarah Feinstein - **Sacrificed**
    Cecil August - *Marries*
    Lindsay Perrone - *Marries*

1972: Third Generation Born

1990: PACT THREE
    Sofia Piccone - *Marries*
    Garrett Hart - *Marries*
    Wendy August - *Marries*
    Thomas Kastan - **Sacrificed**

2005: Fourth Generation Born

2023: PACT FOUR
    Luca Piccone
    Hazel Hart
    Griffin August
    Ariana Shouhed

Below this timeline, Griffin has scrawled shorthand notes on the history:

1924: First four teens defied call to sacrifice. Morrissey Village burned down in wildfire. Dozens of families burned alive. Until Stephen August killed John Weiss in Weiss Hall, the only surviving structure.

1930s: Morrissey Village rebuilt and renamed August Cove. 2nd generation kept apart despite vacationing there every summer.

1956–57: The parents decide to tell 2nd gen one year early, causing a group of camp children to disappear. Only their bones later found, picked clean. When time comes the following year, Cecil August "sacrifices" the first newcomer outside Weiss Hall.

1960s–70s: Cecil August sells campus, which becomes Copper Cove. 3rd generation bond closely as friends. Note: Gino Piccone tries to tell wife about the Pact, unexplained building collapse kills 14 in Copper Cove.

1990: Our parents terrified by prior gen's failures. Cecil August demands Garrett be sacrificed, leading him and our parents to fight. Mom's leg is broken after being thrown off Diver's Rock by Impact, which also rips out Garrett's eye. To stop this, Thomas sacrifices himself by jumping off Diver's Rock and drowning.

2019: Sofia and Garrett consider revealing the Pact to us, causing a pregnant woman to be stung to death by a swarm of bees.

Reading this, it all seems so…unfathomable.

"This explains why all the eldest children in mine and Luca's families were born in the same year," Griffin points out. "It also explains why everyone thinks Weiss Hall is haunted—the first two Pact sacrifices happened there. But it looks like the biggest disasters happened every thirty-three years, when the participants attempted to break the Pact. Things my forefathers thought justified murder."

Griffin's voice is sharp, and angry. But how else

should he sound, after learning his family's legacy is stained with blood?

"It also sounds like your dear old granddad has been trying to make this 'murder the outsider' thing happen for a while," Ariana says, her voice equally barbed. "Good thing he didn't convince the others to off your dad, Hazel, or you wouldn't be here to enjoy your delightful inheritance."

"Right," Hazel says absently, not detecting the edge in Ariana's tone. She's too busy poring over the details of Griffin's timeline. "I'm still trying to process that my dad's eye was ripped out by an evil monster. He always told me he lost it in a freak accident, then he'd change the subject. Now I see why."

Hazel's eyes remain glued to the board—which prompts Ariana to stand and block her view, one hand perched on her hip.

"I don't get why you need to look at some overblown calendar in the first place," Ariana says. "I can feel in my gut this is for real. Not to mention how this Impact thing has obviously been stalking us this summer. It certainly explains the dead animals I've been finding around our cottage, and why I keep finding those gross seedpod flowers everywhere. The Impact must know about my trypophobia, somehow."

"I guess it explains my spider kayak, too," Hazel adds, with a shudder.

"And the dock spiders from our first night," I say, feeling a shiver of my own. "I didn't tell you guys this, but a bug slid in my ear one night when I was…showering. It must have been the Impact, trying to get in my head. Literally."

"That's awful, Luca," Griffin replies. "But there's something else weird going on here. Or, weirder."

Griffin pulls another sheet of paper out of the book, and I wonder how he managed to finish so much in thirty minutes. All I accomplished was placing a stone and trying to process my thoughts. Then again, maybe that's the answer—Griffin is probably moving at warp speed to avoid processing his thoughts. I don't blame him.

"I tried to track the behavior of the Impact, but every generation it seems to shift. For some reason, our version likes to terrorize us. I think—"

"Lucky us," Ariana interrupts. "Griffin, correct me if I'm wrong, but your timeline didn't turn up much your families didn't already tell us, correct?"

"Um, yeah, but don't we need concrete proof this is all real?" Hazel asks, on Griffin's behalf. "What's your point?"

"My point, one again, is that we already know the Pact is real. The evidence has literally been all around us, even if we had no way to make sense of it before," Ariana answers. "So really, my point is that you're all wasting time studying it so you can delay deciding what to *do* about it."

There's still an edge to Ariana's voice, but I suppose there should be given the situation. She's right—we're delaying discussing the inevitable. The impossible. So I know what I have to do next.

"Okay, if we're going to go there, I have something I need to say first," I begin, drawing everyone's attention. "I spent a lot of my time thinking about our parents, and their parents, and how they all handled the Pact. It's so effective at trapping its participants. The rules keep us from running, or talking about it, or choosing not to have kids. And if you think about it, isn't there a certain kind of reverse bravery to following the Pact rules? Our parents sacrificed so much of themselves to save others, to protect this place we all love. But that being said—"

"Just stop!" Ariana suddenly shouts. "You can justify it until you're all blue in the face, but we all know the ending. You've all already made up your minds, just like Griffin's creepy grandfather. I'm the outsider, in every way. I'm the easy target. You'll try to be nice about it, but I'm the one you'll all choose to sacrifice, when it comes down to it."

Once Ariana's voice cuts out, it's replaced by choked sobs. She crumples into a heap, her head falling into her hands. Hazel is at her side instantly, cradling her in a hug. I feel a burst of emotion myself, seeing Ariana break down this way. However, it only doubles my resolve to finish.

"You're right, Ariana. I did make up my mind about the Pact before we all walked in here. And nothing you say—nothing any of you say—can change my mind."

Ariana opens her mouth to speak again, but this time I don't let her.

"We're not sacrificing a damn thing," I say, my voice hopefully full of authority. "Just because I don't think our parents are evil for what they've done doesn't mean I think we should make the same mistakes. I say we don't consider anything other than breaking the Pact and finding a way to fight the Impact. If we all die trying to stop it, then so be it. But we stick together, no matter what."

When I stop speaking, nerves buzz in my rib cage. I know this is the only decision to make, even if facing the potential consequences is a horrifying prospect. I just hope C4 will agree…because if we start walking down the road to even discussing the sacrifice, there'll never be any going back, no matter what we choose.

Ariana still seems too overwhelmed to speak. So Hazel answers first.

"The more I think about it, the more it seems like the generations before us gave into fear, or doing what was expected of them. Maybe they didn't live in a world like ours, with easy access to information and resources. Maybe they just had no choice but to accept things as they came. But I have so many questions and I think it's worth trying to answer them. Who knows, maybe we can find some kind of weak spot, some loophole?

"I mean, it's like Luca said earlier—what are the chances the Pact only happens at Copper Cove? And if this kind of thing *does* happen elsewhere in the world, has anyone ever stopped it? What is the force that keeps the Impact trapped here—could we replicate that somehow? Could there be some clue in the way the Impact's behavior has changed? I don't know about you, but it seems like our parents fell way short, if they don't have answers to these kinds of questions."

I marvel as Hazel's big brain spins around and around, adding her list of questions to my own. Mostly I feel a surge of pride, hearing her defiance.

"I say screw our parents, and screw their failures," Griffin adds, taking his turn. "I say we do whatever we can to stop this, because I refuse to become a murderer. If we're going to kill anything, we kill the Impact."

My heart swells and splinters at the same time, hearing Griffin's reaction. Suddenly I feel more like myself than I have for a long time. It feels good, to regain a shred of agency. The notion spreads through me like a drug: we will resist, or we'll die trying.

"This… That means a lot to me," Ariana says, clearing her throat. "What you're saying is a nice idea, and I want to say I'm with you…"

She pauses again, resetting her resolve. "But what makes you think we can do anything to stop this? I don't think I can stand to have any lives on my conscience. I want to be someone who saves lives, not who puts them at risk. I hate to say this, but how do you know the Impact won't come for your parents? And even if they are off limits, how likely is it that Pact protection would extend to my family? What if, just by having this conversation, we've already loosened the Impact's chains? Why do you assume we're the ones who will pay the price for breaking the rules?"

I can't believe my ears—or rather, I don't want to. But leave it to Ariana to pinpoint the truth, inconvenient as it might be. I'm impressed, too. Who else, despite being convinced she'll be sacrificed, would still push for that same sacrifice to save others' lives? Her poked holes start to deflate my newfound confidence. I instantly think of Glo and Pan. Of Coop, and Blake. Of Manny the lifeguard. Of…our parents. Mom.

Ariana is right. Putting our own lives on the line is one thing, but I can't bear the thought of risking anyone else's.

"I hear you, Ariana. I think we all do," Griffin says,

finally. "But don't you think we have to at least try to see what we can learn? There can't be harm in doing that, right?"

"I don't know. But I do know I'm outvoted. And grateful," Ariana answers. "I won't ever lie about what I really think. So I'll say this: let's do things your way, for now. But shouldn't we have a backup plan for the sacrifice in case something does go south?"

"We have three days until then," I interject, very much not wanting to pick at our collective scabs—or think about what might ooze out if we do.

"I'm with Luca," Griffin says. "Let's learn what we can first. Then we regroup?"

Hazel nods. "Where do we start? I'm trying to remember if there's anything my dad ever told me, something that might help."

"Honestly? Not to be predictable, but I think we start with some sleep," Ariana says. "I don't know about you all, but thirty minutes was not enough time to process all this. And it's late. Cecil said the Impact is usually dormant on the night of the Pact reveal, and it left us alone last night. Since we're probably safe from it coming for us tonight, maybe we take advantage of that and start fresh first thing in the morning?"

I want to argue with Ariana, but the moment she suggests sleep, my gut tells me she's right. I'm tired all the way down to my bones.

Dissecting the Pact is going to take every shred of energy and ingenuity we have. Pulling an all-nighter to take stabs in the dark doesn't feel like the best first step.

"You guys go," Griffin says. "I'll stay here and

double-check my work, see if I can find us any leads."

"I'm too amped up to sleep yet," Hazel adds. "I'll stay and help Griffin awhile."

I can't stop the next thought from creeping up my spine, lodging itself at the base of my skull like a parasite. God forbid it does come to a vote, Hazel and Griffin would never pick one another. My heart begins to hammer against my will again, because I can't help but think...

Where does that leave me?

Chapter Fourteen

I don't want to leave Bellfour, not really, but I can feel it bubbling up my nervous system—the thing I've been trying to prevent this whole time. I thought I had it under control, but tonight has bust everything loose.

Just now, before I walked out of Bellfour, I tried to tell the others I was going back to Hemlock to shower. Instead, what came out of my mouth was, "Shower need."

The first time my speech got scrambled like this during a panic attack, I thought I was having a stroke. I learned afterwards this is common during some anxiety attacks. Your short-term memory is so gripped with unwarranted fight-or-flight adrenaline that words and sentences can temporarily lose their meaning.

Even knowing that, it's still deeply terrifying.

As I made my way towards Bellfour's door, I lost all sensation in my hands. Then my vision spotted and unfocused. And now, walking out of the Auditorium and into the night, panic overrides my entire body.

Fuck. No.

It's like the tide I've been barely holding back this week finally surges. The carefully constructed dam in my brain bursts and panic floods into my system, overwhelming everything else.

Overwhelm.

I focus on the word, but I have a hard time understanding the meaning. *Overwhelm.* Somewhere in the back of my mind I recognize that word, but bizarrely, it holds no weight. *Overwhelm? Overwhelming?* I can't grasp its meaning.

I'm able to heave shallow breaths during my attacks instead of feeling entirely unable to breathe, but I can never really gather my thoughts. If only I could hear something besides my heart thundering in my ears, if only I could feel my fingers, maybe… But all I can focus on is the imminent, pressing, all-encompassing instinct that I am in the process of dying.

It's like my mind has been invaded.

My thoughts consumed.

Like I'm drowning, trapped in my own body.

It's unbearable.

I can't go back to Hemlock, that won't help. I can't face Mom. I can't face anyone, not like this. Which means there's only one place to go.

It's impossible for me to tell how long it takes to make it down to the lake, seconds or minutes. My thoughts are a cyclone that obscures everything else.

The first panic attack I ever had came out of literally nowhere, one night when I was finishing my homework. I thought I was having a heart attack, so I told Mom and we ended up at the hospital. Once we learned what it was, we both thought therapy might be a good idea. That's where I learned most of what I know about panic attacks, that they often come unexpectedly, bubbling up from relatively benign sources. A psychiatrist told me that accumulated and unexpressed stress is like filling up a bathtub with a shot glass—after a while, all it takes is one tiny shot to make everything overflow.

My subsequent panic attacks sometimes come from nowhere, but a lot of them have more specific triggers—little emotional spinouts that balloon and explode. And tonight, I've taken more than a few shots.

From the outside, I know what people who haven't experienced an attack assume: Just stop thinking about it, just rationalize the thoughts and feelings away. But it's impossible to describe how, once I've dropped into this physical space, my body is in charge. Sure, I can chip away at the mass of panic with calm thinking and rehearsed breathing—but only little by little, over time. The only way to kick these episodes permanently is to lower my overall stress level, which I thought I had been doing.

My gut clenches. Something about the attacks always drops my stomach. I wish I could puke, but everything is moving down, not up. Until I realize there is something I can do.

I can swim.

After all, it's the only thing that seems to burn away the panic. To churn and exhaust the anxiety, giving it a place to spin and sputter out. It must be why my body brought me to the lake. And why I'm soon stripped to my boxers, swimming out to the dock. I know it's dangerous to swim alone at night. Normally I'd never take such a risk given my deep fear of drowning—of failing at the one thing I'm actually good at—but it feels more dangerous to stay on land.

Toxic, anxious things litter the land.

In the water, I'm sleek and vital and strong. I'm a bullet hitting a target, I'm a machine made to work, I'm cold and clear. I'm not helpless or on the fritz, I'm not out of control or overheated or rudderless. I'm not...*bound* by anything.

I swim out to the dock and back to shore until my limbs ache and my mind goes blank.

I have no idea how long I swim. When I finally decide to stop, I think I'm at the shore, but find I'm actually at the dock. I climb up the ladder onto the wooden surface and lie on my back, my chest heaving with each breath. As water drips across my body I close my eyes and fight the urge to sleep. To melt into the dock and become one with the lake, where I can remain hollow and numb and at peace.

Like Tommy—just another spirit haunting this maybe holy, maybe hellish place.

When I finally open my eyes, I'm startled by how many stars are in the sky, by how bright they are. My home doesn't have many stars. Now I know why.

It's because Copper Cove kept them all for itself.

And it turns out there's a price.

The need to close my eyes, to make myself something more than I really am, comes over me again. I imagine myself as Echo, Spirit of the Lake, circling forever in laps of my own creation. Swirling and churning through the water's long blue depths, a being of pure emotion and devotion.

When I open my eyes, stars fill my vision once again. During the eight days I've already spent at Copper Cove, it hasn't occurred to me to look at the stars—not once. Just like it hadn't occurred to me before this moment to look across the dock...

Where a row of hairy spiders line the edge—the dark fishing spiders. Shit, how could I have forgotten about them? This close, each one seems the size of a frying pan. Their long brown legs move towards me...

Though the first has already arrived.

I don't have time to scream before it reaches my outstretched hand, rearing to bite. I pull away before the spider can sink its fangs into me. On instinct, I jump back into the lake. But instead of the burst of adrenaline I expect to carry me away, my limbs are spent. I've wasted whatever reserves of panic I had built up. Now that I really need some fight-or-flight juice, I'm a hollowed-out husk.

My head dips under the surface before I can press my lips closed. Water spills into my mouth and down my throat and I think, with a blunt pang, that I might very well drown—the final betrayal of my exhausted body. Or is it the Impact, the wretched mystery thing, orchestrating my demise? Going after my last remaining source of sanity? As water pours into me, a wild smack of fear wrenches alive somewhere deep inside... I can't breathe.

I can't breathe.

I'm not breathing.

My arms must start pumping, because next thing I know my head splashes back into the cool night air and oxygen sucks itself into my choking lungs. I regain my senses just in time to see the enormous brown spiders crawling down the side of the dock, dropping into the water with terrible plunking splashes.

They rest on the surface until, lit by the moon and the stars, the dark spiders begin to streak towards me like silent assassins.

Thankfully my legs find a way to start working again.

My mind fills with images of the swimming spiders reaching me, biting away chunks until I dip into the blackened water, my lungs burning as I'm eaten alive. This vision is enough to get me to shore unscathed, scrambling up the hill with water still running from my nose and mouth in spurts and fits. By the time I turn back to see the spiders rippling to shore, I'm up the hill. But not so far that I don't see the impossible shape they arrange themselves into:

The broken infinity symbol.

The sign of the Pact...or the Impact?

It takes everything I have left to return to Hemlock. As I run, all I can think is, What more does this monster want from me, from us?

Then, as I fall into my warm bed, I think...

These unanswered questions just might be the death of me.

$$\infty$$

When I wake up, it's to a faint knock on my door.

I stir, feeling groggy. At first I hope it's not Mom. Then I hope it actually is her, returned to tell me everything is going to be okay.

Morning sunshine pours into my room as I open the door, backlighting none other than Ariana. She holds two cups of coffee.

"I need to talk to you."

Ariana pushes past me and pokes her head into the bathroom, looking into the next room.

"Your mom isn't there. Any idea where she slept last night?"

"No," I answer, wiping the crusted drool from my cheek. "Shouldn't we be meeting Hazel and Griffin?"

"We will," Ariana begins. "But I wanted to come see you first."

Ariana settles the coffee cups on my dresser and sits on the second bed. I close the door, wishing I had a moment to wake up before being bombarded. But when I turn back around, the look on Ariana's face jolts me awake.

She takes a deep breath before speaking again. The Ariana I know barrels into things headfirst, so this pause sends up an invisible flare in my brain.

"I wanted to make sure you were okay," Ariana says finally. "I don't mean to pry, but something seemed really off with you the other night, even before this…Pact madness. And not in the usual 'Luca can be silently uptight about things' kind of way. This seemed more like the full breakdown kind of way? And then you ran off last night before I could…

"Look, I know you usually talk to Hazel or Griffin about personal stuff, but"—Ariana takes another unusual, extended pause—"with the two of them coupled up, I just wanted you to know you can talk to me. If you want."

Ariana's offer slips past my guard, disarming me. I've always admired her, and I've certainly always had fun with her—but confiding in her? Touchy-feely conversations have never really been her thing. Or is that just another myth I've told myself? I always thought Frances and Ariana had a lot in common—is it possible this summer I built another invisible wall between us? Why shouldn't I confide in Ariana? After all, everything has changed already...

This thought forces another question into my brain, one I'd much rather avoid. Is Ariana's newfound concern genuine...or is this really about the Pact? About the potential sacrifice we have to make? About...shifting allegiances?

I turn my head away, facing the wall. There stand my fantasy figurines, frozen forever mid-fight. I focus on them as I try to clear the little tears from the corners of my eyes. I thought after last night I might have tired out my emotions, but Ariana's gesture has restarted the fountain in me. Suddenly, I don't care what her motivations might be. The words bubble up on my tongue, little hostages begging for release.

When I turn back to face Ariana, it all comes tumbling out.

∞

"I...wow."

Ariana sits and stares at me, failing to form a reaction. I've never seen her struck speechless, but then, I've just spoken more than enough for the both of us. Starting with Frances's outing and ending with last night's panic attack, I tell Ariana everything—even about my feelings for Griffin. I didn't necessarily mean to, but I also didn't really feel like I had a choice. If last night was any indication, it's too much weight for me to carry alone.

"Well, first off, can I track down this Frances

monster for you and pull out all of her hair, or pee in her lemonade, or something equally vile?"

Against the odds, I laugh. Revenge fantasies aren't exactly my thing, but something about all that sounds particularly satisfying. And it proves to me Frances and Ariana *are* different, at least in the ways that matter most.

"Jeez, Luca. I mean, I always maybe thought... Wait, does anyone else know about your thing for Griffin?"

I shake my head. Well, Frances knew, but she doesn't count anymore.

"Damn. Luca Piccone, I always suspected there was a lot going on in that head of yours, but..."

Ariana pauses again, shaking her head before turning back to face me.

"I'm really, really sorry all of that happened to you. I can't fathom what that felt like..." she starts, her voice dropping uncharacteristically low. "But I do kind of know what it's like to feel invisible wherever you go."

I suppress another laugh. The idea that Ariana, big and bold and dripping with confidence, could feel invisible anywhere...doesn't make any sense.

"Okay, well maybe not exactly invisible. But try being the new girl every couple of years," Ariana says louder, catching my reaction. "Or the Persian girl when we lived in the South, or the atheist girl when we lived in Mumbai, or the five-foot-ten size fourteen anywhere on the planet? It's why I've focused so much on getting into the Pre-Med program at Penn, or painting, or singing. Hobbies and goals are usually easier to keep than friends, at least in my world."

"I..." I begin, trying to process this new barrage of thoughts. "I guess that makes total sense. But to be honest, I kind of always thought you were impervious. I mean, you're well traveled, talented, smart, beautiful..."

"Please, do go on."

"No, I mean it. Ever since we were kids, you've always seen what you wanted and just gone for it, without apology. I always wished I could be more like that."

"You can be, you know."

"I don't think so. I'm not really built that way."

Ariana sighs.

"Well, while we're being honest with each other," she says, "if you thought I was intimidating or whatever, I kind of thought you were...content. Not like, in a shallow way or anything. But you just always seemed so happy and like nothing really bothered you. I mean, aside from being tightly clenched about Copper Cove traditions."

"I'm only that way when I'm here. Content, I mean. At least, that's how I want to be," I say. "This feels like the one place I can be myself. Or it used to."

We sit in silence for several beats, letting that thought resonate.

"I feel the same way," Ariana replies. "There's always been something special about Copper Cove. Trust me, I've done the legwork abroad. It's like you can somehow just... be *okay*, here. I guess now we know why. Or rather, now we know what that really costs."

Ariana brings her hand to her mouth, looking emotional herself, now.

"Copper Cove has been the one place my whole life

I haven't had to worry about not fitting in," she adds. "I just... How could that have changed overnight?"

Here, in this moment, I suddenly feel so understood, it nearly overwhelms me. I don't know what to say to Ariana to let her know how much this all means to me, how much it makes me feel seen. And sane.

In response, all I can say is, "It doesn't have to change. We're still us."

"Are we?" Ariana asks. "With Hazel and Griffin now a couple, and with your feelings. I mean, I always thought maybe one of the three of you had a thing for the other, but as much as Hazel and I talk, she never... Well..."

It looks as if something occurs to Ariana just then, but she seems to change her mind about saying it out loud.

"Honestly, I've always been terrified my feelings for Griffin were kind of obvious," I say.

"You hide it better than you think," Ariana answers. "But I've also always thought Griffin likes soaking in attention a little too much."

"So I'm not...crazy to think he sends me mixed signals sometimes?"

"Not at all. But I also think he kind of sends everyone mixed signals. It's like, part of his August charm?"

I consider that. It's both familiar and foreign, comforting and horrifying, to glimpse our unspoken love triangle from Ariana's perspective.

"Hey, why did it take some unthinkable pact to make us have a conversation like this?" I ask.

"I don't know, it's just how things got to be?" Ariana sighs. "You and Hazel have all your little inside jokes and secret languages, and you…have your own thing with Griffin, obviously. And then Griffin and I have our Craft Shop sessions and our duets, and Hazel and I have all this stuff we don't ever tell you boys about. So I guess along the way you and I never really made a thing of our own?

"But Luca, it really means a lot to me, you telling me all this. I know it's not easy for you. Hell, it's not easy for me, either," she says. "So if there's a silver lining to this whole shitty thing, maybe this, right here, can be it?"

Despite everything, I somehow break into a small smile. Maybe it can, indeed. We have so much to untangle, so much to overcome. But right now, after releasing some of this pressure, I feel…not exactly unburdened, but certainly *lightened*.

"And hey, I want you to know, if you have another one of those panic attacks while we're up here, you can always come find me," Ariana adds. "I'm pretty good at cutting through the noise and snapping people out of it. Or just listening."

"That you are," I say. "And you are going to make a very good doctor someday."

I mean this as a compliment, but the idea seems to cut Ariana somewhere deep. It makes horrible sense, suddenly. Because right now, in the face of the Pact, nothing about our futures feels certain.

"Luca, I don't want to say it, I really don't," Ariana starts, causing my heart to drop into my stomach. "But if we really do have to make the…decision. With Griffin and Hazel together now, I just think—"

"It won't come to that," I interrupt, feeling short of breath all over again. "It won't. It can't."

Ariana holds my gaze, intensity burning in her eyes. Her look says the words she doesn't dare speak:

But what if it does?

Suddenly, I can't tell where Ariana's concern for me ends and the concern for herself begins. Can both coexist at the same time? Does this mean I should be thinking about the sacrifice more, that I should...

No, I stop myself again. We may not know much about the Pact or the Impact yet, but I have to remember this much—they're designed to make us feel this way. To breed mistrust and paranoia, to express negativity, to let corruption seep through the surface—all to force us into making that sacrifice.

We can't let that happen.

Which means Ariana and I need to get back to Bellfour, back to Griffin and Hazel. The only way to disarm these questions will be by finding the right answers. And if I can trust in anything, it's that Griffin and Hazel probably spent all night finding some kind of lead.

"We got this, Ariana," I say, crossing the room to hug her before we go.

Then, holding her tightly, more words tumble from my mouth, making themselves known against my will.

"I've got you. I promise."

I wish I knew what this swear really meant.

Chapter Fifteen

Once I'm dressed, Ariana and I step outside to make our way back to Bellfour. This early, campus is still quiet—which is maybe why I'm able to hear Mom and Garrett speaking just above a whisper behind the door to Hazel's Hemlock room. The sound halts me in my tracks, stopping Ariana beside me. If we hold perfectly still, I can make out what they're saying.

"I'm sure she just slept in Bellfour with Griffin," Mom says. "I checked; Luca slept in his bed. He looked so…"

Mom can't seem to finish that sentence. Suddenly, all I want to do is fling open the door and give her a hug. Or maybe scream at her. Both, probably.

But what price would I have to pay for talking to her, now? The parents all warned us it was against the rules to speak to anyone outside C4 about the Pact. What fresh hell would rain down on us if I tried to have an honest conversation with my mother?

Part of me wants to challenge it, to separate any fact from potential fiction. To see *it*, period. I feel like the image of the Impact cooked up by my fantasy brain could be far worse than what it actually is. But then I remember with a crash that I probably already did see the Impact, right here on this balcony, the night it slid that silverfish in my ear. I only got a blurry glimpse, but what I thought I saw was...

Grotesque.

"There's so much I need to tell Hazel."

Garrett's hushed voice swings me back to the present.

"You know we can't," Mom says. "Nothing is worth the risk—we've been down that road. You can say whatever you need to say when...if..."

Mom can't bring herself to finish that sentence, either.

When this is all over, *if* our children survive.

Fear creases my shoulder blades, tensing everything.

"Say it to me, for now," Mom goes on. "What you need to say to Hazel, say to me."

My eyes lock with Ariana's—should we be listening to this? Could the Impact sense this eavesdropping, somehow? There's so much we still don't know about how the Pact works...

"Hazel, you were always wanted," Garrett says, directly. "If you die, I'll die too."

Garrett's whispers take my breath away. Especially as Mom begins to cry quietly.

"I hope the kids feel that much, after the lives we tried to give them?" Mom sobs. "Were they right, Garrett? All these years, I thought we were being strong, being selfless. But have we really just been weak? And selfish?"

"They don't know the things we do," Garrett answers. "I hope they understand, someday."

"I hope they never have to," Mom says. "Do you really think they'll listen to that monster Cecil about poor Ariana? Tommy didn't listen about you, but Wendy—"

Mom stops talking then. It sounds like Garrett moves towards her.

"Stop. This helps nothing."

"What else are we going to do? It's too much. Feeling so powerless."

A thinly drawn silence ensues. I look at Ariana, wondering if we should go...

Until I hear it.

Garrett kissing Mom.

My jaw drops open. So does Ariana's.

New questions flood my mind, the first blaring: How long has *that* been going on? I know Garrett and Mom were in love once, but Tommy's death wedged them apart. Now we know the reasons why. But could this big reveal, this pressure release, be the thing that's pushed them back together?

Ariana places a hand on my shoulder and tilts her head sideways—it's time to go. She's right. As much as it pains me, there's nothing here for us. Now more than ever, it's clear...

We're on our own.

At least that's what I think before we reach the stairs to exit Hemlock and come face-to-face with the last person I expected to see here in Copper Cove:

Wendy August.

She wears a thin cardigan and chic flowy pants, but no amount of finery can hide the look on her face. Wendy is *exhausted*. And just as surprised to see us as we are to see her.

"What are you doing here?" Ariana asks, the challenge in her voice blatant.

It's a valid question—I can't remember the last time

I saw Wendy set foot on Copper Cove's campus. It's an unnatural sight, somehow, like a fish pulled out of water.

"We shouldn't be speaking." Wendy's words are delivered sharply, but they don't match the anxious expression on her face. Especially as she scans the nearby woods.

It's clear she's terrified of whatever this Impact thing is. Or rather, she's terrified of what the Impact might inflict upon her for breaking any rules. It's almost imperceptible, but Wendy's leg bounces nervously under her pants—the leg the Impact broke, once upon a time.

"My mom is up there with Garrett," I say. "That's why you're here, right? Because it couldn't actually be to find your son."

My words surprise me. I don't know where they come from, save for the deep well of resentment I have pooled at the center of my being. Wendy's face freezes over. Suddenly the ice queen cometh, steeped in a glacier of her own guilt.

"I hope this doesn't mean you two have formed some little union," Wendy says. "I'd expect more from you, Luca."

Wendy doesn't look at me when she says this; instead she stares at Ariana with disdain, like a piece of trash to be taken out. I know Wendy must be acting out of some misguided sense of fear or maternal instinct or even self-preservation, but after everything we bore witness to last night...

I've never seen something more inexcusable.

"And I wouldn't expect you to give a shit about any of us." My voice rages with intensity, armed to kill. I glance to Ariana expecting the same fire, but the only expression on her face is pain.

Just then, a door opens behind us. I turn and my eyes connect with my mother's. In that second, I can feel her.

And she is made of fear.

"No. You can't be talking," Mom gasps. "You shouldn't be—"

Mom doesn't finish, because some ragged shape suddenly flashes beside me. Ariana doesn't even have time to scream before she's pulled down the stairs and into the woods behind Hemlock.

I just run. The trip down the stairs and through the outer trees feels like it takes an eternity. It isn't until I've broken fully into the woods that I realize Wendy is running beside me. As unexpected as this is, it's not necessarily unwelcome. I have no idea what I'm about to find.

Until one second later.

We come upon Ariana's body in the dirt, legs thrashing. Something sits on top of her—the Impact. I can't make out much more than a shadowy and foul blur, nor can I make out what it's doing to Ariana.

I charge forward to save her, but to my surprise, Wendy makes it there first. She throws her body into the Impact, shoulder-checking it off Ariana. I expect the thing to howl or reel, but instead it strikes back at Wendy. Some thin, unidentifiable appendage knocks her back onto the root-covered ground.

Just as quickly as it came, the murky Impact then disappears, recoiling across the woods like a bullet.

By the time I make it to Ariana, Mom has also reached her side. And she gasps, just like I do.

Ariana lies in a bed of strange plants made of

dense seedpods. The exposed skin on her arms and face has been…infected. Every inch is set with fleshy divots, pockets of circles filled with tiny particles. Ariana looks like a living disease spore.

"What happened?" she croaks, looking at Mom and me. "What…"

Ariana raises her hand and sees the trypophobia-inducing holes that cover her skin. Mom barely gets her hand over Ariana's mouth before she begins shrieking.

"Drawing attention will only make it worse," Mom says. "Luca, get Ariana to a shower. She will be okay."

"But—" I try.

"None of us will be okay if you stay near us," Mom interrupts. Her frantic eyes lock in on mine, begging me to understand.

I just… I don't want to.

That's when we both hear it—Wendy whimpering behind us. We turn to find Garrett helping her to her feet. Her beautiful clothes are covered in dirt, and blood spills out of a deep gash that mars her porcelain cheek.

"I… I can't…" she stammers, stumbling. "I thought I could, but I can't do this. Not again."

Setting my eyes on Wendy, all I see are the contradictions. Condemning Ariana, saving her. Coming, going. Loving, isolating. Composure, panic. Something below Wendy's perfect surface has cracked through, bloodied and broken. She stands before us, both visible and divisible.

Despite myself, all I can think is, Poor Griffin.

"Luca, you have to go," Mom says, snapping me out of it. "Now."

She's right. I know she is. But I don't—

"Listen to me," Mom says, pulling me closer. "Listen to me carefully, figlio mio."

Mom whispers in my ear, slow and steady: "I'll still be here, when it all burns down."

∞

The day that follows is filled with frustrations.

The only consolation is, after several showers, Ariana's skin has finally begun to clear up. We were all worried she might have been permanently maimed, but much like the Impact's previous hauntings, this one was designed primarily to terrify.

Still, this feels like a clear escalation—and likely only the beginning. When will taunting turn into permanent injury, like the gash on Wendy's face? Or Garrett's lost eye? Or…even worse?

This is the question we were left with when Ariana and I finally made it back to Bellfour, along with a renewed fear of just how deep the Impact can cut us. I didn't want to, but all morning I felt the instinct to distance myself from Ariana, for fear of catching some contagious infection. What the Impact did to her didn't just trigger her biggest phobia—it also made us, her best friends, wary to be around her. How messed up—how on point—is that?

Just what in all holy hell are we dealing with here?

We eventually told Hazel and Griffin about what happened. It shook them just as deeply. Mom and Garrett's confessions, their kiss, Wendy's Copper Cove return, her interference and retreat—the through lines ran deep.

In many ways, these events represented our sincerest childhood dreams coming true, just in the most twisted ways imaginable.

We spent the morning trying to pick apart the final words Mom left me with: *I'll still be here, when it all burns down.* Something about the way Mom whispered the phrase, the way she worded it so specifically, felt like some coded clue. Unfortunately, it meant nothing to Ariana and me. And despite their full night spent in Bellfour reading Copper Cove histories, the best Hazel and Griffin could do was suggest that maybe Mom was referencing the Morrissey Village fire of 1924.

Once it got to be afternoon, we searched the campus. Another visit to the Weiss Crypt turned up nothing except a fresh batch of nerves for potentially tempting the Impact. There was no way to get through the old padlock on the door anyway. Griffin chanced a solo trip back to August Manor to ransack his grandfather's study and scour the internet, but he returned empty-handed—and having missed Wendy. She was evidently rushed to the hospital after "a bad fall," according to the staff.

While Griffin was gone, the rest of us searched the Copper Cove Archive, but we couldn't turn up any references to the Pact. If we learned anything from this first day of research, it was how thoroughly and effectively the Pact has been kept a complete secret. And, of course, that talking to the only people who might have leads for us would just result in being terrorized.

Even now, as C4 sits in Bellfour with the sun setting outside, I can't get Mom's words out of my head.

I'll still be here, when it all burns down. It has to mean something, I know it does. But how will we find out if we can't ask her? Or worse, if we do ask her and she refuses to budge? It's impossible to know what's right here. And after the futile, fearful first day we've had, we're even more collectively lost than before.

"Okay, I'm calling it," Ariana says, breaking our most recent stretch of silence.

Her C4 hoodie covers the remaining imprints on her limbs, but her face still sports some spots, which are thankfully fading with each passing hour. I can't imagine how...violated she must feel.

Actually, on second nauseating thought, I *can* imagine.

"We have nothing," Ariana continues. "I really think it's time we start to consider—"

Ariana is interrupted, however, as Griffin pulls a bottle of whiskey off the shelf and places it down on the coffee table between us.

"Um, what are you doing?" Ariana asks.

Griffin looks up at her and the expression on his face surprises me, like something has shaken loose in his head. His eyes seem to pierce Ariana's, but I can't quite parse why, aside from the obvious.

"If we really do have nothing to go on, if we really can't think of what to do next," Griffin begins, "then we can figure out how we're going to handle...*that*...tomorrow."

Griffin can't bring himself to say the *s*-word—none of us can. He looks so tired, not having slept last night. But it's more than that. He looks...resigned. I can imagine how heavily this family legacy stuff weighs on him in particular, the things his grandfather and mother said. The things they've done.

Though honestly, right now it feels like deception runs in all of our blood.

"Tonight is the Emp Bonfire at Skinny Point," Griffin continues. "If this really is our last chance, then I say we have one final night of...living together."

Griffin pours himself a tumbler of whiskey and downs a gulp. Instantly, he reminds me of Wendy. Shutting down and repressing it all with a drink, the WASP sting of choice. I feel so much for him, it literally hurts.

But is Griffin right? If it really is time to give in, are we all entitled to...what? Get blind drunk together one last time?

"I'm not stopping, even if I have to read every damn book on this godforsaken campus," Hazel immediately reacts, looking annoyed. Then she sighs. "Although, my eyes are starting to cross. I think I've been awake too long. I need to reset my brain. If letting loose is what you all need to do that, fine. But I'm going to get some sleep, if that's okay?"

I turn to Ariana, next. And the same question forms behind her eyes, the same despicable one that crosses my mind: Is this the first rift we're seeing form between C4's golden couple?

Instantly, I reach for the bottle of whiskey.

Griffin is right. If we're going to start going *there*, I need a drink. Several drinks, actually. Because how can we even begin to make a decision like who to sacrifice? Would we put it to some kind of vote? Would one of us volunteer, or more than one of us? Could I volunteer, myself? Would I lay my life on the line for these people, for this place I love more than anything in the world? Could I even survive if one of these three did that for me?

It all feels so…unspeakable.

If we're going to start talking about chosen ones, then I definitely need to get out of my damn mind.

Chapter Sixteen

Standing by the bonfire, the warm swaddle of alcohol wraps around my mind like a blanket, numbing and heightening everything at the same time. It's been awhile since I last got drunk, but tonight I remember why people like it so much. Tonight, it's the escape I desperately need.

Even if I know I'll pay the price for it tomorrow.

I could only handle Griffin's whiskey for so long before switching to Bud Light Limes. He obviously called me out, saying I was opting for light beer as another of my "guise of health" choices. That was right before he and I walked down to Skinny Point, leaving Hazel and Ariana to rest and recover in Bellfour.

I probably should be resting too, but right now this party feels like the only recovery I need. Music pulses across the sand and young people wear easy smiles. It's life, unburdened. Or rather, appropriately burdened by flirting and fitting in.

It even works on me for a while, standing beside Griffin as he charms everyone by the fire. Then, somewhere along the way, my tide begins to turn. Eventually, I want to scream.

Because I want to be normal.

I want to run.

And standing here with Griffin by the firelight, he starts to feel like a reminder of everything I get wrong in my life...

Even if he is still beautiful.

I feel the need to be somewhere other than at his side, so I tell Griffin I have to pee. It might even be true, so I walk off into the nearby woods, appearing to have a sense of purpose. When I get far enough along a trail that the party fades into the background, I stop in place.

Because a carcass lies before me—a possum maybe?

I should probably be grossed out by the gaping hole in the animal's chest and the exposed redness leaking out, but all I can focus on are its eyes: rolled back, beady little orbs that once had life in them, but now resemble grim marbles.

My mind flashes to the Impact, twisted and sharp. Is this its handiwork, too? Some bloody reminder? But for who? And what kind of fate am I tempting, wandering into the woods like this? I'm obviously not thinking clearly, which I guess was the whole dangerous point.

"Oh jeez, another one?"

The voice startles me and I turn, though my reflexes are definitely impaired by the alcohol. My gruesome discovery sobered me up momentarily, but now the buzz sloshes around in my brain again as I set my eyes on Manny the lifeguard. I haven't seen him at any more of my swims, and I completely forgot about our exchange, with everything going on. Manny wears a black T-shirt and dark jeans and looks distinctly better than I remember.

"We've been finding dead animals all over campus," he says, walking to join me. "Different kinds, squirrels and raccoons, all of them with their chests ripped into like that. But want to know the weirdest part?"

I nod as Manny moves closer, pleasantly surprised to find he smells like sandalwood and bonfire smoke.

"Apparently all of their lungs have been eaten," Manny says, looking at the dead animal. "How weird is that? Copper Cove is thinking of reporting it to the state. No one knows any reason that animal lungs would be missing. Assuming it's not a human doing it, this might be some new nature thing to document."

"That's awful," I say, to keep from laughing. Or maybe crying.

No, this isn't some new nature thing. This was done by something decidedly unnatural. Thinking this, all I want to do is get away. To be somewhere else, be someone else, if only for a little while.

"Where were you headed, just now?" I ask.

"If I told you, I'd have to kill you."

Manny smiles, but I don't. It's not funny.

"Tough crowd," he laughs, for both of us. "I was headed to my secret spot, but actually, I was kind of hoping I'd run into you tonight."

I tense. What a preposterous thought. The notion that someone would be thinking of me, looking for me—especially someone like Manny. It makes me feel something...unfamiliar.

"Well, secret Copper Cove spots are my favorite," I reply, not sure what else to say. "Can you show me?"

Manny nods, so we start walking. He leads the way onto another dirt path, one that looks like it's been forged solely by foot traffic. I didn't know there was anything back here in the woods, but leave it to the Emps to have some extra-special spots. Thinking this makes me feel a bit more like my old self, the one who got to cherish every Copper Cove second. Maybe I really can play the part of normal boy again, if only for this one night?

"How has your week been?" I venture.

"Good. They switched my lifeguard shifts around, which is probably why I haven't seen you swimming."

"And here I thought you were avoiding me."

"Not at all," Manny replies. "But I have to admit, as much as I love it here, I'm ready to get back to the real world."

"Where's that, for you?"

"Starting my sophomore year at Catholic University, down in DC."

I scroll back to our first conversation and my overshare about swimming and prayer. Then I experience a fresh surge of embarrassment, learning that Manny goes to such a religious school.

"Oh, you must have loved my swimming monologue from last time, then."

"Actually, it really stuck with me."

"Uh-oh."

"No, it's a good thing." He laughs again. "I didn't necessarily plan on going to a Catholic college, it was just the best school I got into. Though trust me, my parents were beyond thrilled. I've never really found a way to reconcile being queer with the whole Catholic thing, so I've kind of avoided participating in religion as much as possible. Until what you said to me the other day."

Queer. It's the one word I fixate on, baffled by how casual it can sound. Then again, I don't hide my sexuality here in Copper Cove either. Is this really what life could be like all the time, after...?

After what? What does *after* even mean, anymore?

I pull the sleeves of my C4 hoodie over my hands as a breeze from the lake behind kicks up. For better or worse, I've worn it too much for it to smell like Griffin anymore.

Griffin. I left him back at the party. Is he going to think I—

"I mean, it sounds weird now, but no one ever really told me it was possible to look at religion that way," Manny continues, interrupting my thoughts. "I always thought you either had to believe all of it or none of it. I never really thought to focus only on the parts that worked for me."

"That's a lot of why organized religion doesn't work for me," I respond. It feels good, using my brain for something other than worrying. "It can be so valuable if experienced with intent, but I think most people are expected to go into organized religion blindly. To wait to be told what to do by some authority figure claiming to have the answers. But no one has the answers, isn't that the whole point of religion? I mean, if we did, we wouldn't need it in the first place. Really, we only have the questions. So, organized or not, I think a good religion should be about helping us ask the questions that make us better people, not pretending to have all the answers stockpiled somewhere."

"Are you always this eloquent when drinking?" Manny asks, looking at me in a way I don't quite recognize. "Or this passionate when talking to relative strangers, for that matter?"

Actually, no. What is it about Manny that gets me kicked into monologue mode like this? Is it nerves…or the opposite? I can't tell if it's the alcohol or the honesty, but my veins buzz with possibility. Is this what it's like, to be something resembling yourself on the very first try?

Manny walks us into a clearing where a cold campfire is crowded with log benches and discarded beer cans. He keeps going and we head a little farther into the woods, until we come upon what looks like a large dome of clustered trees.

"Welcome to my favorite place in all of Copper Cove," he says, leading me behind a curtain of leafy branches. "One of the older Emps showed it to me a few weeks ago and it's where I've been going to think. Well, I guess I could call it praying, since I met you."

We stand in a circle of trees with twisty, gnarled branches. These branches hang low to the ground, eventually dipping under the dirt, where they seem to grow into the roots of the next tree trunk. This circle of trees, branch to root, is what forms the leaf-walled biosphere.

"None of us have been able to figure out what this tree actually is, but our best guess is that it's an angel oak," Manny offers, stepping up to one of the central trunks. "It kind of looks like a Pirangi cashew tree, but those definitely don't grow on the East Coast. Actually, even if it is an oak, it shouldn't be growing here, from what I can tell. But who knows, I'm not an arborist. I just think it's pretty. And that it's a nice metaphor, the way the branches dip back down and seem to form the next tree."

I agree. In fact, I'm overwhelmed by it—this secret, special place hidden deeper inside my already secret, special place. It's like the tree has formed its own atmosphere, its own radius, existing as an island apart in the middle of the forest. Suddenly it's as if the Pact and the Impact are washed away, like they couldn't possibly touch me here.

"It really is," I whisper.

"They call it the Infinity Tree, because of the way it loops in on itself, how it doesn't really end. Plus, that super-cool old branch there."

Manny points to a thick hanging branch. Instead of dipping back down into the earth, this one has twisted in on itself, forming a crude infinity symbol suspended in midair. I don't know if broken infinity really is the thing that symbolizes the death pact and the deadly Impact. But if it does, this place of complete, circular life feels like exactly the right escape.

"So, I'm getting to hang with a real live member of the infamous Copper Cove Core Four," Manny says, settling to sit on a log. "I'm surprised you came down from your tower to grace us with your presence."

"What are you talking about?" I laugh, sitting beside him. "You guys, the Emps and everyone else who hangs out here at Skinny Point, you're the cool kids. We just do our own thing because we've known each other forever."

"Says the guy in his special hoodie who pre-gamed in his super-exclusive clubhouse."

"Please! You guys have the Emp Rec Center. I've

wanted to go in there since I was a little kid. I promise you, no one pays attention to the four of us."

It's preposterous, what Manny is saying about C4. We're a bunch of misfits who don't fit into the Copper Cove social scene. We don't hang in the Falcon's Nest or use fake IDs to get into the Smokehouse bar a few miles off campus. C4 couldn't be more set apart from all that normal, cool-kid stuff...as we've painfully learned.

"Look, it may be my first time at Family Week, but you guys are kind of legendary around here," Manny says. "The chosen friends of Griffin August, heir to the Copper Cove fortune. You all go to fancy schools and your parents have cool jobs. Everyone knows who you four are, and that your clique is airtight. Not to mention you're all kind of gorgeous."

I'm too stunned to register the compliment. C4 isn't some exclusive club, and we aren't all...*are we?* Being friends with Griffin and Hazel and Ariana has always felt so natural. We've done our own thing for so long, it never even occurred to me we could be viewed like this. But the way Manny puts it...

"Sorry, I didn't mean to call you out or anything," he says, probably catching the look on my face. "I mean, my parents emigrated from Mexico when I was a kid, and we live in a tiny town near Albany. My dad works in a factory, and I went to a giant, shitty public school. So you're all kind of like TV show characters to me. It's why I was so surprised when we talked on the beach that day. I didn't expect you to be so...introspective?"

Maybe it's the alcohol, but my brain is having a

tough time absorbing any of this. I'm not the guy Manny is describing. Well, I am. But not…

"And it's not like Copper Cove is brimming with other gay guys our age," he says, leaning towards me. Our arms touch and it sends an electric current rippling through my body. "If you really want to see the ERC, I'd be happy to show you sometime."

Manny smiles, but I feel like I'm inside a tornado, one where everything has been flipped upside down and things are moving too fast. Is Manny flirting with me? What should I say? I'm paralyzed, like someone has just eaten my lungs and I can't breathe.

I have no idea how to flirt with a boy that might like me.

But I think I would like to try, before I die.

"Hey, are you…um, into me?" I ask.

My pulse thunders in my ears once again, so loudly I think I might not even hear Manny's answer. Oh god, what if it's *no*?

But as a response, Manny just pulls me closer to him.

"I'm not the one who's impossible to read, Luca. This okay?"

I nod, so Manny leans closer, his lips almost touching mine.

"And how about this?"

I nod again, so Manny smiles. And then he kisses me.

I slip my hand under Manny's jacket and his skin feels warm and soft. He gasps a little at my cold touch, but once our lips part, Manny's hand runs through my hair. He tilts my head gently to the side, so he can kiss my neck.

Manny stands and pulls me with him, pressing me against the nearest tree trunk. I let him, even though I can't help but think this is wrong, tonight of all nights. Irresponsible and maybe even selfish. But the most awful thought is the only one that really matters:

I want Manny to be Griffin.

Would it be so terrible if I just...pretend he is?

I close my eyes as Manny kisses me again, letting it all take me away.

When I open them again, something appears behind Manny. Or I don't really see it, so much as *feel* its presence, murky and looming. The Impact stands there, one of its bent appendages holding up another corpse. The rabbit's blood spills forward into the dirt, its entrails leaking all over.

The Impact doesn't want me here. I've broken some unwritten rule and now it's going to make Manny pay the price. It's going to do the same thing to him it has done to that poor rabbit. Because they're innocent.

Which makes me guilty.

"I have to go."

The words fly out of my mouth with such force, Manny instantly steps away from me.

"What's wrong?" he asks. "Did I do something—"

"It's not you," I say, looking behind Manny instead of at him. I don't see the Impact anymore—I don't even see the bloodied carcass.

I can't tell if that's a good sign or a very bad sign.

"I thought I was..." I try, but words seem to fail me as panic bubbles through my limbs once again. "I'm sorry.

I like you, Manny. But can you take me back to the beach?"

Manny looks like he doesn't know what to say about my sudden freak-out, so he doesn't say anything at all.

Instead, he just nods and turns to lead me out, to bring me back to the reality I can't seem to escape.

Chapter Seventeen

"Where did you disappear to?" Griffin asks, standing back in my room at Hemlock. "And why did you rush me out of the party like that?"

Griffin's last question is punctuated by a hiccup because he is absolutely hammered. I knew it the moment I saw his unfocused blue eyes back on the beach, lit by firelight.

"I thought I saw the Impact again," I answer. "I don't know, maybe I didn't—"

"Hey, can we make a deal?" Griffin interrupts.

My heart, thundering as usual, skips a beat. I don't think I can handle any more secret deals right now. What could Griffin possibly ask of me, in the middle of this—

"Can we just pretend the Pact doesn't exist?" he continues, piercing my thoughts. "Just for tonight, until morning. Can we just pretend everything is the way it should be?"

Griffin wears a pleading look on his face and I hold his gaze. This feels like a maybe-irresponsible thing to do, but I'm also still drunk enough myself that it sounds like a good idea.

"Yeah, okay," I sigh. "But you need some water. And something to sleep in."

I should probably be drinking water too. If

anything sounds worse than facing the Pact, it's facing the Pact hungover. I peel myself off my bed and grab a water bottle to refill at the sink. I open the bathroom door as silently as possible and don't turn on the light, but I quickly realize Mom isn't in her room anyway. She must be with Garrett, which is another mind-breaking thought to file away for tomorrow.

When I walk back into the bedroom, I find Griffin has taken off his jeans and T-shirt, his full attention focused on a leftover muffin. I swiped it from the Dining Hall days ago, but Griffin has already bitten into its stale side. I shrug, taking a swig from the water bottle. The tap comes from the lake, so the water is always crisp and clear and cold—all things I'm decidedly not, right now.

Even though I know I shouldn't, I find myself memorizing the exact curves of Griffin's collarbone, the number of freckles visible on his torso, the way you can only see the blond hairs on his stomach muscles at certain angles—important stuff. Who knows when I'll ever get to steal these perfect glimpses again?

"So who was that dude you were with?" Griffin asks, muffin crumbs tumbling from his mouth. "The one you came out of the woods with?"

"One of the lifeguards. We met when I was swimming laps."

"And is that all there is to the story?"

I take another swig, then trade the water bottle with Griffin for the remains of the muffin.

"For now, yes," I answer.

"Is he into you?"

"Well, he's gay."

"Not the same thing."

"Honestly, at this age and at Copper Cove, there are so few of us it kind of is," I sigh. It feels strange, talking about this with Griffin...especially given all the things we're avoiding by doing so.

"That sucks," he says, shuffling into the bathroom to refill the water bottle. "You know, we never really talk about that kind of stuff, you and I."

"Well, I haven't been out that long, especially not in Copper Cove time," I answer. "And there hasn't ever really been much to talk about. If I realized anything tonight, it's that I have zero idea what I'm doing, trying to flirt with a guy."

"Well, if you want to practice flirting with a guy, why not practice on me?"

My stomach flips upside down. Griffin says this innocently enough, but it sets all of my subtext alarms blaring.

"Because you're straight. And dating Hazel," I answer, shoving Griffin's shoulder with a nervous laugh.

"Right." Griffin burps. But then he looks unexpectedly pained. "I'm so sorry, Luca."

"What? Why?"

"You know," he replies, suddenly serious. "I'm just... I'm so sorry. About everything."

I tense. This is teetering dangerously close to the edge.

"You always know, Luca. You're the best."

Griffin hugs me, and even though I don't expect it, I automatically raise my arms to return the gesture. My hands on Griffin's shirtless back feel like fire. His skin is softer than I imagined, even though it's coiled with muscle. This hug is real, too—not one of those straight-guy, pat-on-the-back hugs. Griffin's body actually touches mine, which is suddenly made of glass. I'm sure if someone pushed me, I'd shatter into a million pieces.

"Easy there, killer." I laugh again, but this isn't funny. My heart is racing so fast it might explode.

"No seriously, you've known me longer than anyone, any of my other friends. Well, maybe not longer than my family, but you definitely know me better than… them," Griffin steps back, spitting his last word like a curse.

"That's why I don't want to be the one who hurts you," Griffin whispers, his head hanging.

"You're not," I try, my breath caught in my throat. This is not possible. Where is this coming from?

My mind flashes to Ariana, the tense look she and Griffin shared at Bellfour before the drinking started. But I immediately reject the idea—there's no way Ariana would ever say anything to Griffin about our conversation, about my feelings. Especially not with all this Pact mess tangling us up…

Right?

"You're nice for saying so, but I know you well, too, Luca."

Griffin steps towards me, so he can look me in the eye. He's still drunk, so all his movements are slowed and somewhat exaggerated. It only adds to my sense that, in the last hour, the last day, I've entered some alternate reality where everything has flipped on its side and looks different than before.

"I know that," is all I can manage.

"Seriously, I don't like seeing you hurt."

I could stand forever, right here, eye to eye with Griffin. I never get to just stare at his face like this—it's always through saved pictures or stolen glances. This close, Griffin's eyes are an impossible kind of blue and his pale skin is completely clear. There's a trail of stubble along the line of his jaw, and his lips…god, they're fuller than I remember. It seems absurd to me now, but I've never paid much attention to Griffin's lips, not until they lean in…

And press against my own, with some force.

I'm caught so off guard, my front teeth bang against Griffin's.

I pull back a little, but only to lessen the impact— not necessarily to stop. I open my eyes and see that Griffin's are pressed closed, and then seconds later it hits me. I am actually kissing Griffin August. A full-body shiver ripples through me so violently, I can barely keep myself from shaking. I reach my hands forward to steady myself and grab Griffin's waist, my palms clasping the muscles curved down around his hips.

Then I evaporate. My spirit rises out of my body, and I die right here. What's left behind resembles me, but it isn't really.

Because I'm not the one who anyone, let alone Griffin August, chooses. I'm not the one who gets to decide, who rejects anyone, who kisses two different boys in the same crooked night. I'm not the one who gets to be with the guy I love. Or the one who cheats with my best friend's boyfriend.

I've always been the glue—never the tear.

What remains is some new Luca, the one who kisses Griffin back. The one who knows that, despite the lingering scent of alcohol, Griffin still tastes like nothing I can describe, except with words like *depth*, and *correct*. It's like there's a magnet pulling me in, a tap filtering an ocean of desire through my body. There's no way I can get enough, let alone stop myself.

Instead, I slip one hand onto the flat of Griffin's stomach, while the other hand cradles the small of his back. Griffin's hands stay planted on my shoulders, traveling nowhere.

I wish certain questions would enter my mind and actually matter. Is this something Griffin has always wanted to do? Is this about me, or is this about the Pact? What in all heaven and hell is Griffin thinking? Or is he not really thinking at all? Griffin likes girls. Griffin is drunk— too drunk. Griffin is in love with Hazel. Hazel, our Hazel. Griffin's Hazel. My Hazel.

Somewhere in my mind, I know I have every reason to stop this, but none of these reasons can hold weight. Deep down, I also know this will break things— fundamental things—but what does that matter now? I'm already standing in the mess, already racing over the crossed line, so what else is there to do?

Griffin takes a step back and we both fall onto the bed together, somewhat awkwardly. Griffin almost hits his head on the wall, but he turns and falls onto the pillow instead. We keep kissing. It may be for seconds or for hours—I am stripped of all ability to tell.

Eventually, Griffin pulls back.

"I'm sorry," he whispers. "Can we just…lie here?"

I'm harder than I've ever been in my life and my hormones feel like a literal fire burning through my body. I most definitely want to do more. But I also know Griffin's idea is probably a good one, given everything. Maybe even a romantic one. This last night, maybe this only night.

Lying with Griffin.

I dare not move, instead angling my head on the pillow so we are nose to nose, eye to eye. I want desperately to ask Griffin what this means, but I'm too terrified of the answer.

"Thank you," I say, instead.

He smiles, his eyes still closed.

"You're funny, Luca."

"And you're Griffin."

I'm afraid to budge, afraid to breathe, afraid this will end, afraid it won't ever start. Still, with great effort, I force myself to sit up and turn off the lights. Even this drunk, I decide I can't sleep here in Griffin's bed, because we can't risk being found like this. But in the meantime, I pull off my shirt in the dark and Griffin mumbles something, kicking off his own socks. Then I lie back down beside him.

We will not remove any more clothing tonight. If there's one boundary that might save the many potential outcomes of this story, this is it. Going further together is something to look forward to. Or just kissing is an excuse we can use, a lie we can tell ourselves about how serious this was.

It's a pact we can make. Or something else to break.

Plus, from the sliver of moonlight that falls across Griffin's tight boxer briefs, I can tell he isn't hard.

He rolls onto his back, and I move to rest my head in the nook between his arm and his chest. Griffin's hand rests on the bare skin of my shoulder, radiating circles of warmth outwards. I place my free hand on his chest and run my fingers slowly down his torso, across his stomach muscles to the band of his underwear, then back up again.

Lying here, in the space between awake and asleep, I live in a dream. How many times have I fantasized about this happening? About getting to touch Griffin just like this, about the intense flush of relief I'd feel, about the weight that would be lifted off my shoulders?

But that's only been replaced by a new, unexpected weight.

So for as long as I can, I run my fingers along Griffin's skin like it's gold.

The Golden Prince.

I don't intend to, but eventually I fall asleep here beside him, happier and more confused than I've ever been.

When I wake up the next morning, Griffin is already gone.

Chapter Eighteen

My mouth is dry and my head throbs. Reality rushes up against me, sobering and painful. My body and brain are at odds, the very definition of bittersweet. I have a pit in my stomach and an aching warmth in my chest. Everything hurts, but I'm floating on a cloud.

Where did Griffin go?

And oh god…Hazel.

I turn to look through the crack in the curtains and gray light pours in from the window. There are clouds already covering the sky, and a damp chill in the air signals rain. Of course it'd threaten to storm today.

I close my eyes and can still taste Griffin on my lips, still smell him on the drawn sheets we slept on. My whole body shakes. I have no idea where to begin, or what might have ended. The pain in my head doubles if I think about what I have to face if I get out of bed.

So I pull the kicked-aside blanket over my cold skin, and shove my face into the pillow that still smells like Griffin. I figure, if this is going to drown me, I might as well soak in it for every sacred second possible.

∞

Going back to sleep proves impossible—there's just too much. I know I can't face...anyone yet. So on this most tenuous of mornings, I decide to do the one thing that might quiet my racing mind. Even though my aching skull is not yet dulled by the gallon of water and tablets of Advil I swallow, I slip on my bathing suit, followed by flip-flops, a T-shirt, and my C4 hoodie, then head out. My body protests, but I ignore the sluggishness.

Morning Dip is usually one of my favorite Copper Cove activities, but it's also one my sleep-laden teenage body doesn't allow me to enjoy often. Cove Beach opens every day before breakfast, from 6:30 to 7:30 a.m., and right now I desperately need a morning mass.

This will be my first Morning Dip of this trip, shamefully—a day for firsts, it seems. Or, I think with a shudder, could this really be my *last* Morning Dip? I bury that thought deep down. Which proves easy, because my temples pound not just with pain, but with thoughts and questions and memories.

Griffin kissed me. I kissed Griffin. My skin pressed against his—that was a thing that happened. Griffin had been so vulnerable, so emotional, so... guilty? What does that mean?

What does any of it mean?

And what will it cost us?

It's better to focus on the grass crunching under my flip-flops, wetting my feet with chilly morning dew. I leave the dirt trail down behind the Inn and make my way across the front lawn. At this hour, the campus is completely empty. Usually I love the feeling of having the place all to myself—there's a sense of discovery and promise, in this vacant dawn. But today the gathering clouds cast a grayness over Copper Cove that make it feel deserted, haunted. The charge of a thunderstorm hangs in the air, and wind rattles the trees ominously. It makes me feel like I've entered a ghost town, like there's a time bomb somewhere ticking along with my heartbeat.

In a way, there is.

It's a small miracle I don't feel a panic attack forming, but I suppose the day is still young. And even if I'm not on the verge of physical panic, that doesn't mean my mind isn't unspooling thoughts in every direction. Does Griffin remember what happened? Why did he leave and where did he go? Is he going to Hazel—could he have done so already? What will this mean for the Pact? Did Griffin and I just hit some kind of invisible self-destruct button? Can C4 ever overcome this impossible thing if we stop trusting each other?

How much can I trust Griffin?

He left me alone. Forcing me to twist and churn like this, even for just a morning, is a special kind of cruel. Unless Griffin thought I deserved space? I guess if I really boil it down, there are two explanations for what happened. The first is that Griffin returns my feelings—or at least feels some attraction—and is struggling with what that means. The second is that the whole thing was just a drunken fluke, some crossing of a line that blurred Griffin's affection with his pity.

Then a thought thunders its way into my mind, cracking open a new spiraling crater: Was Griffin so drunk that I took advantage of him?

It's an idea too horrible to consider. Besides, Griffin was the one who kissed me. I only kissed back. Then I respected Griffin's request to stop and sleep. Maybe if I'd been sober myself I might've had the wherewithal to stop the whole thing. To ask questions instead of…taking advantage?

Is that what I did?

Or is that what Griffin did? It's clear now he must have suspected something about my feelings…unless Ariana really did tell him behind my back. But I can't ask her that, not after what we've done—it's too big a risk. Besides, the Ariana I know wouldn't do that. What could she possibly have to gain from telling…

But I don't allow myself to complete that thought.

I always thought being with Griffin would feel like a lingering question finally answered, but this version of things only intensifies the doubt. And that's all before I even allow myself to consider the worst part of this…

Hazel.

"You look like the walking dead."

Pan's voice breaks through my swirling thoughts, and I realize I've already made it to Cove Beach, like a sleepwalker.

"No, I know exactly what that is," Glo adds. "The Emp Bonfire was last night, so I'm betting someone had one drink too many?"

I tap my nose to indicate Glo is correct, at least in part, because the prospect of speaking out loud is still unthinkable. With everything else I completely forgot Glo and Pan are infamous Morning Dippers, here almost every morning. Usually, I'm thrilled for some solo bonding time with both of them, but I'm not sure I'm capable of simulating my normal personality this morning.

"Ah, well there's nothing to cure a hangover like a good Morning Dip," Pan says, stripping her sweatpants and sweatshirt to reveal a one-piece bathing suit worn over her wiry, fit frame.

"And I'd say eat a big breakfast afterwards—Dining Hall food always helps," Glo laughs, causing Pan to emit one of her signature cackles.

It hits me like a sonic bullet. But not just physically. It also aches to hear how *normal* Copper Cove remains to Glo and Pan. Maybe Cecil was right about one thing, maybe we are drafted into some supernatural war like soldiers? Maybe we are the ones who must fight—and sacrifice—to protect this paradise for everyone else?

"Oh, you're looking green already," Pan says, tousling my hair. "We'll leave you be this morning, but we haven't had a proper catch-up. So you have to promise this won't be your only Dip, Mr. Popular."

I nod and attempt a smile, but that nickname also feels like a punch in the gut.

"Okay, time to get into that gorgeous lake," Pan proclaims, turning on her heels. "Especially if it's going to rain later."

Glo goes to follow…but before she does, something makes her turn back.

"You okay, hon?" she asks. "Sure it's just a hangover that's got you down?"

I look up at Glo, who's much broader and fleshier than Pan in her own one-piece, and I want to burst into tears. There's something so maternal about her. I want to bury my head in her chest and sob and have her tell me everything is going to be all right.

Instead, I say, "Nothing a dip and some Dining Hall coffee won't fix."

Glo seems to sense I'm not telling the whole truth, but she also seems to know better than to pry—she raised two teenage boys of her own, after all. She just frowns a little and says, "Well, you can talk to me about anything, if you need to. Believe it or not, I was eighteen once, too."

"You mean you're not eighteen now? Could've fooled me."

I crack an actual smile and Glo laughs. "You've always been too charming for your own damn good."

As Glo turns towards the lake, I think, If only that were true.

But then a different thought presents itself: I absolutely cannot lose Glo. Or Pan. Or Griffin. Or Hazel.

I cannot let what I've done destroy C4—because we have to find some way to protect Copper Cove.

Which means I have one swim to figure out how to shape all these wrongs into something that resembles right.

∞

My flip-flops squish with each step as I walk up the wood-chip path back through campus. I'm still wet from the lake and need to shower and change before returning to the reality of Bellfour, but first I'm going to snag a cup of half coffee half hot chocolate from the Dining Hall.

Unfortunately, Morning Dip did little to calm my frayed nerves—even though I was sure to avoid the spider-dock entirely. The swim did at least clear my mind enough to lead me to another resolution: I need to find Griffin first. Whatever happened between us and whatever else is going to happen, we'll talk about it, and we'll fix it. Griffin and I will make a plan and stick to it—but first, I need to know exactly how he feels…and what he wants.

This resolution gives me the temporary permission to avoid thinking about telling Hazel. She is the one part of this whole equation I truly cannot process. Hazel, who probably spent all night trying to solve the Pact while I slept beside her boyfriend. My best friend, Hazel.

I don't want to lie to her, but I certainly don't want to tell her the truth. Besides, if Griffin does end up choosing Hazel, I want her to have him without the stain of our mistake. But if Griffin ends up choosing me…

Well, hasn't Hazel done the same thing to me already, in a way?

"Shit!"

I hear the shout from the Boathouse as I'm about to pass by. It comes after a loud, crackling pop that sounds like a log snapping in a fire. The first floor of the Boathouse has a fireplace, and they always light it on mornings they expect rain. But something about the tone of the curse, the urgency behind it, tells me I should check on Coop. My blood rushes as my mind flashes to the Impact, gnarled and grisly.

When I walk down the stairs to the first-floor boat-rental level, I indeed find the fireplace roaring—and Coop kneeling beside it, his head in his hands.

"Coop, you okay?" I ask automatically, fearing the worst.

He looks up and, thankfully, his face isn't burned or scarred. But it is racked with something I recognize all too well.

Panic.

Coop opens his mouth to say something, but sound doesn't come out. I put some pieces together quickly. I've heard of veterans' PTSD being triggered by loud noises before, how something like a car backfiring or fireworks can pull them back to combat and cause a physical reaction. Still, even if that isn't what's going on, I'd recognize an anxiety attack anywhere. Some of us don't need phobic monsters to trigger the worst.

"Coop, listen to me," I say, crossing the creaking floor and kneeling beside him. "I think you're having a panic attack."

I put my hand on Coop's shoulder to brace him, and remind myself to use more direct language. One time Mom found me in the middle of a particularly nasty attack, and she managed to talk me out of it that way. Thinking of it now nearly makes me choke, but this moment is not about me.

"I get them too. Has this happened to you before?"

Coop doesn't try to speak, but he does nod.

"Okay, it's actually simple then," I say. "I know it feels like you're dying, but it's just your body overreacting to a trigger. Right now, adrenaline is forcing your heart to race and your hands to go numb, and it's why you can't gather your thoughts or talk. It's very scary and obviously it's unwarranted, but it would actually feel like a totally normal physical response if you were in real danger. But I am right here, and you are not in any danger."

I'm not exactly sure where it comes from, this calm and

authoritative version of myself, but I go with it, nonetheless.

"You also probably aren't breathing normally, but that's actually the key to stopping it. You have the ability to turn the panic off, but only slowly, breath by breath. So I'm going to sit here with you and we're going to breathe very slowly and deliberately. No one is going to interrupt us this early on a rainy day. And hey, do you have a happy place? Mine actually happens to be sitting in one of those rocking chairs over there, looking out at the lake. So maybe picture your favorite place, and let's breathe for a few minutes, and we'll just do that until it passes. Because it will pass, I promise."

I do all of these things, hoping they'll work and that Coop isn't actually having a heart attack or something. But I won't say that out loud, because doubt and fear are the fuel of panic attacks. It's better for me to be calm and spotless. It's what I always fail to be for myself, but for Coop, I will do it.

I sit on the floor of the Boathouse with Coop and breathe. He struggles to get his shallow breaths to match my deeper ones, but eventually he succeeds. I perform the exercise my old psychiatrist taught me—breathing in for four seconds, holding for six, then exhaling for seven, all while imagining I'm breathing through a box with three elongated compartments.

Inevitably, I think about the times Mom sat with me just like this. She insisted I give therapy a shot after our inaugural trip to the hospital, and I did see one for a few months. I didn't really like him—he was old, and his office was overly clinical, his tone was always monotone and unreadable. Plus, he kept trying to diagnose me with panic disorder or OCD, instead of trying to understand why I felt the way I did in the first place. He did provide me some useful tools: a list of rational explanations and panic-stopping techniques, all of which I've just shared with Coop. And a prescription to a mild benzodiazepine. I'm only supposed to take them if my anxiety is particularly bad, but half the time just knowing I have the option to take one can stave off an attack.

A few weeks before Copper Cove, I seemed to have a handle on things, so I stopped seeing the psychiatrist regularly. I've always heard finding the right therapist is kind of like dating, so I figured if I was going to see someone new, someone at college might be better equipped to handle my particular issues. In the meantime, I swam-prayed as much as I could to keep myself centered. I also convinced myself that most of my anxiety was circumstantial, given what had happened with Frances and at school. Which is why the panic attacks following me here to Copper Cove feels particularly troubling. And why I foolishly left my Klonopin prescription back home.

How could I have known that this summer everything I knew about my family, my friends, and my favorite place would explode into a billion flaming bits?

There's no way of knowing how much time passes as I think about these things, but at some point Coop finally speaks.

"Thank you, man. I think it's gone for now."

I pat Coop on the back. "I'm very glad to hear that."

"Can I ask, how'd you know all of that?" he asks, moving slowly.

I stand first and help him up, knowing it's normal to feel physically weak after an attack—and suppressing the memory of almost drowning after my last one.

"Lots of reading. And some therapy. But mostly personal experience, sadly."

"I haven't had an…episode like that in ages," Coop says, not quite able to look me in the eye yet. "But the fireplace has been finnicky for months. Something about that loud bang when it started up…it put me right back…"

Coop stops himself, obviously not wanting to say more.

"That's okay," I say. "We don't have to talk about it. I don't like to, either."

"I appreciate it, man," Coop sighs. "Honestly, I've always hated fire, even before I served. But none of the other Emps showed up to start the fireplace early enough this morning—at least none who know the tricks to get it started. It doesn't help that I tried reading this stupid book from the Library, *When It All Burns Down*. It stunk so bad I didn't get very far, but it had this fire monster thing that—"

"What was that book called?" I interrupt, unable to stop myself.

"*When It All Burns Down*," Coop repeats.

I can't stop my jaw from dropping open, thinking of Mom's coded phrase: *I'll be there, when it all burns down.* If Coop got this book from the Library, there's a good chance it was supplied at some point by Mom. If that's true, could this be the hint she was trying to drop somehow, without untethering the Impact?

"I returned it yesterday, if you want to read it?" Coop offers, clearly puzzled.

"Yes, thank you," I say. "Want me to stick around, or are you good?"

"I'm fine now. Besides, I've got talent-show-emcee-rehearsal duties coming up very soon." Coop pulls me into a hug—the true straight-man kind, complete with a pat on the back. "I can't thank you enough. But hey, Luca..."

"Your secret is safe with me," I answer, knowing what he was about to say. "That is, assuming mine is safe with you, too?"

"One hundred percent guaranteed," Coop says, very seriously.

We nod at each other and don't have to say anything else. I can feel it, the invisible bond we just built. We've been through something together, unearthed a part that's usually buried deep down. There aren't words to communicate that.

Just like there aren't words to communicate the impossible swirl of things I feel right now. Hopeful that I might have just found a lead. Grateful that the universe—or whatever—steered me into Coop's path this morning. Anxious to find Griffin. Dumbstruck with love after last night. Terrified to face Hazel. Proud of myself for helping Coop. Ashamed of myself for betraying my best friend...

And utterly horrified to understand that I'd cheat with Griffin again in a heartbeat, if that's what he wants.

My own pulse starts hammering again as I walk away from the Boathouse. Why can't I do for myself what I just did for Coop? It's just so different when I'm lost in my own head. Like rationality becomes some faraway island I can see but not touch, once I've been swept away on a current of panic. Besides, I suppose every single person on the planet wishes they could be their own voice of reason. But the lovely, inconvenient reality?

    None of us can do it all on our own.

Stone Four

For my fourth stone, I rely on yet another sacred tradition.

I need one, this morning.

After I shower, as I get dressed, I pull open the bottom drawer of the dresser in Hemlock Eighteen.

I take out the *Holy Bible* there and open it to a random page.

Whatever else I think about Catholicism, I've always felt drawn to the Bible.

It's kind of like the original fantasy epic.

After all, it's filled with stories of reflection, tales of how to be generous and kind and better.

Plus, there are heavens and hells and gardens of Eden, resurrections and betrayals and heroic journeys, codes and parables and…sacred pacts.

So I nestle a stone inside, then press the Bible back closed as flatly as I can.

I'm not sure if the stones I've left in the Hemlock rooms of years past still remain, but it doesn't matter.

After the revelation of the Pact and Manny's Infinity Tree and crossing the line with Griffin and being drawn to Coop this gray morning…

It is my annual tribute to the uncertainty of a higher power, and to rules I pray are not set in stone.

Chapter Nineteen

When it rains in Copper Cove, everyone is confined to the few entertaining indoor locations, since the bedrooms are mostly too small and stuffy to do much more than sleep in. As a result, every surface of the Inn's first floor is usually covered with various card and board games, and the Craft Shop overflows with circumstantial artists looking to make enamel charms or copper bowls. I can usually be found in one of two places: with the rest of C4 in Bellfour, watching the well-worn VHS set of *The Dark Crystal* while sipping hot chocolate, or sitting in one of the rocking chairs on the Inn porch beside Hazel.

Today is obviously not a usual rainy day, however, and I am a man on a mission. I need to find Griffin, especially before I tell C4 about this potential new book lead.

After changing I skip breakfast, opting instead for a peanut-buttered bagel from the Store. With my hangover beaten temporarily into submission, I'm determined to track down Griffin. It feels so strange, not being able to just pick up the phone or send a text. But my phone won't work, and even if it did, Griffin keeps his own phone off in honor of Family Week.

Of course, as the universe would have it, on my way across the Inn porch I run into one rather sizable roadblock...

Hazel Hart.

I thought I'd prepared myself to see her, but as it turns out, there's really no way to be ready for something like this. Laying eyes on Hazel, I quickly disassemble. I'm so shell-shocked and tongue-tied, I don't do anything besides accept the rainy-day rocking chair Hazel has saved for me beside her.

I didn't think it was possible to feel much worse than I already do. But sitting beside Hazel breaks the floor open beneath me, plunging me to new and previously uncharted depths of guilt. Is it possible she has already seen Griffin? Did he tell her anything?

"You look like hell," Hazel says, rocking steadily.

I nod. She's probably right.

"Have you seen the others yet?" I ask, my voice nearly cracking.

"No," she answers. "I was just trying to gather my thoughts before heading to Bellfour."

I sigh with…relief? Whatever I feel, I try to breathe as Hazel turns her gaze back out towards the view. Trying to pull myself together, I also focus on the thunderstorm unfurling in front of us. Rain pours in thick sheets, creating a curtain along the Inn porch. Steam rises off everything, especially the lake, and little rivers run everywhere: down the street, through the grass, and out of the gutters routed to the surrounding sustainable gardens. The sky directly above the darkened mountains lights up intermittently with streaks of horizontal lightning, like electric veins pulsing in the sky. I try to let my mind empty and fill only with the rain and the steam and the branching crackles of lightning.

But all I want is out. Out of this nightmare. Out of the guilt. Out of my broken brain. If this is how I'm always going to end up feeling, end up spiraling, how will I ever get through the rest of my life? My heart picks up its pace at this thought, then my senses tingle with that first flush of panic. No, I think. Not again…

I pull off my C4 hoodie, because it feels like it's strangling me. Looking at it, I think of the way Manny must see it, how he must see all of us, wearing our matching hoodies in our bell tower like…

Manny.

I haven't had a spare inch of mental real estate to process the things Manny said the night before. His funhouse-mirror view of C4, or our…kiss. What am I going to say to him? How could I possibly explain myself in the center of this hurricane?

I jump as thunder booms loudly above the Inn, like the sky has been ripped apart.

Hazel yelps beside me.

"Crap, sorry," she gasps, reaching down to pick up the black notebook she dropped. "I've been so on edge. For obvious reasons."

For just a moment, Hazel crystallizes before me. My Hazel, who needs me right now. Suddenly I understand how selfish I've been. How could I do this do her? I just want to tell her everything. She deserves to know.

"Hazel, I need to—"

"Wait," she interrupts, turning in her rocking chair to face me. "Before you say anything, I need to ask you something."

I swallow hard. Today, of all days, what could Hazel have to ask me?

"I just wanted to make sure we're good," Hazel says. "Maybe I'm imagining it, but I kind of feel like there's...I don't know, a disconnect between us? I mean, even before our parents told us about the...you know."

Hazel looks around, lowering her voice for this last part. I stare back at her. Leave it to Hazel to sense that something has been off, no matter how hard I've tried to hide it. I've been bending over backwards to not create distance between us, but...if there was a world where I could've been honest with Hazel about my real feelings for Griffin, it's gone. After what happened, having any right to be upset evaporates like steam off the lake.

"I just can't stand the idea that I might have hurt you," Hazel says. "I can't do any of this without you, Luca."

The truth deflates out of me. Hazel took the words right out of my mouth.

"I love you," I say, tears welling in my eyes. "No matter what else is going on, please don't ever doubt that?"

Hazel fights back tears herself, listening to me.

"Okay. I think I really needed to hear that," she finally sighs. "Especially because I've been up all night trying to think of some way out of this, but—"

"I found a lead," I interrupt, latching onto this scrap of hope. "It's a long story, but Coop told me about a book he took out of the Library: *When It All Burns Down*."

"Oh my god," Hazel says automatically. "That can't be a coincidence, can it?"

"My thoughts exactly."

A look of amazement locks on Hazel's face, thoughts compiling behind her eyes faster than her mouth can speak.

"If Coop had a book like that checked out of the Library, it explains why we weren't able to find it yesterday. But why didn't it turn up in Griffin's internet searches?"

"Coop said the book was terrible, so maybe it's obscure?" I offer. "Or maybe it's something original my mom planted there? There's only one way to find out."

Hazel stands.

"We have to go to the Library. Now."

"Shouldn't we get Ariana and Griffin first?"

Speaking his name feels forbidden, like a curse. Still, I manage not to flinch.

"We can bring it back to them," Hazel insists. "We can't waste any more time."

Hazel's voice hums—clearly, she's relieved to have something actionable on our hands. Whether it's futile or not, I know this must make everything slightly less unbearable. After all, Hazel is at her best when she has a target to hit.

I want to ask her to stop and think a second, to consider the Impact or the others, but I can already tell she's entered one-track-mind mode. I'm momentarily tempted to leave her to go find Griffin, but I know what I have to do now. I have to stand beside Hazel.

I owe her that much, at least.

∞

The Library occupies just one floor in the attic of the Lecture Hall farther up the hill, behind the Store. The building is nestled in the woods, so bursts of green treetops can be seen in every direction through the arched windows, wet with rain that only just stopped. As a result, the Library feels a bit like a tree house, with cloudy light still pouring onto the stacked rows of books at different angles.

I never spend much time in the Library. But being here now I realize if Hazel were to have a secret lair, or magical source of her powers, this would definitely be it. She moves through the aisles with purpose, like she's opened a closet in her own bedroom and is filing through a personal collection. A volunteer librarian is supposed to be on duty, but the Library was empty when we entered. Which doesn't matter, since I suspect Hazel knows her way around here better than anyone.

"Obviously the collection is alphabetized by author's name, which we don't know. Still, there are only two places that book would be," Hazel says, her eyes scrolling over the colorful spines of dozens of books. "Horror or Young Adult."

"Well, that certainly seems appropriate," I sigh. "By the way, this place is way bigger than I remember."

"That's thanks mostly to your mom. She's added so many books over the years, the Library had to expand a few summers ago."

Hearing this opens another current of sorrow inside me. Suddenly, I miss Mom, despite everything. Will we ever be able to come back from this…

Assuming I even survive the next two days?

The idea of dying before I can ever have another real conversation with Mom makes me physically nauseous, along with the idea of never going to college, or graduating, or…the list goes on. Not just for myself, but for all of us.

"We haven't even talked about how crazy it is that our parents are...hooking up?" Hazel says, her eyes still scanning. "You and I did always want to be siblings."

"Well, you know Copper Cove couples rarely last out in the real world," I say, distracted. Until I hear how thoughtless I sound.

"I didn't mean that," I cover. "You and Griffin are—"

"It's fine," Hazel says. "We'll make it. All of us are going to make it."

Staring at Hazel, I wish I could share her confidence. Her remarkable focus. Hazel has always been the queen of tunnel vision and I've always envied that. But now more than ever, I wonder what that might also blind her to?

"I did want to talk to you about Griffin, though," Hazel continues. "How did he seem last night, at the bonfire?"

My body stiffens.

"Why?" is all I can manage.

"Before, when we thought we had nothing to go on, I could tell he seemed...resigned. It didn't make sense," Hazel goes on, thankfully not looking up at me while she scans. "Then I thought about how he just found out about his grandfathers' murderous history all at once. I know him, he has definitely taken on the guilt for it. I thought he'd be raging to fight against this thing, to make it right. But then last night, it clicked. Griffin has already decided how he's going to make it right. If it comes to it, he's going to sacrifice himself, to save us and to make amends."

Hazel's words hit me like a freight train.

Of course.

That's why Griffin suggested one last night of fun.

Not because he'd given up on us, but because he'd given up on himself. That's why he kissed me, one way or another. He was trying to make things right before...

Griffin the Golden Prince, falling on his sword to make sure everyone still loves him. How could I not have seen this sooner? Suddenly I realize Hazel isn't the only one prone to streaks of blindness.

"We obviously can't let him do that," Hazel continues. "The Pact isn't Griffin's fault or his burden any more than it is for the rest of us. But I think he's going to absorb the guilt and he's going to have some idiotic, noble notion of defending our honor. My honor. So he probably won't listen to me about this kind of thing. But I do think he'll hear it, if it comes from you."

I'm speechless. Which is maybe good, because my only urge in this moment, my single blaring instinct, is once again to tell Hazel what happened between Griffin and me. To let her know there's a thick, fresh layer added to Griffin's guilt and that something might have shifted between all of us, forever. My mind flashes, uncontrollably, to Griffin's lips. To our warm skin pressed together, and to all the time I wasted being silent.

My ears burn red. I owe the truth to Hazel, don't I? Or do I owe her more silence, to keep her from a pain she doesn't deserve to feel? The words bubble up and almost tumble out of my mouth...

Until my eyes fall on the broken infinity symbol, practically glowing in the middle of the bottom shelf.

"There," I say, pointing. "What's that?"

The symbol is printed on the spine of a black book

in silver ink, its unfinished curves catching the cloudy light from the nearest window. There's nothing else written on the book's binding. Hazel follows my finger and sees it, then lets out a little gasp. She crouches down and snatches up the book, turning to its cover. There, in sickly green letters, reads the title:

∞ *WHEN IT ALL BURNS DOWN* ∞
BY E. PLATH

"Holy crap, this is it," Hazel whispers, as if she's suddenly holding the lost ark. "What do you think that symbol means? I feel like I've seen it all over campus, but never really remember to ask about it."

"Me too."

I consider telling Hazel about seeing this symbol in the lake, near the stones my grandfather asked me to keep collecting. Or about those dark fishing spiders forming the same shape as they reached the lake's shore. I consider telling her about Manny's Infinity Tree, wondering if there's any connection—but I tell myself I'm grasping. Hopefully this book will be able to clear up some of that confusion.

In the next moment, I have the distinct feeling that someone is behind us. Or some*thing*. The hair on the back of my neck stands on end and every muscle in my body tenses at once. It's the Impact, it has to be, come to punish us for unearthing this lost tome.

"I haven't seen anyone touch that one until this week."

The person's voice causes Hazel and me to spin so fast, we actually scare them. It turns out to be Maggie, her volunteer librarian badge shaking loose as she jumps backwards.

"Oh my goodness," she says, bending down to pick

up the badge. "Sorry, I didn't mean to sneak up on you like that. I got back from the bathroom and you two seemed so intent, I didn't want to disturb you."

My adrenaline ramps down to a light frenzy as I register Maggie's presence. Despite sitting at our Dining Hall table all my life—and having been babysat by Mom and Garrett as a child—Maggie has always existed on the edge of my summers. Still, seeing her frizzy red hair and freckled smile is an unexpected comfort.

"That's okay," Hazel exhales, clutching the book to her chest. "I was just telling Luca about this novel I…never finished. We wanted to see if it was still here."

"I don't think anyone has ever finished reading that one. I got about two pages in before putting it down," Maggie says. "It's a real stinker. Weird premise, and even worse prose. I think it only had a print run of one hundred, if that. Apparently, it was some London editor's die-on-this-hill passion project, which is the only reason it was published in the first place."

"Oh. Well, can we check it out?" Hazel asks.

"No one's going to miss that one, trust me," Maggie answers. "Luca, your mom actually added it to the collection back in 2019. So technically it belongs to you, anyway."

"2019?" I blurt. The details of that year light up my mind, the summer Mom and Garrett tried to tell us about the Pact, causing that fatal beehive encounter.

"I mean, are you sure? Hazel said she read it as a kid." I fudge this last part, trying to cover my overreaction.

"Yes, I'm sure. And let me say for the record, four years ago Hazel would have qualified as a kid. You both still do, at least in my book," she sighs. "Anyway, I guess I remember Sofia dropping this one off on its own, apart from her usual stacks. She seemed to want it off her hands, specifically. I think it might remind her of...well, what happened back when we were all kids, ourselves."

Maggie trails off, realizing she might have wandered into forbidden territory.

"You mean with Tommy?" Hazel asks, causing Maggie to flush with relief.

"Yes. I wasn't sure you two were supposed to know about that. It was the saddest summer I can remember at Copper Cove. Maybe because I looked up to your parents like gods back then. It broke my heart to see how they splintered apart after Tommy's accident. It felt like the end of an era."

Maggie looks somber and contemplative for a moment. Then she snaps back, as if remembering a duty to remain cheery.

"Tommy was such a prankster, we all thought it was one of his practical jokes at first, that he'd pop back out of the water and scream, 'Gotcha!' I remember one summer before, he filled the girls' locker room at day camp with ladybugs. Lord only knows where he found them all. Well, at least he died doing what he loved, for someone he loved."

This information crawls under my skin, unexpectedly. What would people say about me, or Griffin, or any of us, if the worst were to happen? What half-truths would blur the tales of our own demise?

"Well, we should get going," Hazel says, mustering

a smile. "We've got lots of reading to do."

She waves and grabs my hand in the same motion, leading us out of the Library. It's probably too abrupt an exit, but that's fine—we both have some thinking to do.

∞

"Okay, I'm just going to say it, because I know you're probably thinking it," Hazel says as we walk away from the Library. "Do you think your mom came across this book, then whatever she read made her think it was worth breaking the rules to tell us early? At least until that pregnant woman was killed?"

Hazel is right on all accounts, most likely. But it's still a thought too horrible to absorb—the idea that Mom could be responsible, even tangentially, for something like that. Or that C4 could be, too, if we aren't careful… or even if we *are* careful. Selfishly, nothing feels worse than the idea that Mom found a way to end this and then kept it from us.

"I wonder if she even told my dad about it," Hazel continues, her mind still turning all this over. "I've been thinking a lot about the way previous generations handled the Pact. How the first purposefully kept their kids apart, and the next encouraged theirs to be friends, all hoping it would somehow save them. Or how every iteration ended in disaster, when anyone tried to defy it. Is it any wonder our parents were scared into following the rules, after everything? Or do I just want to justify it for myself?"

I can guess what Hazel is probably really wondering: Are our parents right? I've walked down this path in my own mind, but every time I do, I arrive at the same thought: If every generation thought the fights before them were futile, then we'd all be doomed.

There's so much that seems obtuse about the Pact, so much we still don't understand and maybe won't ever. But I also keep wondering why this sacrifice is demanded of us at age eighteen. Is it about being in our physical prime, as the strongest possible tributes? Is it about being in-between, the still-young-but-almost-adult of it all, the power in that transition?

Or is it because some battles require the blind bravery of a young person to be fought and won?

"I was also thinking..." Hazel carries on. When she gets like this she doesn't require a response to keep unpacking whatever problem she's working her way through. "And this is a stretch...but do you think the fact Tommy liked animal-themed pranks has anything to do with—"

Hazel doesn't finish, however, because I grab her by the shoulder and stop her in place. Up ahead, down the trail, is the Emp dorm building—and standing right outside is Manny, talking in a small group.

Hazel looks down the path, then back at me, and puts some pieces together. "Oh...I don't know if we really have time for a stop and chat."

My eyes train on Manny. I don't have any answers for him about my feelings, or about why I freaked out on him last night. Especially not after what happened with Griffin. But if I think it's shitty of Griffin to disappear on me, is it right for me to also ghost Manny?

"I know, but this will only take—"

I freeze into silence, however, once I hear the noise. It comes from the woods behind the lecture hall, or maybe from inside—the echoing makes it too hard to tell. Still, the sound is unmistakably a crash of some kind.

"Maggie."

It's the only thing Hazel needs to say to set my feet in motion. She keeps pace beside me. I'm not sure what we can do if there is trouble, but I do know if we've somehow freed the Impact, we can't let it hurt anyone else. I'm also pretty sure Manny can't hear this sound from all the way down the hill path, so I silently pray he doesn't see me running away from him right now.

Hazel and I sprint around the back of the Lecture Hall, where more woods stretch gradually up into another hill. The back door is left slightly ajar, but there aren't any visible signs of trouble. I look to Hazel, who senses the same, then I scan back around. The wet woods seem empty. Maybe the wind just banged the door open?

Then it steps out from behind a tree, slower and calmer than ever before.

And for the first time, I see the Impact clearly.

Chapter Twenty

It's an angled thing, all murky pus and raw sinew. The Impact stands upright, but I can't make out much more than that. Trying to look directly at it is like looking at the sun or peering through an unfocused magnifying glass. I expected it to be more primal, more animalistic. But this thing is controlled, and incongruous. Like its surface is shriveled and ever shifting, but its muscles are solid and invulnerable. Really, I *feel* the Impact more than I see it. Like I can sense that something vital has been ripped out of it, but the husk that remains is undying.

A hollow pit to fill with dread.

My body sears with acid fear, but my first thought is of Maggie. Does the Impact know what we were after? Has it already gotten to her, or did it just lure Hazel and me back here alone?

I consider screaming for help, but then resist. We can't get anyone else hurt or killed, if we can help it. Hazel seems to be making the same decision beside me. But what do we do next? Run? Fight?

The Impact has never remained so...still before. I blink and although my vision of the Impact does not clear, I swear I see it curl its rancid lips into a crescent grin. Or maybe it's a snarl?

Either way, it suddenly breaks forward, its animal side revealed through its lightning speed and guttural whine. I expect it to rain down a swarm of locusts or something to terrify us, but instead it tackles Hazel to the ground—because it's going for the book she holds.

I can't quite see what happens next as I move to intervene, but Hazel clutches the novel to her chest, refusing to let go. I take one step and the Impact jerks back violently. One more step and Hazel screams, her voice quickly muffled. Another step and the book lands at my feet, tossed aside by Hazel.

I look up and the Impact has already lifted itself off her—high enough for me to glimpse the blood running from Hazel's mouth. I glance back at the book and see splatters of red speckling its cover...

Along with an uprooted tooth, its nerve ending dangling like a raw little tail.

I resist the urge to gag and instead snatch up the book, shaking the tooth loose. I look up and find the Impact has disappeared. Hazel lies in the dirt, the wet leaves around her rustling. One second too late, I realize she's surrounded by cockroaches, thick and scuttling—and zeroing in on her.

Before I can shout a warning, something grabs hold of the hair on the back of my head and pulls. The follicles rip out of my scalp before the momentum forces me backwards. I crash into the dirt, the wind knocked out of my lungs as my back slams into the ground. Through the bolts of pain and loss of breath, I manage to keep the book pressed to my chest. Then the Impact closes in on me, tugging at it.

Still disoriented, I manage to keep my fingers locked around the book. Even as the smell of decay fouls the air I suck in through my teeth. The Impact whines, pressing its body tighter against mine. Somehow, it's both infinitely heavy and incorporeal as a thought. Either way, I can't move. Knowing this blasts jets of very-justified panic through me.

The Impact stops whining just long enough for me to hear Hazel struggling, all sobs and choked yelps somewhere nearby. But she is still far enough away that she obviously won't be coming to my rescue. I can't imagine what horrible thing the cockroaches are doing to her, but then the Impact does something equally disturbing to me. It drops some foul, viscous liquid from its maybe-face. I don't have a chance to close my mouth before I realize it's happening. The liquid fills my nose and clogs my throat. I'm already short on breath from the fall. Now I'm being forcibly drowned.

Tears fill my blurred vision and I struggle desperately. It's no use without my arms, which still clutch the book. My lungs burn and I choke on the liquid, sputtering. *Let go of the book,* my brain screams. *Let go of the book or you're going to die, in the way you've always feared most.*

Every instinct in me shouts to let go, but I'm paralyzed. Trapped. Violated. Blood rushes to my face and the world starts to spin, I'm...powerless.

Just as this thought takes over, I feel a different kind of tug. It's like suddenly, an invisible rubber band snaps, pulling the Impact off and away.

Once free, I scramble back across the dirt, still

pressing the book to my chest with one hand as I brace myself with the other. Vomit comes in violent waves, at first. I don't know how long it takes to sputter out, alternating between dry heaves and gasping gulps of air. Dizzy, I try my best to amble to my feet and look around. The Impact isn't here anymore—just like that.

Where did it go? Did it run out of time? Will it be back?

I let go of these questions when I see Hazel. She swings her arms, still scraping roaches off her skin. They dart away as they hit the dirt, no longer compelled to attack after the Impact's departure. Still, the damage has been done. A stream of blood runs from Hazel's mouth to her chin and her skin is covered in red welts. By the time I reach her side, she shakes loose one final roach and holds her hands to her face. That's when I notice it's not just her arms that are speckled with roach bites...

Little chunks of her fingernails are missing, too.

I almost pass out, but I will myself to hold it together. I pull Hazel into me, gripping the book to her back as I hug her.

"It's okay, it's gone," I croak, my voice hoarse.

Hazel tries to speak, but she only manages some syncopated sobs, like she might be hyperventilating.

I hold her tighter, until she has time to catch her breath.

"Griffin," Hazel gasps, when she can. "Ariana."

Instantly, I understand. We both take off at a sprint. I don't know if running to Bellfour is our best move right now, but I can't think of anywhere else to go—especially not covered in dirt and blood and bites like this. Running actually feels good, like maybe we can outpace what just happened to us.

Because that was not some psychological haunting, or even some phobic prodding.

That was…

I don't finish this thought. Instead, I run after Hazel on the backwoods path to Bellfour, focused only on the feeling of my legs moving underneath me.

∞

The time that follows back at Bellfour blurs together.

Hazel and I return to find it empty.

We don't know where to go next, but our injuries need attention. So we find an old first aid kit, coated in a layer of dust.

I'm about to finish bandaging the worst of Hazel's bites—the ones that broke her skin and cracked her nails— when Ariana appears, thankfully unscathed.

Ariana cries with relief, seeing that Hazel and I are okay, too—relatively speaking, anyway. She'd been filled with dread: on her way up from her cottage, she saw an ambulance outside the Library…

Because a bookshelf toppled over onto Maggie, breaking her leg and leaving her with a severe concussion.

Ariana feared the worst, for the rest of us.

But now, knowing we're still alive, we sit in silence as guilt and fear battle for dominance in each of us. Maggie's injuries are our fault. She could have died.

No one seems to know where Griffin's gone. We resolve to search for him together, next.

But first Ariana takes Hazel into the bathroom with the first aid kit, because her cheek is starting to swell up. I pace Bellfour, having no idea what to do with myself. Until the lock starts turning in the door.

And I finally find myself face-to-face with Griffin for the first time since last night.

My throat goes dry. All of the doubt and pain I felt over the past few hours suddenly evaporates into a fine mist. Griffin wears a T-shirt and jeans, and I can tell he just showered. Seeing me, covered in mud and dirt, he freezes.

"Luca. What happened?"

"We're all okay," I answer. "Where have you been?"

"I went home to change," he says, in an impossibly normal voice.

"I…can we go talk somewhere?" I whisper, almost involuntarily.

Griffin pauses. Recognition plays across his flawless face.

"Not here," he says, his eyes pleading. "Not now. Later tonight?"

Hazel rushes back into the room and directly into Griffin's arms. He hugs her.

"I'm here, it's okay," Griffin says to Hazel. "I'm here."

I feel like I'm suddenly made of paper, ripping to shreds and collecting in a neat mound on the hardwood floor.

Ariana pulls me aside.

"Let me look at your scalp," she says, leading me into the bathroom.

Earthquakes rumble through me as I follow. My

brain can register everything that's going on but it's like I'm watching from somewhere else. Like there's a thin film, a watery screen, separating me from reality.

In the bathroom, Ariana places some gauze on the back of my head. I smooth my hair over the new bald spot, but I'm more worried about the residual burning in my lungs. What did the Impact try to drown me with?

And what do we do about the scars we don't see, the ones that can't be cleaned and covered?

"Luca, are you okay?" Ariana asks quietly. "I mean, you'd tell me if something was wrong? Or I mean, extra wrong?"

This reaction is exactly why I was cautious to tell anyone about my panic attacks. Ariana has switched into protective-friend-slash-doctor-to-be mode, but the truth is that she shouldn't be any more concerned for me than for the rest of us.

"I have to be okay," I say evenly.

If I dwell, I'll fall apart. I'll curl into a ball and never get up again.

So instead, Ariana and I walk back out into the main room and gather around the coffee table. Ariana explains how she cleared and packed Hazel's empty socket—the tooth in question was a small middle one from her bottom jaw. Thankfully you can't even tell it's missing, and Ariana thinks Hazel should be okay until we can get her to a dentist.

After that, all that's left to do is walk Griffin and Ariana through what happened.

∞

"That's...beyond horrible," Ariana says with a shudder once I finish. Hazel still hasn't spoken at all, nestled into the Adirondack chair beside Griffin. "I...do you guys need, like, another minute to process?"

"What I need is to keep moving," I say.

It's true. I can't even bring myself to look in Griffin's direction.

"Okay, because I have about a million questions," Ariana says.

"Me too. Shoot."

"Right. Okay, so did the Impact attack me yesterday outside Hemlock because it didn't want Luca's mom telling us anything?" Ariana begins. "Just now, was it only interested in this book? Is that why it went for you two and not Griffin or me? Also, why did it suddenly go nuclear attacking you two?"

"Yes, I'd like to know what the hell was up with those killer cockroaches," Griffin adds.

I stare at Griffin and find his easiness unfathomable. How can he just...gloss over it all? Then again, I consider my own quiet demeanor, my successful attempts at normalcy. I am once again a calm surface covering a swirling whirlpool, so can I really judge Griffin for maybe being the same?

What did I really expect to happen here, after all?

"Well, roaches don't usually bite humans if there's other food around," Ariana offers. "And normally they prefer dead bodies, stuff like fingernails and eyelashes and calloused skin, but they'll try to eat anything, really."

"Um, how the hell do you know that?" Griffin asks.

"I watch a lot of horror movies. And I want to be a doctor—you have to be just a little bit morbid for that."

"So then what's your theory on why these bugs keep acting so aggressively?" Griffin asks next.

"Obviously the Impact has some level of influence over them, making them do their worst. It seems to be able to tap into our fears and somehow...I don't know, manifest them?"

"Hazel, you've told me you sometimes have that recurring dream, the one where all your teeth fall out?" Griffin asks, prompting Hazel to nod.

Unfortunately, the part we all don't want to admit is how the Impact hasn't just exploited our more tangible fears— it seems to understand how to hit us deeper. Hazel's pursuit of perfection, her tunnel vision. Ariana's fear of being the outsider, being ostracized. Griffin's family guilt, his abandonment issues. My anxiety, my fear of tradition breaking.

Then again, how much of our mess can we blame on the Impact...and how much of it is our own making?

"Whatever psychic mojo the Impact might have, it clearly has to follow as many rules as we do," Griffin offers. "I think maybe it only gets loose temporarily as a result of specific actions: breaking the Pact or trying to talk to anyone outside C4 about it. Taking that book out of the Library must have counted big-time. But on the upside, it does seem like we're safe talking about it here in Bellfour, just between us? Which means, more importantly, we're not endangering anyone else like Maggie."

Griffin rubs Hazel's shoulders as he says this. Against the odds, I still find comfort in his words. The idea of the Impact hurting anyone else is too awful to imagine. The thought of coming face-to-face with it again also sends a shiver through me, radiating down from my torn scalp. What other heinous traumas will it cook up for us, now that it seems to be escalating its efforts? I look at Hazel, one bandaged hand resting on her puffed cheek, and I want to cry.

"Like Ariana said, the Impact obviously wanted to take that book from you guys," Griffin adds. "So why didn't it try to steal it from the Library before?"

"Maybe it didn't know it existed, because my mom stashed it there without telling anyone?" I try. Just pretend you're swimming, I tell myself. Just keep your head above water. "Or maybe the Impact can only go after things if unleashed by a trigger, like you said before?"

"Okay, I have another one," Ariana says next. "Why didn't the Impact just kill Hazel or Luca, or any of us? I mean, it has killed before. And it obviously tried to kill Maggie, in getting to you or the book or whatever. Why only torture and maim us?"

Ariana scratches at her arms as she speaks. Her skin has cleared up, but she's obviously not over her own haunting from yesterday.

"Well, that's easy, now that you mention it," Griffin replies. "Once one of us dies, the Impact is just re-imprisoned for another generation, right? Isn't that the whole point of the Pact? So the Impact must want the four of us to stay alive. It just doesn't need us entirely intact?"

It's a simple explanation, but it clicks. It's also a consolation—but only a small one. Even if the Impact isn't fatal for us, it can still kill others if our actions loosen its chains. My mind flashes to Maggie, pinned under a bookshelf, her safe space turned into a nightmare-scape. I promise myself that if I make it through this, I'll visit her in the hospital. I'll bring a tub of ice cream from the Store and a bouquet of flowers picked from the Inn gardens.

"If we're going to be fighting the Impact, that maybe gives us an advantage," Griffin adds, his knees bobbing up and down with excess energy. "But why do I have a sinking feeling that if it can't kill us, we can't kill it either?"

"Speaking of, even if we do chalk Maggie up to collateral damage for finding the book, that still doesn't explain why the Impact hasn't tried to kill anyone else," Ariana poses. She's on a roll, as if poking holes with her questions and observations might take the air out of this entire situation. "I mean, don't get me wrong, I'm glad it hasn't. But why is it spending its free time haunting us when it could be killing and destroying? Isn't that supposed to be its sole desire? And isn't that a more effective way of getting us to comply, or of stopping us from finding answers?"

"I don't know, I think that's giving it more agency than it deserves," I answer. "It seems to act more on instinct. Maybe it's learning all this as it goes, just like we are? I felt it get whipped back to wherever it came from, like it was yanked by some invisible chain. Maybe its radius or whatever is limited, just like its time seems to be?"

"Right, maybe, but then why—"

"I think we should stop wasting time asking questions when we have a book sitting in front of us full of potential answers," Hazel interrupts, finally breaking her silence. "If Luca's mom led us to it and the Impact fought so hard to stop us from taking it, then there's got to be something useful in there."

"Good call," Griffin says, kissing Hazel's forehead with a look of pride.

What happened between Griffin and me suddenly feels a lifetime away. Like a nostalgic dream in the face of this harsh reality. Because if Griffin has made anything clear...

It's that he chooses Hazel.

Moving forward, I have no idea what that means for...everything?

"Since we only have one copy, Ariana and I can start and give you two a chance to—" Griffin begins.

"There's no time for that," Hazel interrupts again, her voice dry and determined. She stands and grabs the novel. Before any of us can say anything, she flattens the book and cracks its spine. The rest of us watch open-mouthed as she approximates a fourth of the total pages and rips them out in a thick packet. It's an especially violent act coming from Hazel, like watching a priest choke on holy water.

"We each read a section and then we regroup once we're finished," Hazel says, holding out the shredded book piles and noticing the looks on everyone's faces. "What? Like Luca said, I need to keep busy. And we all know reading is my superpower. I saved the biggest section for myself."

"Of course you did," Ariana says, standing. "Only

you could make reading seem badass, Hazel Hart."

"I'll put on a pot of coffee," Griffin adds, kissing Hazel one more time.

I force a smile. Hazel is right. There must be answers in the defiled pages she holds. At least, I hope so.

It's the only hope we have left.

Chapter Twenty-One

We sit in Bellfour over a midnight snack of stale croissants, coffee, gummy worms, and yogurt-covered raisins. There's a buzz running through us, and not just from the caffeine and sugar. Our day of research uncovered some answers—and even more questions.

I look over at our whiteboard wall, which now looks like a war room scene straight out of *Game of Thrones*. It took us all afternoon to read our respective sections of the novel and piece together our most important findings. The entire wall is now covered in transcribed passages and questions scribbled on index cards.

The novel turned out to be as bad as Coop and Maggie claimed, with sometimes-impenetrable prose and a choppy plot racing to a very depressing ending. But none of that mattered as much as the premise, and the setting: a majestic-sounding estate in the English countryside, which sounded every bit as impossibly perfect as Copper Cove. At least, until four eighteen-year-olds from the mansion, in service, and from the surrounding village are haunted by a "curse" that demands one of their lives be sacrificed to keep the estate's peace and beauty for another generation. The consequence of refusing? Unbinding a "demon" that would destroy their home and kill everyone it could find.

Hazel summarized the key details from the novel for us on the whiteboard:

❖ *The three surviving parents claimed this curse (aka Pact) had plagued the estate and bound them to it for generations. Over centuries their ancestors probed and tested the curse, learning some precious accumulated knowledge—which the parents shared with their children on the eve of the reveal.*

❖ *If all four teens agreed, on the night of the sacrifice, they could instead go to the demon's prison (the estate attic) and speak five words to break the curse. Doing so would solidify the demon's form and make it killable, but it would also unbind the still very strong and deadly demon. Which would be free to kill them all, then destroy anything or anyone in the world beyond.*

❖ *The teens were also warned that killing the demon would likely rid their home of its surely magical harmony. But, deciding these were all acceptable risks to take, the teens became the first in their line to ever choose this curse-breaking gamble. They believed they'd find a way to kill the demon by, as their parents instructed, "completing the circle of life, ensuring the demon's death."*

❖ *But after the teens broke the curse and freed the demon, it brutally murdered three of them, their families, and much of the surrounding village in a deadly fire—hence the novel's title.*

❖ *The sole surviving teenager managed to kill the*

demon by trapping and burning it in the fire it had created. Apparently to seal the curse, she had to offer the demon itself as a sacrifice by "returning its body to the place of its birth." So she buried the demon's charred body in the ashes of the estate. Doing so, this surviving teen saved the world from the demon's wrath, but at a terrible price: she lost everything and was badly burned herself.

❖ *According to the novel's bio, the author died before publication due to "sustained injuries from severe burns." Her parting message: "I wrote this novel to show that tempting fate or trying to cheat the system ends in total ruin."*

High on the fumes of learning so much potentially game-changing information, we decided to see if we could find any other books or historical records online that might corroborate this novel. Deciding it was worth a potential Impact attack, we risked a trip to the ancient Copper Cove "Computer Center," which is really just two slow, clunky desktops only ever used in case of emergency. We ended up not having to worry about the Impact, because we turned up absolutely nothing—not even an errant message board comment. It was like the internet had been scrubbed clean of not just of any Pact mentions, but also of the very existence of our obscure novel.

At least this explained why the author chose to write her story as a novel. Perhaps she knew fictionalizing it was the only way to get away with telling it. After all, this novel might be the only piece of writing ever published about the Pact in known history. So, knowing we'd likely armed ourselves with more aggregated knowledge than any previous Copper Cove generation, we returned bleary-eyed to Bellfour to discuss our findings.

"Okay, so we can all agree on this much," Hazel begins, breaking our silence. "The novel is too similar to our Pact reality to be purely fictional. That said, does this make everything in it true?"

"Obviously, that's the question of the hour," Ariana replies. "But since Luca's mom brought this novel here, sent us indirectly to find it, and then the Impact fought so hard to keep it from us—there's got to be some valid stuff in there. And probably some fictional stuff too, as cover. Now we just have to figure out which is which."

And what to do about it, I think. But I know that's a heavy debate we'll get to at some point, so I keep listening.

"Right. Well, now that we know this kind of pact-curse has happened someplace besides Copper Cove, it stands to reason it happens other places too. Maybe even all over the world?" Hazel posits. "If the pacts all demand total secrecy, they could have always existed without anyone ever knowing or talking about it."

"If that's true," Griffin takes over, "then this book might even be the only example of the Pact being broken and the Impact ever being defeated. Which is how the book is able to exist in the first place."

"Yeah, but why Copper Cove, then?" Ariana asks. "Or why this *Downton Abbey* place? I mean, how many pact-fueled beautiful places could there be out there?"

"Few enough the world hasn't ended yet?" Hazel answers.

"Or enough to explain every unthinkable local disaster on the whole planet?"

Both thoughts send a chill crawling up my spine.

"Right," I push through. "So does our pact only exist because the British one ended? Or are we tasked with protecting one of a very few special places on the entire planet? If we free the Impact, will it go on killing and killing until someone finally stops it? Or is it really only going to destroy all of Copper Cove before burning out? It's all very garden and inferno, no?"

And then there's the question I can't bring myself to speak out loud yet. If we achieve the impossible and actually manage to kill the Impact, will Copper Cove just be filled with real-world energy, stripped of its enchanted protection? Are the Impact and the sacrifice a worthy price to have to pay to preserve our private paradise?

Part of me finds a sense of comfort in the symmetry the Pact suggests, the balance of forces. Despite its horrors, the Pact implies some kind of higher order, a larger design that gives things purpose. If looked at one way, the Pact symbolizes the idea that there can never be goodness without accompanying bleakness, sure. But it also means there can never be bleakness without accompanying goodness.

It's a simple matter of perspective.

"I'm not sure I'm buying the heaven and hell vibes, Luca," Ariana replies. "Maybe the Pact seems otherworldly to us, but so did volcanoes and the sun and infectious diseases once upon a time, before modern science. If the Pact is anything, I think it's like an environmental necessity. The way a forest fire resets the soil. There's no greater meaning, there's just the rules we have here on Earth, and our own abundance or absence of understanding."

"You think the Pact is just a natural disaster?" I ask. "Maybe that's how it presents itself, but come on, it demands a ritual sacrifice. How could it not somehow be spiritual?"

"Or supernatural," Griffin jumps in. "It reminds me of one of Luca's fairy tales—"

"Excuse me, they're called fantasy epics," I interject.

And for one blissful second, I actually forget what Griffin has done. What *we* did. But when our eyes connect, it's all there, right under the surface. I have to look away.

"Sure, right. Like one of Luca's fantasy epics or something like vampires, or cryptids," Griffin carries on. "I bet if we're right, if this really does happen in secret around the world, we'd see echoes of it in all kinds of cultural stuff if we start looking."

"I don't know. If we go that far, we could say it's as out-there as aliens," Hazel sighs. "I'm with Luca. Or really, this feels more like mythology, to me. I mean, does it not seem to anyone else like we're facing a version of Pandora's box?"

As usual, Hazel's insight drops a contemplative silence into the research-covered walls of Bellfour. Though our quiet is accompanied by the sounds of the talent show rehearsals taking place on the Auditorium stage below. Absurdly, our research had been set to a soundtrack of mediocre piano playing, flat joke telling, and Coop's booming emcee voice. Right now, a decently sung rendition of "The Hills Are Alive" from *The Sound of Music* comes wafting through the rafters below Bellfour's floorboards.

"As interesting as it is, I don't think we'll get anywhere debating why the Pact happens," Hazel follows up. "Not when we have tangible questions to answer. Like, where is the Impact's prison in Copper Cove? Is it the same as its birthplace? And how do we kill our version of the Impact, once it's freed?"

I glance over at our list of potential Impact weaknesses, which doesn't inspire much confidence: *Likes spiders/bugs? Eats lungs? Fear absorption? Phobic senses? Blurry, shifting physical form? Bound by tethers/ rules? What is the "circle of life"?*

"Okay, let me think this through," Griffin picks up. "This Impact thing seems to love its torture gig, but what it probably really wants… That's the wrong word. Its *instinct* is not to be trapped by another sacrifice. The Impact wants us to break the Pact, so then it's free to kill and maim at will. To destroy this place then go out into the world to do who knows what kind of additional damage. Or to just end its own suffering in a blaze of glory.

"Either way, it wants us to break the Pact. So up until now it keeps our haunting surface-level, to make us confident we can fight it and win. But getting this book, learning how to actually *kill* the Impact for real, that's bad for it. So now it'll do whatever it has to do to stop us— hence the escalating attacks today."

"Yeah, and even if the Impact can't kill one of us without imprisoning itself for another generation, it can obviously still hurt us," I add. "Now if it knows we're learning how to stop it, it's going to want us as wounded as possible for the coming fight?"

"What a lovely thought," Ariana shudders.

The thought forces that awful feeling into my body: My lungs filling up, my throat closing. The deathly panic screaming on a cellular level. But I banish this from my mind. Because I can tell Hazel must be doing the same, absentmindedly picking at her bitten fingernails.

We'll just have to cope with our trauma later...if we're lucky.

"Except we don't know how to kill the Impact yet," Ariana finishes. "Or what this cryptic 'circle of life' nonsense means?"

"I cannot figure out why the author would leave that part out," Hazel starts, shuffling through her portion of the pages once again. "It doesn't make any sense. There must have been something that...holy hell. I am a complete moron."

"What is it?"

"There's a page missing, right here," Hazel says. "See?"

We all rush over to corroborate this potential discovery. Indeed, a portion of the page numbers in Hazel's stack jump by two. Each of the respective pages end and begin on a sentence, so it would be very easy to miss, especially if Hazel was reading fast enough.

"This is the section that talks exactly about how she killed the Impact," Hazel says. "How could I have missed that?"

"You have a few other things on your mind," I say. "But hey, maybe the page fell out into one of our stacks when you divided the pages?"

It's a hopeful notion, but one thorough check of

our individual sections doesn't turn up the missing page. Neither does a general search around Bellfour. After both, Hazel reexamines the ripped remnants of the missing page. And that's when she shows us that it seems to have a different pattern than the rest of the pages...like it was a single page torn out earlier.

So who removed this crucial page?

My stomach churns, because the most obvious answer is not one I want to vocalize.

"What if it was your mom, Luca?" Griffin asks for me. "She's obviously conflicted about us having it. Maybe she saved this one page to stop us from fighting the Impact?"

The idea burns in my gut. I haven't yet been able to reconcile Mom's place in all this. Obviously, she went out of her way to find answers about the Pact, just like she obviously planned to give us the book when she learned the truth. But then that pregnant woman died, and Mom lost her nerve, understandably. Still, she stashed the book nearby in the Library and gave me that hint about the title... Would she really have taken out the one page that matters most?

"If that's true, she must not have liked whatever we have to do to kill the Impact," Ariana says.

"Or my dad took it," Hazel adds. "We don't know how much Sofia told him about the book. But they're potentially the only two who understand its significance."

"Yeah, my grandfather would probably have burned the book if he knew about it," Griffin says, disdain coating his voice. "And there's no way your parents told my mom."

Ever since Wendy's surprise appearance, it has been all quiet on the August front. None of us can talk to our parents, but as always, the Augusts feel particularly…distant.

"Maybe Sofia or Garrett took the most important page for safekeeping, in case someone got hold of the book before us?" Griffin tries.

I'd certainly like to believe that—but there's only one way to find out. The idea stings me someplace deep. I'm not remotely ready to confront Mom about any of this. From the look that crosses Hazel's swollen face, it seems she feels the same about talking to Garrett.

"You know, I bet they don't just have the missing page," Griffin continues. "I bet if anyone knows where the Impact is imprisoned, it'll be one of them. But for the record, my money is on the prison being in Weiss Hall— and on one cryptic spot in particular."

"Well, that would explain why my dad was so weird the night of my birthday dinner," Hazel considers.

"Yeah, but how do we get them to talk to us?" I ask. "My mom and Hazel's dad still believe they caused that woman's death. You all saw how much it still haunts them. After what happened with Maggie today, there's no way they're going to want to chance hurting anyone else."

"But if it means saving everyone by ending this thing for good?" Hazel asks. "We're still their kids. If we tell them we have a shot to save ourselves, they'll hear that and want to help. Or at least cough up the missing page."

"Will they?" Ariana asks, her face pained. "You're assuming we've already decided to free the Impact, but is doing that really worth the risk in the first place? This is clearly why your parents didn't rock the boat. If we break the Pact and fail, everyone dies. Game over. The message of the novel couldn't be clearer."

White-hot emotion flashes through me. I want to dismiss Ariana's pessimism, but part of me knows she is probably right. And it's frustrating as hell.

"Listen, I'm not saying we don't keep learning," Ariana follows up. "Maybe we can figure out how to save our own kids, someday. That's obviously worth doing. I just don't know if it's realistic to assume we'll learn how to beat this ancient thing in one day, especially now that we know there's so little information out there beyond the novel. Three of us living on to stop this in the future might be the win we go for? It's certainly better than all of us being responsible for the deaths of thousands of people and the annihilation of Copper Cove...or even worse."

I wish I had a rational argument lined up, but all of mine seem too rooted in emotion. Griffin looks especially conflicted as well.

"Is it, though?" Hazel counters, debate mode clicking into place behind her eyes. "I hear what you're saying, Ariana. But I refuse to act out of fear of the unknown—not when there's a chance to overcome the odds. I say we learn everything we can and save making a decision until tomorrow afternoon. Then, once we have all the knowledge we can gather, we can vote on what to do."

Ariana considers this for a few beats.

"I can live with that," she says. "Especially because tomorrow morning happens to be the annual Shouhed Breakfast BBQ. I know this is a weird year for it, but I bet

Sofia and Garrett will still make an appearance."

Given the past few days, I totally forgot about Ariana's yearly family barbeque. She's right—I bet Mom will probably cling to any shred of comfort or distraction she can.

"I think that's smart, especially given how late it's gotten," Hazel says. "If we're going to break any more rules, I'd rather not do it in the middle of the night. Not if the Impact…"

But Hazel doesn't finish this sentence, wincing as a shot of pain seems to fire through her jaw.

"Agreed," Griffin says, rubbing Hazel's shoulder again. "We can all sleep here together tonight and take guard shifts to look out for the Impact. But I'm hoping it stays in hibernation as long as we don't give it a reason to come out. Then we wake up fresh and get more answers first thing in the morning."

I'm not convinced we should be wasting any time with sleep, but I also don't want to go out into the night after this horrible day. Nor do I want to face Mom when I'm this exhausted. Griffin and Hazel are probably right—at this point, we need all the perspective we can get. Getting some rest is the only thing that will provide that…

Or, maybe, rest is the only thing that will provide *them* perspective.

Maybe there's a way I can make up some of this misery to Griffin and Hazel and Ariana while they sleep. Maybe I should go on my own to find my mom. The thought petrifies me for so many reasons, but there's also no good reason all four of us should take this big a risk together.

This is one burden I can shoulder alone. Or at least, one *more* burden.

I look at Griffin and realize that conversation we were supposed to have "later" isn't going to happen. Not tonight…and maybe not ever?

So I make my silent decision. I will get the answers we need from my mother. I tell myself I'm being selfless.

But deep down, I know the selfish truth.

I just need to get the hell out of Bellfour, now that it feels like it's rotting at its core.

Stone Five

It's a few hours before dawn and fear has seeped deep into my muscles, tensing them like coiled springs.

I took the last of the night watch shifts, knowing it would be easiest to slip out undetected the later it got.

I didn't sleep very much, being so close to the truth, yet still so far.

Being this near to Griffin and still feeling worlds apart.

The Impact hasn't shown itself, but I almost wish it would.

Something about the anticipation, waiting in the deathly silence to make sure everyone else is fully asleep, is perhaps even more frightening.

Before I go, I decide to leave a stone here in Bellfour.

I can't help but wonder if this stone tradition is some ritual my grandpa wanted me to finish.

Or could it all just be more inherited nonsense, another empty gesture for my grandpa to try and atone?

Adding these questions to the pile, I leave my fifth stone

in the jewel case to a Taylor Swift CD, which houses my favorite song by her, "All Too Well."

It has a line in it that always resonates with me, about being paralyzed by time.

So I suppose it is my tribute to turning into stone.

Chapter Twenty-Two

I slip out of Bellfour as silently as I can, though the others seem to be sleeping pretty heavily. Fear courses through my veins. The idea of roaming Copper Cove's campus at night to break the Pact rules by talking to the one person I feel most betrayed by suddenly feels quite stupid.

But punishment is probably what I deserve, anyway.

I try desperately to steady my breathing as I descend the stairs and enter the Auditorium's outer hall. It's a short walk from here up the hill to Hemlock, but right now it feels like it might as well be a million miles. What could the Impact do to me, alone in the dark like this?

I can't think about that now. All I can think about is moving.

"Luca. Wait."

The hushed voice nearly makes me jump out of my skin. Especially when I realize who it belongs to.

I turn around to find Griffin coming down the stairs behind me, wearing only a pair of gray sweatpants. The sight of his curved V muscles, his broad chest, the moonlight catching on his shoulder blades…

It's devastating.

"I knew you'd try something like this," he whispers, approaching me.

Why does he make it so hard for me to think clearly?

"Griffin. Please. Don't."

"I know you, Luca."

Griffin says this just before he kisses me again, his stubble scraping my chin. This time there's nothing clumsy about it. Griffin's hands grasp my back, and he maneuvers me sideways. He keeps kissing me, deep and steady.

Before I know it, he opens the door to a utility closet at the base of the stairs and moves us inside. He closes the door. He must understand what will happen if we get caught. Still, he pulls off my shirt. He pushes me against the wall and presses himself against me, knowing I won't stop him.

Griffin knows *exactly* what he is doing.

But I am lost.

Gone in Griffin's lips, his smell. Dropped into the feeling of his muscles flexing all over me. Leaning into the idea this wasn't some drunken fluke, that I didn't cross this line alone.

I want this so badly. It's all I've ever wanted and it's so much better than I imagined it would be, because it isn't just physical. I can feel how much Griffin wants me, wants this. There's love here, and not just mine.

Griffin is right, he knows me. Better than almost anyone. Better than everyone, except...

Except for Hazel.

Hazel.

When Griffin reaches to pull down his sweatpants, I somehow summon the will to stop him.

"Griffin, wait," I gasp.

"Please don't stop," he says, his hands still all over me, his lips on my neck. "Please. I need to."

"Griffin."

Pushing him away feels impossible, but I manage to do it anyway.

"Luca, please," he whispers, coming closer. "I can't lose you."

There's a small window in this closet. It lets in just enough light from the full moon for me to see the tears in Griffin's eyes.

"Listen to me." I try to get some kind of grip. "I need to know what this means. Because I love you."

The words just fall out, simple and messy as hell.

I study Griffin. I study his gorgeous face as it freezes. For the first time since this all started, I see him so clearly.

Griffin doesn't have any answers. That's why he avoided me, avoided dealing with this all day. He doesn't know what this—what any of it—really means. What he wants is eating him alive, same as me.

And more than anything, Griffin needs to be loved.

So I kiss him again. My hands reach into his underwear. We gasp together. I give Griffin what he needs.

What I need?

It's all so *wrong*. Still, it feels better than anything has ever felt in my entire life. Maybe that's why I don't hear it at first, the sound outside the door. The...familiar sound.

Whining.

"Oh god, Griffin—"

I don't finish my warning before the door swings open in a silent fury. One single crack reveals the Impact again. It must be here because I was going to talk to my mom. It's here because of me.

Maybe that's why it rips me out of the utility closet first, sending me skidding across the wooden floor. I expect it to pounce next, to hold me down and drown me out.

But maybe the Impact understands the quickest way to hurt me is to hurt my people. It reaches out with slick appendages for Griffin's face. Before I can say anything, the Impact's antennae slide up Griffin's cheeks. The ends split in half, twisting and writhing…

Aiming to pry Griffin's eyeballs out.

In the next second, I hear a slicing sound…

And I sputter with relief, seeing that Griffin has slashed the Impact with a rusty knife. Its antennae fall to the floor in a wet splat, still twitching.

The Impact rears in retaliation, bucking and knocking Griffin back into the closet with shocking force. It opens some deep rift inside its body and spews liquid, yellow and curdled. The vile regurgitation pours out faster than ever, drenching Griffin and filling the small closet quicker than should be possible.

By the time I'm back on my feet, Griffin is fully bathed in the Impact's…blood?

Then it closes the door with him still inside. Griffin, claustrophobic and answerless, trapped in a tiny closet filled with some rancid fluid. The Impact has entombed him in the very building his family bought with its murder money.

And it's then I understand.

The Impact is evolving.

It turns to me, its sad excuse for eyeballs swirling

with an ink-black pulse. A void wrapped in evil. A monster of our own making.

I charge at it before I even know what I'm doing.

The second I tackle the Impact to the floor, two things happen. It is pulled away in a blur, retracted by its bungee-cord snap. Then Griffin tumbles out of the utility closet, choking and gasping. He falls to the floor beside me, covered in foulness.

I reach out for him, to help him or hold him. But before I can, Griffin pushes himself up to his feet.

And then he runs away. Without a word. Griffin just runs.

I don't know where he's going or what he's thinking. I just know that once again, Griffin disappears on me.

What else could I expect?

Chapter Twenty-Three

I check on Hazel and Ariana upstairs, but they're still both asleep, safe and sound. Heavy door, heavier sleepers—especially after these last few sleepless nights.

I try to find Mom next, tempting fate once again. But she and Garrett aren't sleeping in Hemlock. I have no idea what that could mean. Are they safely removed from Copper Cove's campus? Or are they dead in an Impact ditch somewhere?

I realize I'll have to wait until the barbeque to find out, after all.

I don't even bother looking for Griffin. He's made it very clear I can't reach him when he doesn't want to be found.

So with nothing to occupy this final dawn, I go to the lake. I'll return to Bellfour after, but first I must swim.

The moment my body enters the lake, with water warmer than the air at this hour, it still feels something like a baptism. The lake washes me clean and renders me weightless, if only for a short while. I try to imagine it's protected by an invisible shield, rippling and wavering like the water itself. In this lake, no one and nothing can reach me…

That is, as long as I don't break any more rules…or go anywhere near the dark-fishing dock.

This morning I have the whole beach to myself. I

forgot there's an early call time for the annual sunrise hike to McDonough Peak, so not even Pan and Glo are Morning Dipping. Without any boats or other swimmers, the lake is almost completely still. Totally silent. I settle my shoulders under the water and look out at the mountains, where the sun is just beginning to show over the peaks. Sunlight breaks through the few low-hanging clouds to shine over the lake, like a golden scar bursting across the calm blue surface.

Despite this sight, I feel the power of prayer and reflection won't be enough this dread morning. I'd have to swim the entire lake to begin sorting through the wreckage. Still, I dive forward, cool water rushing across my face and through my hair. I open my eyes underneath and sunrays streak down through the water, stalks of light floating with particles. I reach my hand through the nearest beam, and it shines across my skin in a kaleidoscope of refractions. I feel not unlike the light, broken into pieces, a thousand beads of brightness lost underneath miles of water.

What am I going to do?

I realize I'd better decide quickly, because when I turn to swim back to shore, Griffin is standing there. He waits several feet away from the lifeguard stand, which is still empty. Griffin's feet dig into the sand and the sun catches on his blond hair. He is like a vision, an actual golden boy bathed in the light of dawn.

Whatever else the Impact bathed him with earlier, that's gone now.

The familiar early warning signs of panic creep into my limbs, but I try to ignore them. This is too important. I've waited too long to fall apart now. I need to know if this thing between us doesn't matter to Griffin. Or if it matters more than ever, given the deadline we face.

I take a deep breath, then swim towards shore. I stay under the water as long as possible, still somehow self-conscious about being shirtless in the daylight in front of Griffin. Wading through the shallows with my arms crossed, I settle at the shoreline. I stand next to Griffin, both of us looking out at the lake instead of each other.

"You ran away," I start. "Again."

"Have you met my mother?" Griffin tries.

"That's not funny."

"I know," he sighs.

My wet skin feels frosty against the morning breeze. I want to grab my towel, but I'm not going anywhere now that we're here. Questions run across my mind in a never-ending ticker-tape scroll, but one keeps repeating itself, over and over: "Why?"

"I don't know. I was…"

Griffin clears his throat. I try to steel myself against the cold, and whatever Griffin is about to say…or maybe not say.

"I couldn't deal," he says finally. "With all of it. I need time to process, but we don't have any time to spare. I told myself I didn't want to say anything until I had the perfect words. I wasn't joking, just now. I've grown up with a black belt in avoidance. But if I've learned anything these last couple days, it's that I don't want to be anything like my mom. Or my grandfather. It makes me sick, thinking I've repeated their mistakes."

"You haven't. We haven't," I say. "But Griffin, you…"

The wind picks up, and I'm sure it will blow my

fragile bones away. I plant my feet deeper in the sand.

"I think you know what you...what this means to me," I go on. "So I need to know what this means to you."

Griffin pauses, turning from the horizon to me.

I match his gaze and, even after all the turmoil, a sickly burst of love pulses in my chest. My body betrays me yet again, pulled into Griffin's magnetic field. I want to reach out and touch him, to be wrapped up in him again.

But instead I hold my ground.

"Okay, I'm just going to say the things I came here to say," Griffin finally sighs. "The truth is, I was oblivious to how you really felt until the day of the Emp Bonfire, that awful day after we learned about the Pact. Looking back, I don't know how I could have missed it. I think each one of us has realized how much we've been missing all these years. Still, when it comes to Copper Cove, I knew something was wrong here much longer than you all. I could just never put my finger on it. Learning about the Pact... It wasn't a relief, exactly. But it did lift this fog I've lived inside my whole life.

"When it comes to you though, Luca, your feelings—I truly didn't know. When Ariana told me how you really felt about me, how you've been hiding it for so long...*that* hit me like a brick."

Wait. Ariana... What?

My brain throbs once again, tilting the world sideways. All of the emotions I felt after being outed suddenly come flooding back, strangling me into silence.

"Ariana didn't even mean to tell me," Griffin adds. "She was trying to get me to give you some space when I said I was planning to sleep over these last few nights, but I didn't get why. So she kind of hinted at it. And then once she did... She was just trying to help. I know she feels terrible about letting it slip."

Trying to help. The things Frances, and Mom, and now Ariana have done to protect me, to *help* me... I choke on all of it. A familiar tightness tugs at my throat and I beg my body to leave me be, even if only a few minutes longer.

"But do you really think she 'let it slip'?" I say flatly. "Our so-called outsider, on the day we find out we have to vote someone off the island?"

"I..." Griffin begins. "I didn't think of it that way."

No, of course he didn't.

"I just, I couldn't believe I didn't see your feelings before. I mean, maybe it crossed my mind, but I didn't think it was so..." Griffin continues. "Anyway, I felt so guilty. About everything that happened with Hazel, how we rubbed your face in us being together. The idea of hurting you, I couldn't... You're one of my best friends, Luca, and the thought I had been causing you all this... hurt, for so long. I just kind of froze up. I know how hard this Pact thing must be hitting you, out of all of us. I wanted to make something better. I felt like I owed everyone that. It's why I pulled out the whiskey that night. I was going to say something to you at the bonfire. I think that's why I got so drunk, to build up some courage."

"Are you gay, Griffin?" I speak the words, but they sound like they come from someone else. Disembodied, somehow.

I know I should be asking Griffin if he plans to

sacrifice himself, if that's what he thinks he "owes" us, but I can't go there. Not yet.

"It's more complicated than that," Griffin answers. "I'm straight, but not all the way?"

He takes another breath.

"I know what you're going to think, that I'm gay and I haven't accepted it yet. Because this is the way it starts for most gay guys, right? The truth is, I've messed around with some guys at school. Like, you know how a girl can make out with another girl even if she is straight, or have a crush or something, and it doesn't have to mean she's gay, or even bisexual? That happens for me. I can find a guy... interesting. It doesn't gross me out or anything. But if you admit to anyone you're even a little bit attracted to a guy, everyone just assumes."

"So, you're bisexual?"

"Yes, I... Being bisexual is sort of it. Or maybe pansexual? I just... It doesn't feel like there's space for what I really am to exist? None of the labels sound...

"Sorry, I'm rambling," Griffin sighs again. "Yes, I can be attracted to guys. But it's not an equal-opportunity thing. You know how sexuality is supposed to be a spectrum, or whatever? I feel like I'm 80 percent straight, but there's no... I can't say that to anyone and have them believe me. But yes, pansexual is the best label we have for it right now, I guess."

"Then why..." I begin, clearing my throat. "Why didn't you ever tell me?"

"I don't know," Griffin answers. "I guess I'm not ready to have everyone else put their labels on me. I respect you so much for coming out to us, Luca. But for me, it doesn't feel like something everyone needs to know."

I think of Frances again, of what happened to me, and find it hard to blame him. We're supposed to be living in a different world, one where being queer is eventually accepted and it all gets better. But that promise sometimes just makes the lingering indignities feel worse. Suddenly, I realize how self-absorbed I've been. I was so wrapped up in my own feelings and fears, I hadn't ever stopped to think what Griffin might be going through underneath it all.

"But I did tell Hazel. About my sexuality, I mean."

Then a sickly feeling, green and festering, creeps into my chest. Hazel…knew?

"That's part of what I came here to say, I guess. What I should have said earlier, when I…stopped you," Griffin continues. "Yes, I've messed around with a couple guys, but I've never had feelings for one. At least, not the way I do for Hazel."

The words are like knives, each one cleaving a chunk off me. I stare at the horizon, even though the sun is getting brighter. Trees and grass, water and sand, *Griffin and not me*.

"Then what was it, the other night?" I ask, even though I already suspect the answer. "Why didn't you tell me this a few hours ago, when you…"

I can't finish the sentence, because once again, I was so wrong. Before, I thought Griffin didn't have any answers. But clearly he did all along. He just seemed so conflicted because he couldn't bring himself to *tell me*.

"I don't know. When I realized what you really wanted, maybe I just wanted to make you happy. Fuck, that's not what I mean. I don't know how to—"

"Twice?" I interrupt.

"Yes. This isn't fair to you, but...here it is. I am attracted to you. There's a world where we could have been more than best friends."

Griffin looks back out at the water, searching for more words.

"But I love Hazel with all my heart."

I expect the things he says to keep hitting me like sledgehammers, but instead I don't feel a thing. I've dropped into that numb space, coated in a thick and protective layer of shock.

"Luca, don't get me wrong. I love being around you. And not just because of the way you see this place, but because of the way you see me. It makes me feel good, better than I am," he starts. "But it's also like you put me on this pedestal, and I always want to be that person you see. I feel pressure to be this shining example, because I don't want to disappoint you. But that's not all of me. Sometimes I'm really spoiled, and I can feel really alone, and I shut down when I shouldn't, and I'm not as smart or funny as you or Hazel or Ariana by a mile. Around everyone else I try to keep up, but Hazel—she sees all the bad parts. And she seems to love me anyway."

This doesn't feel right to me, at first. But then I think about the way I saw Copper Cove before, all the things I missed. Did I somehow do the same with Griffin? And what if I had said something to him earlier about my feelings? Would it have broken down some invisible barrier between us, given us a chance to talk about all these things, these secret selves, we have in common? Would it have changed anything? Would I have seen him more clearly, like Hazel? Could Griffin have maybe loved me too, if I had given him the chance?

Then I remind myself that the world isn't always safe outside the closet. Can anyone really blame me for keeping it all in a vault, locked in my head where the risks were only potential? It doesn't matter. I missed my chance, so the what-if's don't count. What does count is that I made my friend, one of my best friends, feel like he couldn't be himself around me.

I can already tell I'll be adding this to the list of things that will haunt me from this dreadful day—however long I have left.

I look back over at Griffin and there he is. The same impossible boy, evolved and sensitive enough to acknowledge his emotions, even if his first instinct is to run from them. The same boy who just wants to be good. But who, in trying to make it better, has only made it far worse. In this version of things, Griffin isn't off-limits because he's straight. In this reality, Griffin has a choice to make.

And he doesn't choose me.

In that moment, I drift further out to sea. It's like my life is a continent I've been severed from and now there is only water, uncharted, in every direction.

Instead of feeling panicked, I'm surprised to feel calm. I feel alone, sharply alone, but I also feel something else. I realize I'm about to lose something vital, an entire limb...but maybe instead of claiming my life, this will save it?

Save.

"Griffin, did you kiss me because you plan to sacrifice yourself tonight?"

The question hangs in the air between us, cold and piercing.

"We agreed we wouldn't discuss that unless we have to."

Griffin's non-answer speaks volumes. This is *exactly* his plan. It's why he wanted to give me this last… gift, sloppy as it was. If it all falls apart today, Griffin is going to sacrifice himself, just like Hazel said. She really does know him best. But she isn't the only one who won't let him give up on himself.

"Hazel can't know," I say. "About us. Because we're all surviving this. Together."

"Yes," Griffin answers. "I mean, I agree. But are you okay with that?"

I laugh. I can't help it.

"I am so deeply not okay with anything right now," I say. "But not telling Hazel is the right thing to do. This was our mistake. And if it's really done, telling her would just be selfish. We can spare her this. It's the least we can do, now."

I say the words, hoping that might make them true.

Griffin is silent, but I can tell there's something hiding in that.

"What?"

"Nothing, it's just"—Griffin pauses, turning over something in his head—"you kind of sound like our parents, when you say it like that."

"I…know."

What else is there to say? We've officially lost the

ability to judge anyone else's bad decisions, or the sins of our families. Something tells me we never really had that right to begin with.

Griffin takes another moment. "Listen, I know you're probably mad at Ariana for telling me and you have every right to be. But can you also not say anything to her, for now? I mean, after what my grandfather said about targeting her…"

There it is, that trademark Griffin kindness. Held up, as always, by that trademark August pressure.

"I won't," I promise.

Griffin is right. Confronting Ariana won't do any good, even if the river of her transgression runs deep. The fight we face today is too important. So once again, I bottle this spike of emotion, swallowing it down like another jagged pill.

We stand there for a while, Griffin and I.

I'm not sure yet, but I suspect he might be ruined for me, just like Copper Cove. They're still beautiful things, but now they're also broken. Perhaps irreparably.

Before, all I wanted was answers.

Now that I have them, I just want to be more careful about what I wish for.

Stone Six

For my sixth stone, I return to the Infinity Tree.

I don't mean to at first, but I find myself walking there on my way to Bellfour and the barbeque.

I need a place to gather my thoughts.

Or lose them.

I pray I don't run into Manny there, for his sake.

For my sake?

Still, I return to the Infinity Tree, hoping to find it empty, yet also looking for something.

Instead, I leave a stone.

It is my tribute to folding in on oneself.

And to circles, to stone rings with no beginning and no end.

Chapter Twenty-Four

I sit on a tiny strip of sand, the sun warm on my face and the water cool on my bare feet. I discovered this secret little beach in August Bay ten years ago, playing with Ariana in the backyard of her family's rented cottage. The beach is tucked behind a thicket of bushes and brambles, occupying the only five feet of sand on this entire section of bay. I haven't thought to come here in ages. Back then, it filled me with a sense of magic, that same summer I discovered both *Lord of the Rings* and Stevie Nicks. It was also the first time I ever thought to close my eyes and imagine the nearby archery course as a castle's courtyard, or the Boathouse as a bustling port. Ariana and I played princes and princesses on this little beach, where we had a kid wedding to join our imaginary kingdoms.

I snuck here to escape the barbeque and the social niceties that feel physically impossible. And maybe to savor a slice of the paradise I suspect I'm losing? I can't outrun the idea I've been a fool to see everything so blindly, believing in my distorted daydreams. Though maybe I should be grateful for having so many perfect summers here. I just wish someone told us we'd be paying for them on borrowed credit.

I breathe in—an act I no longer take for granted,

sitting here by the lake. And I try to remind myself I can be strong, especially as Ariana appears beside me. She sits and a flash of fury bakes my bones. How could so much have gone wrong between us all so quickly, for the first time? I know I could blame the Pact. But what we need—what I need—is to remember that we're friends, no matter what. I might be running dangerously close to empty, but I just need to hold it together for one more day. Until the sunset that will bring our final showdown, one way or another.

"I knew I'd find you here," Ariana says. "I was going to freak out back there if I had to endure one more second of chitchat. Not when I want to scream at everyone to run and hide, to tell my family to leave right now and never look back. But warning them would only doom them, right? Set the Impact free for real, to do goddess knows what? This is…"

Ariana presses her eyes closed. She silently counts to five, some kind of mental reset I've never seen her do. I suppose stress-relieving techniques are a new thing for all of us here in Copper Cove.

"How's your anxiety level doing?" Ariana asks.

"At a constant eight, I guess." My heart swells in one of its cracked corners. Still, I don't know how much more of Ariana's *concern* I can handle. "I only have an attack at ten."

"I'm so impressed you haven't had a full episode yet, honestly," she says. "This is all so…"

"How are you doing?" I return when Ariana doesn't finish.

"Me? I'm…everything at once, right now. But I

also feel kind of…reduced to nothing? Does that sound melodramatic?"

"No. Not at all."

"Mostly I keep thinking about stupid stuff, like what if I never get to use the ugly pink shower caddy my mom bought me for college that I said I hated. Or who is going to feed my pet fish if I—"

"No one is dying, Ariana," I interrupt.

She doesn't respond to that. Instead, she hands me something.

"I saw this in my room. I meant to give it to you earlier."

Ariana has handed me a watercolor painting the size of a postcard. It's a blurry yet beautiful rendering of the Auditorium, with Bellfour's tower standing tall against a blue sky. Something about the watercolor doesn't capture the reality of the scene, but rather the emotion I always remember feeling inside our secret hideout. It's like a magic trick—Ariana's personal power at work.

"When did you have time to make this?" I nearly choke out. I'd forgotten I even asked Ariana for a painting.

"I was mostly done with it before all this hell broke loose, but I did sneak into the Craft Shop the night of the Emp Bonfire to clear my head. I thought you'd still like to have a piece of Copper Cove, of us, if you went off to college."

Ariana looks out at the lake—which has grown choppier than usual, all whitecaps tossing in the wind. *If*. It's the only word I absorb.

"At first I was going to paint one of those fantasy places you've always said you wanted to travel to, maybe New Zealand because I've been there a couple times,"

Ariana continues. "But then I realized something. Places, even beautiful places, are just that—just postcard pictures, if they're not filled with memories or people you love. That's what makes a place like Copper Cove really special. Not magic, or ancient pacts. I guess I wanted to remind you of that, because you always do that for me."

Tears roll down Ariana's cheeks.

I want to say so many things. *Thank you. I love it. You're right. This means the world to me. I'll treasure it forever, however long that ends up being.* Instead, something about the painting unravels me.

"I don't know why you told Griffin about my feelings," I say, tears staining my own cheeks.

I feel it all bubbling up and suddenly I lack the capacity to contain anything. So here, on the strip of secret beach, I melt. Ariana turns and hugs me as I sob, emotion burning through me.

"I'm so sorry, Luca," she says. "I swear I didn't plan to. I heard Griffin going on about sleeping over with you and I just thought, maybe if I told him to back off, it would make things easier for you. But then once I said something he wouldn't drop it. And I just hate lying."

"That's funny," I reply. "Frances used to say something similar. I didn't realize my best friends all thought of me as a liar."

I don't know where these words come from, but they leave with a push, tearing something loose. I'm furious. At Frances. At those monsters back in high school. At Mom, and the Pact, and Ariana, and Hazel, and Griffin...

And myself.

We're all just clumsy caretakers, aren't we? Ripping things open inside each other in the name of healing.

"I don't know if that's fair, Luca," Ariana says, sensing the shift in me.

"No, it isn't." I want to stop, but I'm possessed. I've opened the floodgates and now my toxic waste is going to raze us both. "While we're on the subject of unfair, please tell me you didn't do that to try and tear us apart, to save yourself in this nightmare?"

Ariana recoils.

"How dare you say that to me."

"Griffin kissed me, the night you told him about me," I say. "He did it because he felt bad for me. Why do you think that is?"

"Wait, what?" she sputters. "Griffin is gay?"

"No, he's…" I start, suddenly realizing what I've done.

"I shouldn't have…" I try. "It's not my place to tell you."

"I don't…" Ariana begins, pulling further away each second. "Does Hazel know?"

"She knows he's pansexual, yes. But not about what happened. Griffin didn't mean to do it. He loves Hazel—he made that very clear. It's never happening again, so it's not something Hazel needs to know about."

"Is it really your place to decide that?" Ariana asks.

"Was it yours?"

This hangs in the air between us for a few seconds. Until I add, "Griffin just pitied me. Everyone seems to."

"God Luca, then maybe you should stop being so pitiful. I'm sorry, I don't mean to be a dick, but someone needs to say it. Can't you see, all the secrets, the not speaking up—it's poison. And now you tell me this, today of all days? And, what—now I keep this from Hazel, one of our supposed best friends, too? Then I'm supposed to march with you all to the death, to risk everyone I love to protect…what, our friendship? The one filled with hiding and cheating and—"

"I don't care if it's hard for you. You can't tell Hazel," I say, my anger flaring again. How dare Ariana react like this, how dare she blame me when she's the one who…

The one who…

Is completely *correct*?

"I need to clear my head," she says. "Or…I don't know."

Ariana stands and walks away, leaving me with only the watercolor she made. And my doubts.

Now that I've drained a drop of my guilt, I realize just how deeply I've been drowning in it. If Griffin loves Hazel the way he says he does, the guilt must be even more suffocating for him. How could I… How could I not have…

How could I have failed so spectacularly at the one thing that matters most to me?

And what will Ariana do next?

I barely have time to process these questions when someone takes Ariana's place on the sand…

Mom.

Chapter Twenty-Five

"We thought you kids might be here," Mom starts. "Or we hoped, I guess."

"Isn't us talking against the rules?" I ask, trying desperately to shove what just happened out of my mind.

"I don't know. I'm hoping if we don't talk about *it* directly, everyone will be okay," Mom answers. "But honestly, I'd risk just about anything to be able to have this one conversation with you. Garrett too, with Hazel."

"And Wendy?"

"Griffin asked the same thing," Mom sighs. "No. We haven't heard anything from the Augusts since Wendy's visit. I want to judge them for keeping their distance, but neither Garrett nor I could stand speaking to Ariana's parents for very long just now. Not being able to... Maybe distance isn't... You know, I could barely bring myself to visit Maggie in the hospital without... She's okay, thank god, but... Luca. Hey. Can I give you a hug?"

"Yes," I answer.

I wish I didn't, but at this moment, I just need my mom. Screw the risk. She's right. If I'm going to survive this, I need to have this conversation. Burying my face in Mom's shoulder, I feel the urge to cry again, but I have so little left in me.

"Can we walk?" I ask. I don't want to be on this soiled beach anymore.

Thankfully, Mom nods and we begin moving, making our way towards the nearest building, which happens to be the Boathouse. We're halfway there by the time I realize I'm still holding Ariana's watercolor. I shove it in my pocket, before I finally work up the nerve to ask my first big question.

"How could you keep this secret, all these years?"

Mom takes a deep breath, but she's ready with an answer. This is obviously a question she has asked herself countless times before.

"It was easier on the days I could convince myself we were really protecting you. I still pray that's what we were doing. But Luca, you have to understand, as the years go on, you just push it down. File it under things to deal with later. It's hard to justify when you ask me out loud like this…but it's like flipping to some trashy reality TV after watching news about some disaster across the world. You know it's happening, but there's nothing you can do to stop it, so you detach. It's so much easier to repress than you think."

I suppose I can understand that much, at least.

"But somewhere along the way, I made a choice. I could be full of dread and shame, or I could savor every moment I got to spend with you. I could try to save you and smother you, or I could let you live whatever life you had left, because nothing is ever certain. I never knew if I was giving you the greatest gift or the worst kind of curse, but it was all I had. The letting go, despite the never-ending fear."

Mom pauses, like she needs to regather her

strength—and her focus, to make sure she chooses the right words.

"I used to think Wendy was evil, she and her monster of a father. The way she closed herself off from this place, and from Griffin. I used to think it was inhuman of her to stay so isolated. Maybe I was jealous of how easy the Augusts seemed to make it for themselves. But that was until our visit the other night. I see now that palace they built to protect themselves is really just a prison. Lord knows I'm in no position to judge, but at least I don't envy Wendy a single thing. Not anymore."

I can tell Mom's last thoughts are more for herself than for me. After all, she doesn't have anyone to talk to about this—except for Garrett, who prefers his syllables in mono. Despite everything, I still want to be there for Mom, for us to be there for each other.

But time is short. And whatever else might be broken, I still have a job to do. I just hope I can choose my own words carefully enough to not trigger the Impact.

"Mom, I know you think you can't, but you have to tell me what else you know," I say, while she might not see it coming. "We read the book. But there's a page missing. And I think you have it."

Knowledge flashes behind Mom's eyes, in that familiar way I now fully recognize. At the same moment, we reach the Boathouse. I follow her lead as she settles onto a rocking chair overlooking the choppy lake. After one tense glance at our surroundings, she begins again. I force myself to listen to her instead of the hopefully normal whirs and clicks from the woods all around.

"After what happened to us, I decided to devote my life to finding answers. I didn't tell anyone. I vowed I'd find a way to stop it myself. But college, grad school—I had access to all that information and still I couldn't find a lead. Even long after you were born, I was starting to believe I'd never find anything."

Mom swallows, eyeing the tree line beyond the Boathouse again. We both know how dangerous this conversation could be. Once her eyes fall on a flower bush buzzing with bees, she starts speaking a little faster.

"Then I finally came across that awful novel on an obscure book listing. The author was dead, but I tracked down her editor at this tiny press. She said she only published the manuscript out of pity, fulfilling the last wish of an old friend's daughter after she lost her family all in a fire. I must have read that book a hundred times before I came to three conclusions.

"First, there were no reports of horrible incidents in Copper Cove since I found the book, so my research must have somehow been inbounds. Second, there was nothing we parents could do anymore—that would have to be up to the next generation. Third, I had to tell Garrett. He agreed that we should arm you with the information in the book early, consequences be damned. Any price was worth paying to save you all, or so we thought. We were going to tell you the night of Hazel's fourteenth birthday. And then that woman, and her unborn child…"

Mom trails off again, unable to bring herself to say the rest out loud.

"That night I realized how stupid we'd been to

ignore the warnings from our own parents, to ignore the clear message of the book. We realized too late how selfish we'd been, prioritizing our own children while damning other parents, other families, to the same fate. But even if we couldn't give you information, we decided we could give you four more years of innocence and Copper Cove happiness. Because Luca, living with those kinds of losses, the innocent lives..."

Mom turns away from the lake to look me right in the face, tears brimming in her eyes.

"Everything I've ever done has been to try and protect you, the best way I know how. You have to believe that if nothing else, figlio mio."

I look at Mom and suddenly she is just a person, someone who was eighteen herself once. I'm tempted to close my eyes and picture her differently, but I force my eyes to stay open. All I can think about are the things I've kept to myself this summer, too, in the name of *protection*.

"I believe you," I say. "But if that's true, why did you leave the book at the Library? Why did you drop the clue if you didn't want me to do anything with it?"

"I don't know anymore," Mom says, in a voice so small I can barely hear. "I just can't lose you, Luca. That's all I do know."

"You've already told us this much. We've already taken the risk just having this conversation," I try again. I hate pressing when she's like this, but I don't have a choice. "If we're going to make the right decision, we need all the information you have."

Mom sighs deeply. She doesn't say anything more. She

doesn't need to. Instead she reaches into her pocket and pulls out a folded-up piece of paper. Then she hands it to me…

The missing page from the novel.

"I still don't know if I meant to keep it from you or save it for you, even after all these years," Mom says. "But that's it, I've given you everything I know. It's up to you and the others to figure out the rest. I just hope I've given you enough to do better than we did. Than I did."

Mom reaches out to take my hand, but then suddenly freezes in place. She must smell it one second before I do.

Smoke.

I turn around and am stunned. The roof of the Boathouse is ablaze with silent flames, shooting high and clear into the cloudless sky. When did this fire start? We were so preoccupied with—

"Luca, run!"

I turn back around and there is the Impact, glitching into existence beside Mom. It reaches across her for me, so I shove the missing page into my pocket. Then I brace myself for whatever horror is coming. Within the next second, the Impact has me in its clammy grip.

Then it tosses me off the deck like a rag doll.

As my body hits the hillside grass, I see the blue sky marred by plumes of black smoke. I see the Boathouse flashing red and orange.

And I see Coop on the deck, engulfed in flames.

Then I black out.

∞

By the time I regain consciousness, I've been moved

to the lawn of the baseball diamond. People fuss over me, but I only look for one particular person.

When I see Mom, I cry out with relief.

She hugs me, asking a string of questions that are indecipherable through her sobs.

"I'm fine," I say, because it's true. Physically, anyway. "Are you okay? Is Coop okay?"

"Emergency workers are already here," Mom answers. "I only got hit once before…"

Mom doesn't have to finish the sentence. *Before the Impact was pulled away and I dragged you here.*

After all our talking, was the Impact finally freed by Mom handing me that missing page? Did it come after us in that moment? Or was it freed sometime before, triggered by something we said? Did the Impact start the fire in the Boathouse?

We were sitting right there. That can't be a coincidence.

I check my pocket and the Impact hasn't taken the missing page. But I'm not exactly capable of relief right now. Instead, I brace myself to look at the Boathouse…

Which is half-collapsed, still flickering with flames as firefighters work to extinguish the dying blaze.

I scan the crowd and see dozens of familiar faces, all of them stunned with silent shock. Most of Copper Cove is gathered here by now, and no one is accustomed to this kind of horror touching our place.

Except for Garrett, whose face I see pushing through to reach us—followed by Hazel and Griffin.

"We're okay," Mom says as they arrive. "You?"

"It didn't come for us," Garrett answers, dropping

his voice to a whisper. "But I spoke to one of the officers. They're already blaming a faulty fireplace. Everyone got out of the Boathouse in time. Everyone except…"

I go slack with disbelief as this news hits me. Because I understand before Garrett even says anything.

"Coop saved everyone. But his burns…"

My eyes land on Hazel and she looks so pale. Suddenly I feel like a fire has just engulfed my own heart, melting my flesh translucent.

That final vision of Coop sears itself into my mind.

I almost pass out again.

Chapter Twenty-Six

We all want to stay here, standing frozen with grief in the grass. None of us want to move a muscle, to accept what has happened. What we *allowed* to happen. The fireplace might have been old and tricky, but we know only one thing could have caused it to ignite so violently…

The Impact, feeding on Coop's fear of fire.

And if he really died because of the truths printed on the piece of paper in my pocket, then we'd sure as hell better do something about it.

"We have to go to Bellfour," I say, my voice coated in steel. "We have to end this."

No one, not Griffin or Hazel, not Garrett or Mom, argues with me. Because we all agree. There will be no more blood on our hands unless it's our own.

One way or another, this nightmare dies tonight.

Ariana is waiting there by the time we make it to Bellfour. She looks just as ashen as the three of us. We C4 don't hug each other. We just sit in a circle, silent and shaking in our seats.

All I can think of is Coop. How he isn't in

the Boathouse where he belongs. Because there is no Boathouse anymore. There is no Coop. From now on, there will only be the memory of him. Of the same opening line he gave every summer. Of him filling out the boat-rental log. Of him hosting the talent show, his favorite thing in the world. Of him crippled with anxiety that cloudy morning over the fireplace.

Of him running across the deck wrapped in his greatest fear come to life, but still sacrificing himself to save everyone else.

It should have been one of us.

Now I understand what Mom has been trying to save us, save me, from. I understand so deeply, nothing inside me will ever be the same again. It will always be spiked with this…guilt.

"It's our fault." Hazel is the only one brave enough to speak out loud what we all must be thinking.

But it's not *our* fault. It's *my* fault, mine and Mom's.

At least that's what I think until Hazel pulls something metal out of her pocket and places it on the coffee table between us.

"This is the key to the Weiss Crypt, to the padlock with Tommy's name on it," Hazel says. "My dad gave it to me, right after he told me what he thinks the Impact really is. That's how it got free. That's why Coop is…"

Hazel can't bring herself to finish the sentence— while I can't move to stop her fast enough. In the next second I pull out the missing page and unfold it, then place it on top of the key.

"My mom had the missing page all along. She gave it to me while we were sitting at the Boathouse. *That's* what freed the Impact."

I look away, feeling the disgust chew through my insides. That's when I realize Ariana's watercolor postcard has also fallen out of my pocket. It sits on the floor between us like a loaded weapon.

I raise my eyes to meet Ariana's, but she looks away. Given everything that happened this awful morning, I wish I knew what that meant.

"We don't know anything for sure," Griffin says, his voice shakier than I've ever heard. It breaks my heart all over again.

"It could have been the page or the key or both or neither," he continues, trying to steady himself. "It doesn't matter. We all chose *together* to talk to your parents, to try to learn more. So if the Impact killed Coop, it's because all four of us decided to take that risk."

Ariana's entire body tenses, like this is a notion she refuses to accept. I wish I could say Griffin's words make me feel any better, but they don't. Hazel either, likely. Back outside, we decided to separate completely from Mom and Garrett—no more risks. Are they blaming themselves too, wherever they are now?

Ariana resettles in her chair, trying to take a beat before responding.

"What's done is done." There's fire in her voice, which seems fitting.

Bellfour suddenly smells like smoke—the wind off the lake must have shifted in our direction. My clothes will probably reek of ash all day, but that feels like an appropriate reminder of what we've wrought.

"We paid the worst possible price for the answers sitting on that table," Ariana continues. "So we'd better make them fucking count."

∞

We start with the missing page. It doesn't take us long to list the most relevant details on our wall.

❖ *The curse/Pact keeps its haven pristine and harmonious by forcing the demon/Impact to absorb ugliness, fear, and doubt. As a result, the Impact is driven to destroy its haven-prison and ruin the generational circle of connection.*

❖ *To break the Pact and destroy the Impact, a generation must prove their connection is strong enough to overcome everything drained into the Impact.*

❖ *The "circle of life" means the Pact-breakers striking the Impact at the same time with the "weapons that makes them strongest."*

❖ *In the novel, only the author/sole-surviving teen was left to strike. Her weapon was a cage, because her greatest fear was being trapped.*

Looking over our work now, I have many thoughts.

"So we know how to kill the Impact, by going to its prison and breaking the Pact. That makes it both unchained and mortal, and we have to kill it by striking at it together with the right personal weapons. To prove the strength of our connection."

I am tempted to dwell on this last part. Just a week ago I would have argued the four of us have the strongest connection on the planet. But now...? I don't want to go there.

"The author didn't mention any weapons besides her own," I continue. "So how do we choose the right ones? And how do we find the Impact's prison?"

"If we're satisfied reviewing the page," Hazel takes over, "then I think my dad answered that last question for us. It's why he gave me the key. He believes the Impact is imprisoned in the Weiss Crypt."

We shift our eyes from the key to Griffin, because he certainly called that one. But he looks far more miserable than proud.

"Like Luca's mom, my dad spent his life looking for answers," Hazel continues. "Just different ones. He always had a suspicion about the Impact, about what it really might be. He spent every summer trying to learn more as discretely and carefully as he could. He said it took a lot of trial and error, but he eventually confirmed the Impact is contained in the Weiss Crypt. He found a way to watch it get unleashed from there. Just once, but that was enough. And there's a reason he thought to investigate there in the first place."

Hazel takes a breath, like what she is about to say is too difficult to express out loud. Given how dark this day has already been, it liquefies my stomach with fear.

"Dad believes the Impact is born every generation of the sacrifice. Literally," Hazel says, finally. "Dad believes the Impact is *Tommy*. Or what's left of him."

This theory rolls like thunder through my entire body. Then one image strikes like lighting in my brain.

My nightmare vision of the Impact, with the broken infinity symbol branded into the side of its head…the same place of impact from Tommy's fall off Diver's Rock.

I try to remember if I've seen this on the Impact in our physical encounters, but it's always been too fast and too blurred. Besides, this potential detail would have been easy to miss on its body of defects.

"Didn't your parents say Tommy was always spooking everyone with animal pranks?" Ariana asks first, the same look quaking through her face. "Knowing how to scare people… Doesn't that sound familiar?"

"That would also explain the way the Impact's behavior has changed every generation," Griffin says. "I bet if we did some digging, we'd find John Weiss was a gluttonous overeater, or that Sarah Feinstein was direct and no-nonsense. You know, to match with those Impacts' patterns of behavior."

It's not lost on me that Griffin has memorized the names of the past sacrifices—the peers his forefathers murdered. But his logic does track.

"And the dead animals everyone keeps finding around campus, the ones with their lungs missing," Hazel adds. "Tommy did ultimately drown to death, right?"

I don't even need to speak my nightmare-vision out loud. Once again, the proof is all around us, now that a missing puzzle piece has slid into place. But that doesn't make me feel one bit better.

This new aspect of the Pact feels equally unthinkable.

Dying for the Pact seemed bad enough—but being sacrificed only to *become* the monstrous Impact? It's obviously a fate far worse than death.

This foul new layer must be sinking in with the others as well, because we all fall silent for a few beats. I don't want to, but I can't help pondering what kind of Impacts we'd make. Would Ariana slice her victims open? Would Griffin rip out their beating hearts? Would Hazel just be about clean shots to the brain? I then try to project my own potential damage, but I can't conjure any images.

What does that mean about me?

"My dad said he never risked telling your mom all this, Luca," Hazel says eventually.

"My mom said she never risked telling him about the missing page, either."

We sigh. We understand the reasons why now more than ever.

"But this is why my dad pushed for the job at Weiss Hall this summer. And why he freaked out my birthday night, when Griffin brought us to the crypt."

Thinking back on that night, it almost shakes loose a bitter laugh. It seems like a lifetime ago. Those naive kids who heard that whining through the stone... Now that we know what it truly was, will we ever be those people again?

"Dad said he still wasn't fully sure about his Tommy theory, not until he heard about the way the Impact had been haunting us," Hazel goes on. "He said Tommy was fearless. And he was always pulling pranks to try and show everyone they could be too, if faced with their worst fears. Back when the Pact was revealed to our parents, Tommy believed if one of them volunteered instead of being singled out or murdered, it would break the Pact. After Wendy's fall and what happened to my dad's eye, Tommy jumped off Diver's Rock. He thought being selfless would mean he'd live, being fearless enough to call the Pact's bluff. Obviously, he was wrong."

A chill seems to pass through Hazel, but she shakes it off.

"My dad gave us that key because he wants us to end the Impact, so Tommy can rest in peace. And so his sacrifice won't have been for nothing. But Dad also said it's up to us to choose what to do, because now only we have the power to break the Pact."

"My mom said the same thing about it being up to us," I say.

"How generous," Ariana says, to no one in particular.

I avoid looking at her, like she's a trip switch and glancing her way might trigger an explosion. Then again, Ariana hasn't said anything about our conversation on the secret beach yet, so maybe she won't.

"Well, if each sacrifice becomes the next generation's Impact, it does raise another question," Griffin says, rolling a tennis ball between his hands. "Who was the very first Impact? Could it have wandered off from some other pact and taken root here in Copper Cove? Maybe that's what happens if we let the Impact go free?"

"Right. We know what happens if we make the sacrifice," Hazel builds. "But if we do nothing, the Impact is set free, still immortal, to cause carnage. Or if we break the

Pact and fail to kill the Impact, does that mean no one else can kill it? What does it do once it destroys Copper Cove? That's the million-dollar question, right? Even more than how the Pact starts—where does the Impact end?"

"And when a new Impact is born from a sacrifice, what happens to the old one?" I add. "What if it's like, for every sacrifice, the person's goodness, their soul, is what protects or fuels the beauty of Copper Cove for another generation? Then what's left behind, the discarded physical husk, becomes a vessel for all the fear and darkness? And it dies when the new Impact is born?"

This feels right to me, but then it would, leaning into the idea of a graceful soul within and the damned devil without. I know the moment I say it, the others will disagree. But I'm also starting to think maybe we're all wrong about the origins of the Pact…and yet little bits of right, too.

"Maybe," Griffin answers. "Or maybe the Impact is just some kind of zombie and the first one was patient zero. Maybe it…I don't know, ate Tommy or something, so it's not really him. Maybe Copper Cove is beautiful all on its own, and this Impact thing just leeches off it, like a parasite or a cockroach? Sorry Hazel, bad word choice."

"No, I know what you mean," Hazel says, swallowing a visible wave of disgust. "I'd like to believe that. Or that maybe the ritual sacrifice is actually meaningless, aside from creating a new Impact?"

"How many times do I have to say this?" Ariana finally says, her voice raw. "It doesn't matter what fantasies you all cook up. It doesn't change the reality that there is a deadly creature coming to kill everyone and everything unless we find a way to stop it. And our time to do that is rapidly running out."

"Ariana is right," Griffin says. "Luca summarized the first part. But after we free the Impact from its prison and kill it with our weapons, we have to return it to its place of birth to close the circle. Now we know that birthplace has to be where Tommy died—Diver's Rock. So all we have to do now is figure out how to choose the correct weapons, right?"

"Wrong," Ariana replies. "We need to do what we know works to stop this, here and now."

"Why do you keep pushing for us to turn on one another?" Hazel responds, frustration seeping out of her voice. "We're not going to pick you. We're not going to pick anyone."

"Tell that to Coop."

Ariana's words hit us like a gut punch.

"I'm just so tired of the lies," she sighs. "Even to this day, Sofia and Garrett didn't tell each other everything they learned, not until we forced their hands. The lying only multiplies, it only spawns more lies. I want us to start telling the truth."

"No," Hazel digs in. "I refuse to go there. We're better than this."

Hazel crosses her arms, so Ariana looks to Griffin. But he just reaches to place his hand on Hazel's shoulder in support. Ariana looks to me last, her eyes sharpening. Her stare slices into me finely, but all I can do is silently plead with her: *Don't do this. It won't help like you think it will.*

"That's the thing, Hazel," Ariana says. "We're not better."

I am paralyzed. It's like I'm watching the start of a car crash from the sidewalk, powerless to stop it. Dread plants me into the floor, taking root.

"I'm sorry, but I can't let us risk so many more lives because we think we're 'better.' Not when we haven't been honest with each other all summer, not really. We have to face the facts, ugly as they might be."

"Ariana, don't do—" I attempt, too late.

"Look out at the Boathouse! Think of Maggie. We can't let all of Copper Cove pay for our inability to have a goddamn difficult conversation!"

Ariana's voice echoes through Bellfour, but she doesn't even try to rein herself in as she continues.

"Luca, you've been in love with Griffin all this time and you didn't say anything, at least not to the people it mattered most to. And Hazel, you told me you suspected Luca's feelings all summer. But instead of being honest with each other, you shut each other out and only told me."

I turn to Hazel. She...*suspected*, all along? The realization slams into me. But this truth pales in comparison to what I know must still be coming.

"And I kept your secrets, because I finally felt like I had entered your inner circle," Ariana keeps on. "I'd finally become one of the three musketeers, after all these years. But then I go and open my big mouth and tell Griffin, who can't stand the thought of losing an ounce of someone's affection. So he goes and kisses Luca to try and make it better. And then you both decide to keep that a secret from

Hazel, but not from me. Can't you see it? We keep trading secrets and telling lies to protect each other, but it's killing us. And we can't let it kill anyone else."

I look only at the floor. This can't be happening.

Ariana pauses, but only for a moment. "None of us are perfect, and we're all equally to blame. No one here is better than anyone. So maybe the best thing we can do now is let fate decide which one of us pays for all that's happened, for all the pain we've caused. I'm not saying we take a vote— I'm saying we draw straws. We let the universe pick our cosmic draft number. We can make this stop, if we just stop digging our heads in the sand and pretending it'll get better."

As Ariana finishes, I find the nerve to look up. She appears to hate the things she's saying as much as the rest of us, but she clearly feels them resonating with us all the same. Except with Griffin, who moves to look Hazel straight in the face, tears pooled in his eyes.

"It's not, it wasn't..." he tries, grasping for the thing to say. "It was a mistake—Luca and I were both so overwhelmed and confused. When Ariana told me about Luca...I felt so terrible for not seeing it, for not doing better, and it just happened. But we only kissed. I love you, Hazel. Please, it was just a mistake. We didn't want to hurt you."

Hazel pulls away from Griffin, one blemished hand drawn involuntarily over her mouth. Then she turns to me. I nearly black out again.

"Is this why you've been so... Why didn't you just tell me about your feelings when I asked?" Hazel pauses, trying to make sense of these new facts. "And then you both decided to not tell me? Together?"

"I didn't know how to tell you any of it," I say, as if the truth will be enough now.

"So you told Ariana?" Hazel asks, turning to her next. "Then you kept it from me, after all the times I told you I was worried? You thought it was a good idea to tell Griffin, instead?"

"Hazel, no, it wasn't like…" Ariana falters. "This isn't what I wanted, it's not what I meant when—"

"God, then what exactly did you mean to do, Ariana?" I finally fire. "Go ahead, be honest! You just wanted us all to hate each other so you wouldn't feel like the outsider anymore? Well, mission accomplished."

Ariana opens her mouth to protest, then presses it back shut. Whether or not she agrees, she's still the one who just split C4 with an axe.

"Stop it. We don't do this," Griffin pleads, standing and stepping into the middle of us all. "It doesn't matter, because I already made up my mind. I decided days ago if we didn't find a way to stop the Impact, I'd volunteer to sacrifice myself. It's my responsibility, the only way to pay for what my family has done."

"No, you can't do that," Hazel says, reacting on instinct. "We knew you'd say that. Luca and I… We…"

Hazel freezes. Then she starts crying.

"How could you… How could you spring this on me now, when we have to…?" she tries. "I just… I need a minute."

Hazel walks towards the door, pushing past Griffin.

"Hazel, no, please, we have to…" he says, trying to stop her. "You can't be out there alone, not while…"

But Hazel leaves.

And all my sureness goes out the door with her. Realizing Ariana has been right all along sucks the air out of my lungs. There is no overcoming this. We aren't better than our parents, than anyone who came before. We're just as human, just as beaten. We don't have a clue what we're doing—we never have.

I follow Hazel out, walking in the opposite direction when I see her heading up the hill.

I don't know where I'm going or what danger might await me wherever I end up. But right now, anywhere feels safer than Bellfour.

Chapter Twenty-Seven

I walk for what feels like hours. It can't be, not really, but then there's the sun, advancing farther across the sky than it has any business doing. The time must have been taken somewhere. And it's not like I have any to waste.

Maybe this is really just my final tour, a bitter goodbye to my favorite place. But maybe I'm still looking for answers, too. Looking for weapons to fight…everything. When my head finally clears enough to realize where I need to go, I can't believe I didn't think of it sooner.

I end up back at the Infinity Tree. It feels almost like I was called here, after what we learned today about the Impact. Deception and isolation versus connection and continuity. If the broken infinity symbol we keep seeing really does represent the Impact, then maybe a complete infinity symbol could represent its opposite? And there's only one place on campus I've ever seen one of those…

It's also the one place on campus I happen to find Manny, sitting on a dipping branch on the central tree.

"Oh," I say, startled as I pass through the leafy curtain. "I didn't mean to—"

"And here I was thinking you might have actually come to find me," Manny says.

For a terrible moment I consider turning and

sprinting. Haven't I endured enough emotional turmoil for one day? But I'm too exhausted to keep running. And I owe Manny more than that, even if the timing is awful.

"I came here to pay my respects to Coop," Manny adds. "He was all the Emps' favorite."

I nod—Coop was everyone's favorite. I expect stabs of grief to cripple me, but I can't even seem to process that Coop has been taken from us… Maybe I'm still in shock? Or am I clinging to denial? Either way, it feels deeply wrong—as wrong as the pounding in my head. Chances are I have a mild concussion from my fall earlier, but dealing with that will have to wait. One crisis at a time…

"You know, this was my tree before you made it yours too, Luca," Manny adds, when I don't say anything. "You're not the hero of everyone's story."

I flinch. The sentence barrels into my skull, destroying things as it crashes around.

It turns out I'm not the hero of *anyone's* story.

"I saw you run in the other direction yesterday, outside the Emp dorm," Manny sighs, disappointment baked into his voice. "Before that I was doing a decent job of convincing myself you weren't actively avoiding me. But then you still didn't turn up…until now. Unintentionally."

I want to tell Manny about fearing for Maggie or seeing the Impact back when we kissed, or about every other excuse I have for not being honest with him or paying him enough attention. But the awful truth is that, in a way, I used him to distract myself. If I really wanted, I could have treated Manny differently, even with all the other horrors swirling around me.

"Manny, I'm sorry," I try, but my hands go numb. I know my speech will go next.

Another anxiety attack has been...inevitable.

"I didn't mean to—"

"Honestly, I don't need to hear the excuse," Manny interrupts. "Look, it's obvious you have something personal going on, and it probably has nothing to do with me. But still, what you did, ignoring me after...it hurt. You're the first guy..."

Manny stops himself. "You know what, it doesn't matter."

His thoughts dismantle me, like a wrecking ball tearing through whatever is left of my foundation.

"I think you could be someone..." Manny begins, standing and approaching me. "I think you could be one of the good ones, Luca. Maybe for someone else. Just try to remember you're not the only one walking around with some big, secret pain?"

Manny kisses me on the cheek. Then, before I can say anything, he walks away from the Infinity Tree.

His final words level me. I slam into the cold flatness of rock bottom. In that moment, I prepare myself to lie there. To curl up and let the river of panic sweep me away, to wash off the last traces of my existence. Maybe it'll be best for everyone if I just...

But this time, as anxiety cripples me yet again, I experience something unexpected. What happens next isn't quite explicable. It's kind of like I crash through some hard mental floor—one that's been rotted through with tears and liquid panic. Weighted by the truth, I drop into some new headspace that's empty and unfamiliar. A chamber where one single realization resounds.

Maybe I'm not quite the person I intend to be.

I've always believed my first instinct was to put others' feelings, especially the feelings of those I love, before my own. That might still be true, in part. But it's also true I probably tell people what I think they want to hear for my own sake. Maybe because if I say what I really think, if I am really myself at all times, unguarded…I'm not sure anyone will love me the same way?

It's a question that runs so deep, my legs go weak. I tuck myself into a low hanging branch and let my drained-out mind fill back up. Hearing Manny, I suddenly understand how my silence has hurt so many others, how it nearly consumed me.

So maybe pleasing the people I love isn't the same thing as taking care of them?

Tears brim in my eyes. It's like, all of a sudden, the little shreds of perspective I get from swimming have multiplied. Like this moment of grace just burst the sky wide open. It's hard to pinpoint the emotion exactly, but despite everything, I find myself centered. It's not just that I can think it, or intellectualize it—I can actually *feel* it. I've read about this kind of thing happening to people: an epiphany, or a breakthrough, or whatever you want to call it. I didn't know it'd feel so…personal. And infinite, at the same time.

I already suspect this moment will be fleeting, but that's okay. I used to think the tragedy, the suffering, the sadness, it would always lead back to the panic, to the anxiety.

But what if, instead, the pain could guide me back to this calm source?

To this state of mind where the right questions align. What if I stop waiting for some fantastical future to be myself? What if I just take the risk to come all the way out, in every way? Maybe I'll lose some people—people I really care about.

But maybe my real friends will stand up and cheer?

Griffin. Hazel. Mom. Even Ariana, the one to remind me it's not the place that's special, but the people who fill it up. Then it hits me like a bolt of lightning, the thing that makes me strongest: This family, the one I've chosen for myself. And this place we all come together, Copper Cove. Connection, continuity—community. *That's* my greatest weapon.

This is also when I realize I'm sitting right in front of that gnarled branch, the twisting infinity symbol hanging in the air. This failed root, made beautiful only by its imperfection. Just like my friends, or Copper Cove, or... me. I suddenly understand this is my weapon, this infinity branch. Not because it holds any inherent power, or because the symbol has any secret meaning—but because it holds exactly as much power as I give it.

This is what will kill the Impact. Not magic or relics or fury, but *faith*. These weapons will have strength proportionate to the belief we place in them. If there was ever a fantasy epic lesson to be learned, that sure as hell must be it.

I stand up, my legs improbably sturdy, and I reach for the infinity branch. Perhaps because it's so old, it snaps off with jagged edges. For a weapon, it will do quite nicely.

Which is good, because in the next second the Impact steps out from the other side of the tree trunk. I tense, my body re-pooling with dread. Holding the branch, I try to remind myself that the Impact can't kill me—it can only hurt me, or frighten me. And that once upon a time, I thought I felt more fear than anyone.

Perhaps that's why the Impact has stalked me here, instead of the others. Perhaps that's why it lurches at me now, screaming its guttural cry and pushing me down with its burnt-up excuses for hands. Once again, it traps me on the ground underneath its sharp body. This close, I can smell its putrid, bloated core. I can feel its hunger, ceaseless and pining. Most of all, I can see it— the broken infinity symbol seared into its skull. *Tommy's* impacted skull.

My instinct is to cry out, to struggle and sob. But things can be different, I now know.

It's a simple matter of perspective.

Instead I scream back at the Impact, imagining myself as the side of an epic cliff, resolute against the battering of a storm. Or better yet, a giant shark, moving with the raging current. I imagine I am Coop, an avenging phoenix rising from the ashes. Throwing this determination out at the Impact, I sense something unexpected seeping from its toxic pores…

Fear.

In the very same breath, the Impact reaches out for the branch-weapon I've secured—but I already know I won't let go of it, no matter what. Not even when I feel the Impact tug, or howl…

Or when it grasps at my hand, twisting at the fingers it can pry loose.

As my bones snap, I finally react. Enough is enough.

I swing my other hand around and knock the Impact off me. Touching it is like hitting a rock, but also like trying to grab a gust of wind. Using my momentum, I roll over and switch the branch to my unbroken hand.

Then I strike.

The Impact shrieks the moment the branch hits it. So I strike again, for Coop. For Mom. For Hazel. Then, before I can strike again, the Impact recoils. It is pulled away, hopefully returned to the chains of its crypt, just like that.

I fall into the dirt. My temples pound. Both the pinkie and ring fingers on my right hand are definitely broken, but the pain doesn't compare to the feeling I have now. The Impact's attempt to stop me had the opposite effect.

It only proves I'm right about the weapons.

At first, I don't move. I want to remain grounded, even if only for a few more seconds, in this place where the surface has shattered. Where I've gotten to the heart of the matter.

Then I stand, because there is so much work to do.

Stone Seven

On my way back to Bellfour, I pass the burned remains of the Boathouse.

I am tempted to throw a stone into the ashes, but I know what they say about glass houses.

Instead, I walk around the side to the lakefront.

There, I skip the seventh stone across the water, watching it dance on the surface before sinking beneath.

It is my tribute to things lost—and to things found.

To Coop.

And to knowing exactly what to do with my eighth and final stone.

Chapter Twenty-Eight

By the time I make it back to the Auditorium, the sun hangs even lower in the sky and the annual Family Week Talent Show has begun. It's an event I usually look forward to religiously, but this year it has barely even registered. Ignoring the invasion of showgoers that now occupy the Auditorium, I hope I can find the rest of C4 before it's too late.

Then I hear the sound coming from inside, on the stage.

It's the unmistakable tenor of Ariana's voice, accompanied by an acoustic guitar. That can't be possible—there's no way I've missed the entire talent show. Then I realize that Griffin and Ariana must have switched their finale spot to become the show openers. People are still settling into their seats as I arrive at a side door, all of them stunned into silence by this surprise change. They also likely grow reverent seeing the large picture of Coop displayed farther up on the stage.

Blake must have printed it as a special dedication. Coop always said hosting the talent show was the highlight of his year. That must be the reason Copper Cove didn't cancel the event—to carry on in the face of tragedy. Without a doubt, Coop would've wanted the show to go on, even without him. It's so much less than he deserves, and the talent show will be greatly diminished without his jokes and cheesy introductions. But at least it's something.

I look over the somber faces of the audience, all reeling from the tragic incidents of the past few days. I can't decide if it's worse or better for them, to think Maggie and Coop were victims of random, terrible accidents…the way I used to.

Griffin's lilting voice sings next, full of pain and meaning. I know this song, the one Griffin must have chosen, perhaps better than any other: "Up to the Mountain" by Patty Griffin. It's who Griffin himself was named after. It's…perfect.

So, before doing what has to be done, I join the silent audience to pay my respects to Coop. Listening to the song Griffin and Ariana sing in his honor, I try to soak up all the strength I can from this performance.

Coop might have died because of us, but he also died trying to save others from the Boathouse fire. He died trying to save the place he loved most.

Now it's our turn, whatever that may mean.

∞

When I go upstairs to check Bellfour, Hazel is already there. Griffin and Ariana arrive right behind me. I look out the window to see the sun dipping dangerously low on the horizon. It's almost time.

None of us sit in our seats. Instead, we stand apart around the room.

"I know you all probably have a lot to say, but I'm going to start," I say. "Because just now I learned what kind of weapons will kill the Impact."

Ariana is first to notice the broken fingers on my

hand. Then she sees the branch bludgeon resting against the wall next to me.

"Luca, what happened to—"

"I'll tell you everything, but you need to hear me out first," I interrupt. "This weapon works on the Impact, trust me. But you need to understand why. After we split up, I went out to this place in the Skinny Point woods. It's a tree, and my...friend told me the Emps named it the Infinity Tree, because of the way it seems to loop back in on itself. I thought it might have something to do with the Impact and the broken infinity symbol. But while I was there, I realized some more important things. Mostly how weak I've been all summer. And that what makes me strongest is Copper Cove, despite its flaws. And all of you."

I know if I pause for a moment there will be questions and disagreements, so I soldier on.

"There are a few things I need to make clear," I continue, turning my focus to the deep blue of Griffin's eyes. "Griffin, listen—you aren't an August, not really. You haven't been for a long time. You've become your own person, apart from them. A person who can face the Pact and volunteer himself and do the right thing in ways they obviously never could. So the August mistakes don't belong to you. Their debts are not yours to pay."

Griffin looks back at me and I can tell instantly—he hears me on this, deeply. An understanding settles between us. I'm not sure what it means, but it's a start.

"And Ariana," I continue, turning to face her next, "you're one of us. Period. You're not an outsider and you never have been. Really, you're more like our leader. You were right to call us on our bullshit—mine especially. I'm sorry for the impossible position I put you in. You've been a better friend to me than I deserved this summer."

Ariana appears surprised, but also touched. This obviously isn't what she was expecting to hear from me.

"And I'm sorry I told Griffin behind your back," Ariana answers, before I can go on. "Not when I really should have just encouraged you to tell him yourself. It was silly of all of us, to think Griffin and Hazel dating wouldn't change anything. But change doesn't always have to be a bad thing."

Ariana nods at me, and I return the gesture. But I don't linger too long, because I still have the most important part left.

"Okay, Hazel. I need you to know—"

"No. I'm sorry, but no," she interrupts, her fists clenched. "I know I'm supposed to accept your apology and say we're good, because we're about to face death. But that's all the more reason not to keep lying. The truth is, I need more time. It's all too much to gloss over with some insightful words."

Hazel pauses, trying to ease herself a bit. "I'm happy you're trying to express yourself now, Luca. But there were so many times you could have—should have—said something to me, instead of sweeping it under the rug. I just… I'm not sure how to trust you, after all that. And after…"

The sentences blow holes in my chest like cannonballs, but they aren't unfair. I know I'll have to do more than apologize to Hazel to earn back the trust we've lost. But will we ever get that time?

"Hazel, I—" Griffin tries.

"No, the same goes for you," Hazel interrupts again. "I want to make something clear. You should know I'm fine with your sexuality, however you choose to define or express it. I always have been. But the betrayal of trust…"

Hazel trails off, unable to bring herself to speak the words. Griffin seems to wither away beside her.

"Maybe Ariana was right," Hazel sighs. "Maybe we should just—"

"No," Ariana interrupts now, with some force. "I owe you an apology too, Hazel, when you're ready to hear it. But aside from that, I had time to think about what I said before, about the sacrifice. I think…I was just talking out of fear. Sacrificing one life for the sake of many can't be right—at least not after all we learned, not when we have a chance to save every life. However slim."

Ariana pauses to let that thought sink in. "Listen, Luca might not have been exactly his best self this summer. But no one knows Copper Cove better than him. And no one loves it more. If he thinks he found the last answer… Hazel, can you trust in that, if nothing else?"

Hazel still seems unconvinced. But she also seems to be considering Ariana's question.

"I'm not saying everything is magically okay between all of us. Or that it will be ever again," I try. "But this is still my favorite place on the planet, and it's full of my favorite people. I wouldn't make us take the risk if I wasn't sure. We can do this, I know it. So we do it for us. For our parents, whether they deserve it or not. We do it for all of Copper Cove, and the generations to come. For our futures, and most of all for…Coop."

There are a few beats of grim silence after this.

Until Griffin takes his turn to weigh in.

"I know it's scary, but I don't actually want to die. And I don't want any of you to die, either. I just want to save all of Copper Cove. And there's only one way to do that. But if we agree to it—if we agree to break the Pact and free the Impact—we have to do whatever it takes to kill it, no matter how it terrorizes or threatens us. We can't let it get out to the campus…or beyond."

"So then you're all agreed?" Hazel asks, looking around Bellfour.

Ariana nods, and so do I, and then Griffin. We are scared shitless, but we agree.

So, in the end, it's left to Hazel. To properly break the Pact, it needs to be all four of us. But she still looks so unsure, standing on unsteady feet after her whole world has been flipped upside down, over and over again.

She closes her eyes and takes a deep breath. "What you all did…" Hazel begins. "I don't know about things ever going back to the way they were before. But maybe that was never meant to be after the Pact changed everything. Still, I know this much—you guys love me, even if you have terrible ways of showing it. I could never think, not even for a second, about sacrificing one of you over the other. So yes, I agree, we fight—we stop this. If not for ourselves, then for everyone else who comes after us."

I'm not sure I'd call it relief, but I feel something. Lots of things, all at once.

"Okay," I reply. "Now that we're in agreement, here's what happened."

"So…you're saying it doesn't matter what weapons we choose?"

Griffin asks the question after I've filled the rest of C4 in on my latest Impact encounter.

"I'm saying it matters a lot, but that it's different for each of us," I correct. "For the author of the book it was a cage, because it represented harnessing her greatest fear. For me it's this infinity branch, because for me it represents the community we have here in Copper Cove. But we all have to decide this for ourselves—I think that's the real point."

"So Griffin is sort of right," Hazel tries. "The weapon doesn't matter—what matters is how strong it makes us feel?"

"Exactly," I answer. "I know it sounds strange, but you should've seen how badly the Impact didn't want me to have this branch. And how much it hurt when I hit it."

"Then we have all our answers," Griffin says, walking towards the whiteboard list. "We free the Impact from its prison—the Weiss Crypt—by breaking the Pact. Then to kill it, we all strike at it with our chosen weapons. Then we feed its body back to its place of birth—Diver's Rock—as a final sacrifice, to close the circle?"

Everyone nods in agreement, a bit stunned we've managed to piece all this together. But none of us is in the mood to feel impressed with ourselves.

"If that's the case, then we just need to pick our weapons?" Griffin finishes.

"Well, I think I've actually already got mine," Hazel says, pointing to the corner of Bellfour, where a crossbow and a quiver of arrows rest against the wall. "I went down to the archery range to clear my head. I figured it couldn't hurt to swipe that, if we did decide to break the Pact. Nothing makes me feel stronger than being on a mission, working towards a goal—or hitting a bullseye."

Ariana considers this for a moment. "Well, I always feel strongest when I'm cutting through bullshit. So if anything weaponizes that, it's a knife? Or maybe a scalpel?"

"I know just the thing," I say.

I motion for Ariana to hold on, ignoring the dull pulsing in my broken fingers. I walk over to the letter-writing desk and rifle through the drawers until I uncover an old pocketknife. I bought it at the Porch Sale years ago, fancying it an imaginary sword.

But as Ariana takes the dagger, there's nothing imaginary about it anymore.

"Great, I know my weapon, too," Griffin says, taking his turn. He walks across the room and picks up an old wooden baseball bat collecting dust near the CD tower. "Baseball Star Griffin is the strongest Griffin there is."

Griffin fake-swings the bat, but something doesn't sit right with this choice. That's maybe because I have a thought of my own, one I cooked up earlier.

"I think I might have a better idea," I say, walking over to him. "I know you're good at baseball. But I don't know, doesn't that kind of feel like the Griffin everyone else wants you to be, just a little?"

"I guess," he says, frowning. "But a guitar or a history book aren't exactly handy as monster-killing weapons, are they?"

"No, but this is."

I reach into my pocket and hand Griffin the eighth stone, which also happens to be the largest from my collection this year. I was saving the best for last.

"It's a long story, but finding these stones is a tradition I inherited from my grandpa. They stand for family, at least to me. And the older we get, the more I see we really get to *choose* who we consider family. But Griffin, you've already done that with us, every summer of your life. You're also the one who saw all this haunted stuff first, and the one who gave us this home in Bellfour. So I'm giving you this stone because you're our rock—you always have been. I know things are weird right now, but I think you will be again, someday."

Griffin takes the stone in his hand, looking like he's processing a million thoughts at once. He stares down at it, tears forming in his eyes.

"Now there's a weapon I can get behind," he finally says, seeming to hold his breath as he grips the stone.

We all hold our breath, in a way—the fateful heroes assembled in our private war room. But the time to imagine us as anything more has passed.

We will have to be enough, just as we are.

I let out a breath of my own, but it isn't filled with the swell of confidence I'd hope for. As our final moments tick away, all I can do is pray I really am right about the strength found in these chosen weapons. After all this, if I'm not...

The death of Copper Cove and everyone I love will be on *me*.

Chapter Twenty-Nine

The sun is just about to set, so we approach the padlock to the Weiss Crypt without delay. It was a silent walk here— we all needed to prepare ourselves. Besides, nothing we can say will change what's about to happen on this dark hillside behind Weiss Hall.

Bronze rust falls onto Hazel's hand as she uses the key Garrett gave her to open the old padlock, Tommy's padlock. The key sticks halfway and, for a horrifying moment, I think it might not open. But Hazel twists harder and the lock finally clicks.

Then she turns to us to see if we're ready. That isn't exactly the word I'd use to describe any of our expressions, but our time is up.

Hazel removes the padlock, and we all push the heavy stone door open. We step back, bracing ourselves... but we can't see anything, except some blurry barrier, the same murkiness that always seems to obscure the Impact. The unfocused sight is unsettling, like being in a dream where you want to scream but can't make a sound.

Then we hear it coming from inside the crypt, the shrill wailing of the Impact. Instinctively, we fall into formation, clutching our chosen weapons. The fingers in my right hand still throb and my head aches, but I tell myself to push through. Hazel's injuries must be bothering her just as much, but she's still fiercely determined.

I push all the pain, every single shred of fear and doubt, resolutely out of the way. Because my friends need me. And all of Copper Cove, maybe even the rest of the world, needs us.

So then, standing there locked in a row, we Copper Cove Core Four utter the five words we came here to say, in perfect unison:

"This pact is not ours."

At first, there is only silence.

Until suddenly, the blurry barrier pops like a bubble. In the same instant we break the Pact, the Impact is upon us.

It happens so much faster than we could have imagined.

The Impact is nothing but a smear that goes for me first, ripping the branch from my hand and tossing it away. It jerks to thrust its appendages through my rib cage, but Ariana jumps forward to stab it with the pocketknife in the smashed side of its skull. It makes a squishing, damp-leaves noise. The Impact whines with something. Surprise? Pain?

Either way, I scramble away. Because we need all four of our weapons for this to work.

"It threw the branch farther up the hill!" Ariana shouts, just before the Impact clamps down on both her arms.

There's a sickly suctioning sound. When the Impact lets go, the familiar pattern of deep grooves once again imprints in Ariana's skin, this time blistering with blood. There's something else there, too. New seedlike pods set in the fleshy divots, some kind of writhing, flaking particles that begin to fester.

Ariana freezes. Her skin looks foul, dusted again with these crop circles of decay. But this time the Impact has no restrictions, no rules to follow. It's so much worse. This deathly sight stuns Ariana just long enough for the Impact to slam her aside, sending her tumbling down the steep edge of the hill.

I want to help Ariana, praying the contamination and the fall don't kill her. I consider running down to save her, but I know I need to find my weapon first. Besides, this must be what the Impact wants, to keep us scrambling and disorganized, when what we need to do is remain focused on the final strike. So I run up the hill to find the missing infinity branch.

"Stay away from them!" Griffin shouts from somewhere behind me.

The sound of his fist connecting with the Impact rings out. It's a hollow clang, like pounding on a cellar door. This sound repeats as I search the dirt, desperately trying to distinguish the branch from the woodsy hill. But it's getting dark out—too dark in this unlit place.

"No!"

Griffin screams and I turn to find the Impact knocking him into the winding hill. The Impact dashes forward, then makes quick work of collapsing the hillside earth.

I watch in horror as it tumbles apart under the Impact's brute strength, covering Griffin in an instant...

Burying him alive under several feet of packed dirt.

In the next second, an arrow shoots directly into

the center of the Impact's rotten mass. Then another, and another, as Hazel fires away. The Impact staggers and loses its footing, sliding down the side of the hill. It claws to try and stay on the path, but it tumbles down into the woods below, not far from where Ariana fell.

Hazel bought us some time to regroup, but probably not much. We're the only ones capable of killing the Impact. So it will no doubt come back to kill us first.

I turn frantically and nearly cry out as my eyes fall on the coarse loop of the infinity branch resting among the fallen leaves. I snatch it up and race back down to find Hazel digging madly, in the spot where Griffin is buried.

"He'll suffocate if we don't—"

But Hazel doesn't finish, or I don't hear the rest, as I begin to help scoop out the collapsed hillside.

Dirt cakes under my fingertips as I fling it away. It covers my clothes and my skin, it flies into my mouth, but that doesn't matter.

Because Griffin is somewhere in the ground below, buried alive.

Griffin—our Griffin, my Griffin—is trapped underneath several feet of tumbled, packed earth. Dying a custom-designed death, unable to move, unable to see, suffocating as the air is crushed from his lungs. He can't even scream, his mouth filled with earth.

So I scream for him.

I dig and I scream and I dig, even with my broken bones, because I will not let Griffin die. Not this way, with his worst fear realized.

In my frenzy, this moment folds in on itself like the

worst kind of déjà vu. I swear I've been here before...or maybe I've just always been hurtling toward this terrible conclusion? The waves of doubt make a thunderous return as my arms keep scrambling and the clumps of dirt keep flying. This has always been the ending to our story, hasn't it? The moment it all goes to hell.

We should have made the sacrifice, I think with a leaden drop. We were never going to win, not when we couldn't even fix the things that broke between us this summer. Now we're all going to die, *everyone*—but first it'll be the four of us, drowned and diseased, infested and crushed...

We never really stood a chance, did we?

I picture Ariana at the base of the hill, her diseased limbs broken into impossible angles. Her skin will rot, sliding off her muscles in wet clumps. Griffin will be crushed, his beautiful skull rendered unrecognizable. Then the Impact will murder Hazel, sending a line of fire ants streaming down her throat, choking her as her insides are infested. Finally, it will be my turn. The Impact will gut me with my own weapon, then use it to hang me from a tree. The life will be drained out of me slowly as I am forced to watch the Impact descend upon the rest of Copper Cove, still gathered neatly together in the Auditorium.

Suddenly I realize I was wrong.

I played right into the Impact's hands. This was exactly what it wanted all along. It stalked me to the Infinity Tree and helped me find what I thought we needed, because it wanted the Pact to be broken. It wanted to be free, because the Impact knew four teenagers would be no match for its fully unleashed fury.

I did the wrong thing again, hurting when I only meant to help. Panic pools like vomit in the back of my throat as I dig, all of our lives flashing before my eyes.

But the things that scroll by aren't memories. Not highlights of the past, but rather glimpses of the future, of its unfulfilled potential: Of me moving into my dorm and finding my place, and my purpose, and maybe even another boy to love. Of Ariana's very first surgery, her talent show finales, and finding one place to call home. Of Griffin's music and his history, all the games he will win, and his chance to make things right with the girl he loves. Of Hazel awarded for her writing, losing countless more pens, and discovering whether things with Griffin really were built to last…and maybe even forgiving him.

Maybe even forgiving me, too.

It's this thought that finally makes me swallow my doubt. That forces me to drop into my newfound headspace, the safe center of myself where I feel right. *I can reroute the inevitable*, I tell myself.

It's a simple matter of perspective.

So I dig and I scream, sucking in deep breaths. In this moment, I refuse to make this the ending of anyone else's story.

Just then, my hand knocks against something solid—something that belongs to Griffin. I keep scraping and suddenly Griffin's hand breaks free, appearing from under the piled earth. Griffin claws his own way out once we clear some leverage for him—but that's also when the Impact snatches Hazel away.

She shouts and I turn to find the Impact stretching above her, plucked arrows gathered in its jaundiced mouth like splintered teeth. It screeches and reaches to clamp down on Hazel's throat…

Until I push her out of the way.

The Impact pierces my arm instead, puncturing straight through to the other side in a red burst. I'm so full of adrenaline I don't feel the pain—but I watch as the Impact pulls Ariana's pocketknife from its own skull. It holds me in place while it brandishes the knife, smudged with something viscous and yellow.

It's going to cut my throat first, drown me in my own blood. Then it's going to slice up the infinity branch that's…not in my good hand?

Oh god, what did I do with…

This thought vanishes, however, as Griffin appears behind the Impact, a muddy vision of dirt and fury. He pushes forward with the infinity branch in hand and wraps it around the Impact's thick stalk of a neck.

He pulls back, rattling the arrows loose.

The Impact tries to howl, but what comes out instead is a gurgling sound. It struggles to move, attempting to claw at Griffin with whatever it can.

But Griffin's choke hold has crippled the Impact. This is it—this is our window to strike.

I work my way out from under the Impact, burrowing through the dirt. As I do, I look across the path to see Hazel pulling at something. No, not something—someone. Hazel pulls Ariana back up onto the hill. Her skin is a sickly yellow and her left arm hangs limp and broken at her side, but she is alive—and she is back.

I look to Griffin, still strangling the Impact with the

branch. He stays strong, but his teeth grind together. He won't be able to hold forever. But he will hold a little bit longer, to repay the August debts still weighing so heavily on him.

It only takes Hazel and Ariana a few seconds to collect their weapons, but then I panic. I don't know what to do. Griffin has my weapon, he...

But then I snap myself out of it.

Because if Griffin seems stronger than ever using the infinity branch, then why can't the eighth stone, this token I've revered so very long, make me strong enough, too?

I scan the upturned earth and see it, the stone I once gave as tribute to Griffin. I run towards it and the moment it's grasped in my good hand, it feels right.

Hazel must understand, because she lets another arrow fly, ripping into the Impact's dark mass. It howls as much as it can.

Ariana is up next, shrieking as she runs forward to plunge her dagger into the Impact's body, right beside the arrow.

In the next moment I take my turn, without hesitation. I smash the stone forward, my hand pushing deep into whatever counts as the Impact's mouth.

For a second, the Impact freezes. Strangled by Griffin, shot by Hazel, stabbed by Ariana, and drowned by me, as I drive the stone down its tortured throat.

It is my tribute to the Impact's death...

Which the four of us now witness together, moment by breathless moment, cradling our broken parts.

Chapter Thirty

After the Impact dies, one last task remains in front of us. But first we take a few moments to make sure we're all okay. Well, okay enough. Hazel ties her C4 hoodie around my wound to stop the bleeding. Griffin helps Ariana fashion a sling for her broken arm. She returns the favor by brushing off some of the dirt caked on his face.

Then it's time to drag the Impact's limp carcass up to Diver's Rock. Its blurred lines have cleared in death, but what remains—the raw tendons and globs—doesn't resemble anything that makes sense. It's a thing of pointed arms and legs, of head and body. There's no visible trace of Tommy, the person it used to be—but maybe that's a relief.

Even though C4 is exhausted and drained, shaken to our cores and walking wounded, none of us complain as we march uphill. We all want this to be over, and every second we delay is another chance for the Impact to come back to life—or whatever you'd call its terrible existence—and finish its deadly run.

When we finally reach Diver's Rock, we're surprised to find Garrett and Mom waiting for us there. Mom bursts into tears, but Garrett remains silent. He fixes his gaze on Hazel, then on the Impact that was once his best friend.

Perhaps because C4's work is not yet done, or because we're still angry, or because Garrett and Mom understand how wrong they've been to hold us back, they don't hug their children.

Or maybe it's because we're not children anymore.

As I do my part to one-handedly drag the Impact to the edge of Diver's Rock, I notice Mom holding Garrett's hand. I'm pretty sure I know what that means, so I can't stop my eyes from finding Mom's. They are full of relief and shame, deep pride and deeper apology. And a look that says we'll have to talk about this later, before bed, in our pajamas.

Suddenly it hits me. There will be a later, for all of us. The notion pours through me like warm water, heating me from the inside out. It gives me the last push of strength I need to reach the end.

Diver's Rock consists of two flat stone ledges jutting out above the water, one about forty feet and the other nearly twice that high, now roped off behind rows of warning fences. Obviously, this place has always held a strange weight for my family, even before I knew the truth. But that's also because of the view.

Diver's Rock is set farther up on Lake Charlie, so it offers a complete view of Copper Cove's campus. It lies before me now, dropped into place on the mountain's side, glittering and alive with evening light. Skinny Point and the ERC, the Store and the Dining Hall, the Inn and the Auditorium—where the talent show is likely just letting out. August Bay and, of course, Hemlock, which has always felt like my true home. Then there's the dark spot where the Boathouse once stood, a reminder of the black hole that has always loomed just underneath the gleaming surface of Copper Cove.

Coop died for this. Now that I have an unburdened moment to process this fact, it seems so random, so unfair. Then again, nothing about the Pact, for all its balance and consonance and rules, is fair in the slightest. Will the burned Boathouse remain a blemish, a stain upon the shining face of Copper Cove now and forevermore?

No, I know better. We will rebuild. And then we will rename the Boathouse something like Coop's Dock. The generations that come later won't know why it's called that, because all of this will become a footnote, a line of text highlighted in one of Griffin's history books.

But not for us. I can tell C4 has barely touched the grief surrounding Coop's death—the kind that will stay with us for the rest of our lives. Coop's death was violent and senseless, yes—but it was also an inspiration, a call to arms. Both sides of it will live inside us, no matter where we go.

As the four of us stand on the edge of Diver's Rock, we turn from the view to look at each other. In this moment, an exhausted triumph settles in. *We did it.* We took our fates into our own hands, ignoring the old rules once laid out for us. Unlike the fearful generations that came before, we fought for what was right. Or maybe we just got some fierce kind of lucky, benefiting from the mistakes and knowledge we inherited.

Either way, the Copper Cove Core Four changed everything.

But we've also broken so much to get here. There's no telling, not yet, if we're truly any better for it. At least we've earned the chance to keep trying. After this kind of experience, there will be lingering traumas, unexpected aftershocks. But there will also be power. The things that stopped us before, the fears that once paralyzed us, have been beaten into submission.

What will we be capable of doing next, without them?

That's a question for later, because in this moment we have only one job remaining: To push the Impact off the ledge and return it to the depths from which it sprang forth. To complete the circle of life and ensure the death of the Pact.

It is a quick and difficult gesture, one completed without ceremony. We watch as the Impact drops through the open air, a ruddy watercolor bleeding around the edges. It sails noiselessly, landing in the lake with a thick splash.

For a moment, I swear I see the lake pulse and fill with dissipating particles, like stars in a constellation…

In the shape of the broken infinity symbol.

But then I blink and the vision disappears.

It's over.

Before any of us can turn, before we can separate and face the inevitable aftermath, Hazel takes my unbroken hand.

"We still have a lot to talk about," she begins. "But after what you… After almost losing…"

Hazel seems ready to break open with emotion, but instead she braces herself, not needing to say more.

I look back at her, and even though there are still oceans to swim between us, I am determined to get there, in time. I nod and squeeze her hand.

Hazel turns to face Griffin next. Despite the dirt and mud still caked on their faces—despite everything and anything else—she kisses him. It looks like it pains her a little to do so, but still, she does it.

I hate that it still stings me to watch, even after all this. But it stings a lot less than I expect. I resist the urge to close my eyes once again. Instead, I open that newly discovered channel inside myself and imagine the sting swept away on a current of calm. Maybe someday, I hope, that feeling will be enough—that I will be enough. And that maybe I'll find someone else who thinks so, too.

Until then, plain old Luca will have to do—though maybe just a little bit louder, and prouder.

Ariana moves to hug my side, careful to grip my unpierced arm with her own unbroken one.

"Feeling left out of the world's worst love triangle?" I ask, surprised to find my voice steady. I even laugh a little, and so does Ariana. Griffin separates from Hazel—but only slightly—to look at us.

"Oh, I'll take a hard pass on that one," Ariana says. "But after we fix ourselves up, I think we've earned as much ice cream from the Store as we can physically stomach."

"Really?" Griffin asks. "I'm actually in the mood for a quick dip. Anyone want to jump off Diver's Rock with me?"

Hazel slaps Griffin's chest, finally releasing a nervous burst of laughter.

"That is not funny," she says. "But I could really use a shower."

"I could use ten showers," Ariana adds, shivering

as she passes her good hand over the imprints in her skin, which have already begun to fade. "And probably a cast."

I smile and look over my friends, over C4, and feel that maybe—improbably—we will be all right.

I take the first step to leave Diver's Rock and return to Copper Cove. I'm not sure what we'll find there, now that the Impact is gone and the Pact is broken, but I'm very ready to find out.

I try to see it, what will happen next...

We will return to Copper Cove with Mom and Garrett. With the time we have left, we will talk about all of the forbidden things we couldn't before. Ariana will be able to stop lying to her own family, she will tell them the whole truth. And then we will invite them into our new, enlarged inner circle. Maybe this will even inspire Hazel and Griffin and me to start over with our own parents.

And with each other.

Maybe, just maybe, we'll be able to fix ourselves, after saving our own little corner of the world. Then... maybe we'll get to save another?

After all, if we are really only the second group ever to stop the Pact—and the only ones to ever survive the experience—what is our responsibility, moving forward? How many other families are privately trapped in the binding web of the Pact? How many other beautiful, charged places are locked in its silent cycle?

And when we return next summer to Copper Cove, the same way we do every year, what impacts new and old will we face?

I know these questions are infinitely worth answering.

Just like I now understand how capable we all are of writing our own stories, of changing our own endings. Not because we won't ever face terrible obstacles or fierce battles in the future—but because at least now, we know how to fight right.

So in this final breath, looking over Copper Cove's imperfect campus, I decide.

Every summer, it will be about change.

And maybe *that* pact can be ours.

Acknowledgements

First, to you the reader, thank you for picking up this book. Just the fact that it made its way to you already feels like a miracle. I first conceived of this novel as a new step in my career back in 2017. Since then, the manuscript endured three rounds of submissions, two Revise & Resubmit near-deals, a TV studio option that survived three rounds of corporate acquisitions, a pandemic slate-clearing, a new agent search, and my attention pulled to two other published print novels. But this story came straight from my heart and I never gave up on it—a seemingly-unwinnable battle and some broken pacts of my own to contend with. So I hope this book has inspired some hope or faith or fortitude for you, dearest reader, the way it has for me.

To Joshua Dean Perry, I remain in awe of you and your incredible work with Tiny Ghost Press. When it comes to This Pact Is Not Ours, no one else has ever understood this novel the way you have—thinking of your acceptance letter still gives me chills to this day. You also knew exactly how to elevate the weaker parts of this book with all your brilliant edits. I couldn't be more grateful or honored for you and Tiny Ghost Press to be bringing this book to readers, for so many wonderful reasons.

To Lucy Carson, who fought for this book for years before opting to leave the YA space—I owe you more thanks than I could ever give! To Moe Ferrara, who (after a very painful querying year) showed up quite literally the same day as Josh's acceptance letter—I have learned how rare and special it is to find partners who really understand the work. I'm beyond grateful to have found two creative partners with this book, and excited for all we have in store together. And a very special shoutout to Lindsay Tolbert, TV development exec extraordinaire, who saw this story's potential before just about everyone else.

Enormous thanks to Dana Keller for a brilliant set of copy edits that went above and beyond. And to Ailish Brundage for formatting this novel--it's always a bit of magic to see a word doc suddenly transform into a book.

Special thanks to Kylie Koews, Reuben Davies-Hoare, Jeremy Gibson, and Lewis Hughes for all your hard work promoting and packaging this novel. And an extra special thanks to Dri Gomez for our truly dynamic cover and jacket art, which successfully channels the Sarah Michelle Gellar trifecta: Cruel Intentions, Buffy The Vampire Slayer and I Know What You Did Last Summer.

As you might have noticed, this book is queer and indie—so to every reader, bookfluencer, and bookseller out there who helps this tale reach new eyes, I thank you from the bottom of my heart. Your work remains valuable beyond measure, now more than ever.

There are too many early readers and fellow writers to list by name here. You know who you are, and I thank you for keeping the faith when mine runs thin—

and for enduring my constant cycles of self-promotion to stay in business as a writer. I'm especially thankful to the community of (often queer) YA authors who have accepted my interactive/indie self with open arms. And I need to shout out super-readers Mia Van Matre, Justin A. Menorath, and Qymana Botts, whose support both on Patreon and in our pen-palling keeps me afloat and constantly inspired.

To Silver Bay (the real Copper Cove) and the extended family there—I dedicated this book to you, but it bears repeating. Thank you for every summer past, for telling me your ghost stories, and for every beautiful summer yet to come.

To my ever-growing immediate family—this one's for you. For us.

And finally, to my teenage self: You can finally let go of some things that haunt you. They'll never really leave you, but those ghosts will help make something really beautiful someday.

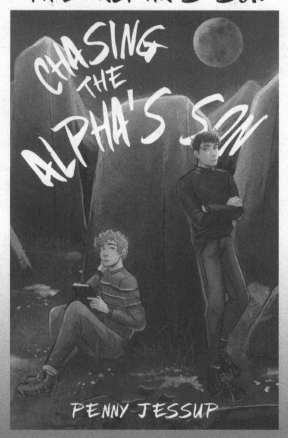